Heart of the Season

Laurel Ridge Series, Book #17

Tara Baisden

Sterling Ridge Press LLC

Dedication

For every heart that has loved, lost, and wondered if second
chances are more than just beautiful dreams—
And for the nurses, caregivers, and quiet heroes who show up
every day to tend not just wounds that can be seen, but the
deeper hurts that require patience, compassion, and the kind of
gentle strength that believes healing is always possible.
Most especially, this is for those who understand that coming
home isn't always about returning to a place—sometimes it's
about finding your way back to the person you were always
meant to be, in the arms of someone who sees your worth not
in what you can provide, but in who you are when you're brave
enough to be truly, beautifully yourself.
May you always believe that love is worth the risk, that God's
timing is perfect even when it doesn't feel safe, and that the very
best chapters of your story might just be waiting to be written.

With love and hope,

Tara

Contents

Prologue

The wind shifted southwest at exactly the wrong moment.

Wyatt Gibson adjusted his radio headset and squinted through the haze of smoke rolling across the ridge, his trained eye tracking the orange line of flames as it carved its deliberate path through the dry underbrush of the Monongahela Forest. The controlled burn had been progressing perfectly for three hours—consuming accumulated deadfall while leaving the mature oak and maple canopy untouched—but that sudden wind shift could turn routine forest management into catastrophe in minutes.

"Miller, pull your crew back fifty yards," he called into his radio, his voice calm despite the adrenaline coursing through his veins. "Wind's picking up from the southwest. Let's give ourselves some breathing room."

The October afternoon hung crisp and clear above the forest canopy, the kind of perfect autumn day that made West Virginia's mountains look like a postcard painted in scarlet and gold. At thirty, Wyatt had spent enough years fighting wildland fires to read weather patterns in the way leaves trembled and smoke curled, and everything about today's conditions had screamed ideal for prescribed burning.

He keyed his radio again. "Collins, how's your eastern flank looking?"

"Burn line's holding steady," came the crackling response. "Moving nice and slow, just like we want it."

Wyatt nodded, though Collins couldn't see him through the trees. The satisfaction of a well-executed burn never got old—the careful planning, the precise timing, and the delicate balance between destruction and renewal that kept forests healthy. This particular tract hadn't seen fire in over four years, and the buildup of undergrowth had created a tinderbox waiting for lightning or human carelessness to set it ablaze. Better to burn it now, under controlled conditions, than wait for nature to do it catastrophically.

He pulled his worn leather glove down and checked his watch. One twenty-five in the afternoon. They'd been at this since dawn, and the burn was ahead of schedule—always a good sign. His crew moved through the smoky haze with practiced efficiency, some tending drip torches that painted careful lines of fire along predetermined boundaries, others manning hoses and hand tools ready to suppress any flames that jumped their designated path.

The radio on his belt crackled with the routine chatter of men who'd worked together long enough to communicate in shorthand. Weather updates from the base station, progress reports from section leaders, and the occasional joke that helped maintain morale during long, tedious hours of work. Wyatt half-listened while scanning the burn perimeter, his attention focused on a section where the flames seemed to be moving slightly faster than he liked.

"Jackson, keep an eye on that slope near the old logging road," he said into his headset. "Looks like it might want to run uphill on us."

"Copy that, boss. I'm on it."

The familiar weight of responsibility settled across Wyatt's shoulders like a well-worn jacket. As burn boss for today's operation, every decision filtered through him—where to set the next fire line, when to pull crews back, and how to adjust tactics as conditions changed. It was the kind of pressure that had driven him to volunteer to work for increasingly dangerous assignments over the past several years, the weight of other people's safety somehow easier to carry than the weight of his own thoughts.

A red-tailed hawk circled overhead, riding thermals created by the rising heat. Wyatt watched it for a moment, envying the bird's perspective on the controlled chaos below. From up there, the burn probably looked exactly like what it was—careful, measured, and necessary. From ground level, surrounded by smoke and flame and the constant potential for things to go wrong, it felt more like controlled madness.

His radio crackled again, but this time the voice belonged to Captain Rogers, his supervisor back at the incident command post a quarter-mile down the mountain.

"Gibson, I need you to come down to my location. Now."

Something in Rogers' tone made Wyatt's stomach tighten. In all the years of working under the captain, he'd never heard that particular edge in the man's voice—urgent, but carefully controlled. Not the sharp bark of immediate danger, but something else entirely.

"Copy that, Captain. Miller, you've got command until I get back."

"Roger, boss. We'll keep the fire happy for you."

Wyatt began picking his way down the steep slope, dodging patches of still-burning underbrush and stepping carefully over logs that smoldered like giant cigarettes. The acrid scent of wood smoke clung to his yellow Nomex shirt and filled his lungs with every breath. His boots found purchase on loose and slippery rocks as he descended, using roots and saplings for handholds when the grade got too steep.

Captain Rogers stood beside the white incident command truck, his weather-beaten face grim beneath the brim of his hard hat. At fifty-five, Rogers had been fighting fires since before Wyatt was born, and nothing much fazed him anymore. Seeing worry lines creased around the older man's eyes sent ice through Wyatt's chest.

"What's wrong?" Wyatt asked before he'd even reached the truck.

"I need you to call your sister." Rogers handed him a satellite phone, his expression carefully neutral. "There's been a family emergency."

The words hit Wyatt like a physical blow. Family emergency. In his line of work, that phrase usually meant one thing—someone was hurt or dead.

With hands that shook slightly, Wyatt dialed Lauren's cell phone number. It rang once, twice—

"Wyatt?" Lauren's voice came through the speaker thin and strained, barely recognizable.

"Lauren, what's going on?"

"It's Jake." The words tumbled out in a rush, accompanied by sounds Wyatt couldn't immediately identify—mechanical beeping, urgent voices, and the slam of doors. "There was an accident with the tractor. A tree fell during last night's storm, and he was trying to move it alone, and the tractor rolled—"

"Is he alive?" The question came out harsher than Wyatt intended, cutting through his sister's rambling explanation.

"Yes, but Wyatt, it's bad. Really bad. They're loading him into the ambulance right now, and they won't tell me anything except that I need to follow them to the hospital."

Through the phone, Wyatt could hear men shouting medical jargon he didn't understand, the mechanical whine of hydraulic equipment, and someone calling for more IV bags. The sounds painted a picture his mind didn't want to accept—his little brother, the one who'd followed him around the farm as a kid begging to help with everything, broken and fighting for his life.

"Which hospital?" Wyatt was already moving toward his truck, Captain Rogers falling into step beside him.

"Charleston. The trauma center. They said something about possible spinal injuries and internal bleeding, but I couldn't understand everything—there's so much noise, and the paramedic keeps asking me questions I don't know how to answer."

"Lauren, listen to me." Wyatt forced his voice to stay calm even as his world tilted sideways. "Drive to Charleston. Don't try to keep up with the ambulance—drive safely. I'm leaving right now, and I'll meet you there."

"He looks so pale, Wyatt. There was so much... Oh, my gosh... when I found him, and he wasn't moving, and I thought—" Lauren's voice broke into tears that tore at Wyatt's chest.

"Lauren, breathe. Get yourself together before you start driving. He's going to be okay." The words felt hollow even as he spoke them, but Lauren needed to hear them. "Jake's tough. Tougher than both of us put together. Just get to the hospital safely, and I'll be there as soon as I can."

"The ambulance is leaving. I have to go."

The line went dead, leaving Wyatt staring at the satellite phone while smoke from the controlled burn drifted down the mountainside like a funeral shroud.

But all Wyatt could think about was Jake lying broken beneath a rolled tractor and how the world he'd built for himself had just burst into uncontrollable flame.

Captain Rogers was watching him with the expression of a man who'd delivered too much bad news over the years. "Go," he said simply. "We'll handle the burn."

Wyatt nodded, unable to trust his voice. He stripped off his hard hat and radio headset, dropping them into Rogers' capable hands. In all his years of Forest Service work, he'd never abandoned an operation mid-burn.

But Jake was his baby brother, the kid who'd tagged along during every farm chore and begged to help with everything from planting trees to fixing equipment. The one who'd inherited their father's gift for growing things and their mother's head for business, turning Gibson's Tree Farm into something their parents would have been proud to see.

Wyatt's keys felt foreign in his hands as he unlocked his truck. Through the windshield, he could see smoke rising from the ridge where his crew continued their careful work, following protocols he'd drilled into them through years of training and experience.

He started the engine and pointed his truck toward Charleston, leaving behind the controlled destruction of the forest for the uncontrolled chaos of whatever waited at the trauma center.

Jake had to be okay. He had to be.

If something happened to his brother, he wasn't sure how many more pieces of his family he could handle losing.

Chapter 1

The coffee had gone cold twenty minutes ago, but Robin Fitch barely noticed as she studied the medical file spread across the break room table at Mountain Valley Home Health Services. Jake Gibson's chart read like a textbook case of what could go wrong when farm equipment met autumn storms—spinal compression fractures at L1 and L2, crushed pelvis requiring surgical reconstruction, lacerated spleen, punctured lung, and multiple broken ribs. The kind of injuries that changed lives forever.

She traced her finger down the discharge summary from Charleston's trauma center, noting the precise language the orthopédic surgeon had used to describe Jake's spinal damage. Significant nerve involvement with an uncertain prognosis for motor function recovery. Medical speak for "We don't know if he'll walk again." At twenty-eight, Jake Gibson faced months of painful rehabilitation with no guarantee of returning to the physically demanding work that had defined his entire adult life.

Robin reached for her coffee mug, grimaced at the lukewarm contents, and set it aside. She'd been twenty-two years old when she'd completed her nursing degree and chose to specialize in trauma recovery, drawn to the challenge of helping people rebuild their lives after catastrophic injury. Eight years later, she'd learned that the medical file never told the whole story—behind every surgical report and medication list lived a human being grappling with loss, fear, and the terrible uncertainty of an altered future.

The Gibson family had been part of Laurel Ridge's fabric for three generations, their Christmas tree farm providing holiday magic for families throughout West Virginia. Robin could picture Jake as she'd last seen him at church in the beginning of October—strong, confident, and moving with the easy grace of someone who'd spent his life working outdoors. The contrast between that memory and the broken man described in these medical reports made her chest ache.

She'd known Jake through church and community connections, the way everyone knew everyone in Laurel Ridge. He was Lauren's younger brother, the one who'd inherited their father's gift for growing things and had transformed Gibson's Tree Farm into a thriving year-round operation. Lauren often spoke proudly of Jake's innovations during their casual conversations after church services, mentioning his expansion into nut tree cultivation and the greenhouse complex that had made their poinsettia business profitable.

Robin flipped to the pain management protocol, noting the complex schedule of medications required to keep Jake comfortable while maintaining enough mental clarity for decision-making and physical therapy participation. The narcotic requirements alone indicated the severity of his ongoing discomfort, while the list of potential complications read like a medical emergency waiting to happen. Blood clots, respiratory depression, infection at surgical sites, pressure sores from immobility—any one of which could derail his recovery or threaten his life.

Her phone buzzed against the table, displaying Charlotte Allen's number. Robin answered on the second ring, putting her on speakerphone while she poured a fresh cup of coffee.

"Morning, Charlotte."

"Robin, I wanted to confirm you're prepared for the Gibson case." Her supervisor's voice carried the brisk efficiency that had made her one of the most respected nursing administrators in the region. "This is going to be an intensive case."

"I've been reviewing his file. The spinal injuries are going to require careful monitoring, and the pain management protocol is complex enough that I'll need to coordinate closely with his physicians."

"The family specifically requested our most experienced trauma nurse, and frankly, Jake's going to need every advantage he can get, which is why I assigned you to this case." Charlotte paused, and Robin could hear papers rustling in the background. "The ambulance transport should arrive at the Gibson place in about thirty minutes."

Robin glanced at the wall clock—9:30. "I'll leave in a few minutes. Do we have confirmation of the medical equipment delivery?"

"Hospital bed, wheelchair, and shower chair were delivered yesterday. The family's been scrambling to convert the downstairs master bedroom into a medical suite, but Lauren Gibson strikes me as the type who gets things done."

That was accurate. In the years since the Gibson parents' tragic death, Lauren had stepped up to manage the business side of the farm operation while Jake handled the agricultural aspects. Robin had always admired the younger woman's grace under pressure, the way she'd transformed grief into determination and built something meaningful from loss.

"Any family dynamics I should be aware of?" She asked as she sat back down.

"Lauren's been Jake's primary family spokesperson during his hospital stay, and she's understandably exhausted. The older brother, Wyatt Gibson, is managing the farm during Jake's recovery. Apparently, he's some kind of forestry specialist and wildland firefighter stationed up in the Monongahela Forest. The siblings' parents are deceased."

Robin's coffee mug slipped from her suddenly nerveless fingers, clattering against the table and splashing coffee. She grabbed paper towels from the counter, her hands moving automatically while her mind reeled.

Wyatt was home.

"Robin? You still there?"

"Sorry, Charlotte. Just spilled my coffee," she said as she blotted up the coffee. "When did Wyatt arrive?"

"According to Lauren, he's been home since just after the accident. He and Lauren both alternated between running the farm and hospital visits."

Robin tried to picture Wyatt sitting beside Jake's hospital bed, but the image felt foreign. In her memories, he remained frozen at eighteen—tall, serious, and driven by dreams that required leaving everyone behind, including her.

"The family seems capable of handling the emotional support aspects," Charlotte continued. "Your job is keeping Jake as comfortable as possible while his body heals. This is going to be a marathon, not a sprint."

"Understood. I'll call with an assessment after I've examined the patient and reviewed the home setup."

Robin ended the call and stared at Jake's medical file, though she was no longer seeing the surgical reports and medication schedules.

Instead, her mind filled with memories she'd thought she'd successfully buried—Friday night pizza dates watching movies with his family in their living room, Saturday afternoons spent at Gibson's Tree Farm, when Wyatt had taught her to identify different tree varieties and explained the careful timing required for optimal harvest. She could still remember the pride in his voice when he'd described his forestry school plans, the way his eyes had lit up when he'd talked about protecting wilderness areas and fighting fires.

She'd been so young and stupidly in love, convinced that love could overcome obstacles like geography and divergent dreams. The breakup had been mutual—or so she'd told herself—but Robin had spent the better part of her freshman year at community college nursing a broken heart and learning that some wounds took longer to heal than others.

Robin gathered the medical charts and slipped them into her bag alongside the specialized supplies she'd collected from the medical supply room. Wound care materials for Jake's surgical sites, calibrated pain medication in a locked container, mobility assessment tools, and the dozen other items that might be needed during a complex case transfer. Her hands moved with practiced efficiency, but her mind kept circling back to the uncomfortable reality of seeing Wyatt again.

She'd built a good life in Laurel Ridge—meaningful work, strong friendships, and active involvement in her church community. She'd dated occasionally over the years and had even been engaged once, though no one had ever quite measured up to the memory of first love. At thirty, she'd made peace with the possibility that some people were meant for independence rather than partnership and that her calling lay in caring for others rather than building a family of her own.

The November morning was crisp and clear as Robin loaded her medical bag into her Ford SUV and began driving through the Appalachian foothills toward Gibson's Tree Farm. Early Christmas decorations had begun appearing on a few homes she passed—wreaths on front doors, strings of lights outlined against rooflines, and the occasional inflatable snowman that made her smile despite her nervousness.

The route to the Gibson farm was as familiar as her own street.

The road began climbing into genuine mountain terrain, winding through forests painted in the gold and scarlet of late autumn. Each landmark she passed triggered memories she'd thought had lost their power to affect her. She passed the turnoff to Sunset Point, where she and Wyatt had spent countless evening hours talking about their futures and making plans that had seemed so certain as teenagers. The memories felt like viewing someone else's life through a telescope—distant, slightly out of focus, but undeniably real.

Gibson's Tree Farm appeared around a familiar curve. The farm sprawled across hundreds of acres, with orderly groves of evergreens marching up small hillsides in precise rows. Modern greenhouses gleamed in the distance, and a large restored barn bore a hand-painted sign reading "The Christmas Shop."

The Gibson siblings had expanded the farm into something impressive since they had taken over after their parents' death.

The ambulance sat on the circular gravel drive beside the Gibson farmhouse, its rear doors open while EMTs wheeled a stretcher toward the front steps. Robin parked beside a black pickup truck and grabbed her medical bag, her professional instincts taking over as she assessed the transfer situation. Jake was conscious, his face pale against the ambulance linens.

The farmhouse before her, a two-story white clapboard structure with a wraparound porch, had provided the setting for so many conversations during her teenage years. The same rocking chairs sat grouped near the front door. The same flowering bushes lined the foundation, now dormant for winter.

Robin took a steadying breath and shouldered her medical bag, drawing on eight years of professional experience to calm her suddenly racing pulse. She was here as a nurse, nothing more. Whatever personal history existed between her and Wyatt belonged to the past, irrelevant to Jake's medical needs and recovery requirements.

She approached the porch steps with confident strides. The front door stood open, and she could hear Lauren's voice directing the setup, medical equipment being positioned, and the controlled chaos that accompanied bringing a critically injured patient home.

Robin took another deep breath and entered the home.

Chapter 2

"Easy now. Watch that IV line." Wyatt stepped back as the EMTs maneuvered the stretcher through the doorway of what had been his parents' master bedroom, now transformed into something resembling a hospital room. The hospital bed dominated the space, its chrome rails and mechanical adjustments a stark reminder of how catastrophically everything had changed in three weeks.

Jake's face was pale against the white sheets, his eyes half-closed but tracking the movement as the transport team positioned the stretcher alongside the bed. Wyatt's stomach twisted at the sight of his brother's carefully immobilized form.

"On my count," the lead EMT said. "One, two, three—"

They lifted in unison, and Jake's sharp intake of breath cut through Wyatt like a blade. His brother's hand clenched against the sheet, knuckles white.

"Almost there, buddy," Lauren murmured from her position near the headboard, her voice steady despite the worry lines creased around her eyes. She'd barely slept during Jake's hospital stay, and the exhaustion showed in the way she gripped the bed rail like it was the only thing keeping her upright.

Wyatt found himself counting Jake's breaths, watching for signs of distress beyond the obvious pain that came with moving a body held together by surgical hardware and desperate hope. The doctors had used words like "significant nerve involvement" and "uncertain prognosis" —medical speak that translated to a future nobody could predict.

"We're going to lower you now, Jake." An EMT's voice carried practiced calm. "Deep breath if you can."

The transition from stretcher to hospital bed seemed to take hours, though Wyatt knew it was only seconds. Jake's jaw clenched, tendons standing out in his neck, and Wyatt had to look away. He'd seen colleagues injured during wildfire suppression, but watching his little brother suffer hit differently.

A thousand thoughts raced through his mind. What if they'd damaged something during the transfer? What if Jake's pain meant complications the hospital had missed? What if his brother never walked again, never ran the farm the way he'd planned, and never lived the life he'd built so carefully after their parents' death?

The EMTs adjusted Jake's position, and Wyatt forced himself to focus on the immediate present rather than the uncertain future.

One moment at a time. One breath at a time.

"That's the worst of it," the lead EMT said, stepping back to assess their work. "How's your pain level, Jake?"

"About a seven now." Jake's voice came out rough. "Maybe nine when you guys decided to play toss-the-patient."

The EMT grinned. "Sense of humor's intact. That's a good sign."

Lauren moved to Jake's side, smoothing the blanket across his chest. "You're home now. That's what matters."

"Good morning, Gibson family, it's Robin with Mountain Valley Home Health Services."

The voice hit Wyatt like a physical blow—familiar despite twelve years of silence, carrying the same warm clarity he remembered from a thousand conversations. His head snapped toward the entrance, and the careful composure he'd been maintaining shattered.

Robin stood in the doorway, medical bag slung over one shoulder, with a professional demeanor firmly in place.

His tongue felt thick in his mouth. Words scrambled in his brain and refused to form coherent sentences. Twelve years. Twelve years since he'd last seen her, since their mutual decision to go separate ways had carved a hole in his chest that he'd spent over a decade trying to ignore.

He managed a nod, but his face must have shown everything he was feeling because Lauren's eyes widened in obvious surprise.

"Robin!" His sister moved past him in a rush, arms opening for a hug that Robin returned without hesitation. "I didn't know you'd be Jake's nurse. Charlotte just said they were sending their best trauma specialist."

"That's me, apparently." Robin's smile was genuine, though Wyatt caught the slight tension around her eyes as her gaze flicked toward him and away again. "Though I suspect Charlotte was being generous with the compliments."

"I doubt that." Lauren stepped back but kept one hand on Robin's arm, as if anchoring herself through physical contact with someone who represented competence and control. "Jake needs the best, and if Charlotte says that's you, then thank God you're here."

"Hey, Robin." Jake's voice was weaker than Wyatt had ever heard it, but his brother was trying for his usual friendly tone. "Sorry about the dramatic entrance. I'd shake your hand, but I'm a little tied up at the moment."

"Rain check on the handshake." Robin moved toward the bed with the easy confidence of someone comfortable in medical settings. "Let's see what we're working with here."

Wyatt watched, still frozen near the window. She spoke quietly with the lead EMT, asking questions about Jake's pain levels during transport, medication timing, and any complications during the ambulance ride. Her hands moved with practiced efficiency as she checked the IV line, adjusted the flow rate, and made notes on a tablet she'd pulled from her bag.

"Did he have any respiratory distress during the drive?" Robin asked.

"Breathing stayed steady," the EMT confirmed. "Pulse ox maintained above ninety-five percent. His last dose of pain medication was right before we left the hospital."

Robin made another note, then turned to Jake with a smile that somehow managed to be both professional and genuinely warm. "How's your breathing feel right now? Any tightness or difficulty?"

"A little tight," Jake admitted. "But that might just be from trying not to scream when they moved me."

"Fair enough. I'm going to listen to your lungs in a minute, but first let's make sure you're as comfortable as possible."

Wyatt found himself cataloging the small changes twelve years had wrought. Robin moved with more assurance than the girl he'd known, her medical expertise evident in every gesture and decision. But underneath the professional competence, he could still see traces of the person she'd been—the quick intelligence in her eyes, the gentle humor in her voice when she spoke to Jake, and the instinctive kindness that had drawn him to her when they were teenagers discovering what it meant to care about someone beyond yourself.

"Lauren, could you grab me that extra pillow from the chair?" Robin gestured toward the corner.

His sister moved to comply, and Wyatt realized he should probably be helping instead of standing uselessly by the window. He forced his legs to carry him closer to the bed, though he made sure to stay on the opposite side from where Robin worked.

"Jake, I'm going to need you to tell me if anything I do increases your pain beyond what you're already feeling," Robin said. "Rate it on that one-to-ten scale the hospital probably drilled into your head."

"They mentioned it once or twice." Jake managed a weak smile. "Or maybe a hundred times."

Robin's laugh was soft but genuine. "Medical professionals tend to be repetitive. It's one of our more annoying qualities." She glanced up at Lauren, who'd returned with the pillow. "I'm going to lift his shoulders slightly, and I need you to slide that pillow behind him."

The EMTs had stepped back, giving Robin space to work while they gathered their equipment. Wyatt watched the coordination between Robin and Lauren, the way his sister seemed to relax slightly now that someone familiar was taking charge of Jake's immediate care.

"Ready, Jake?" Robin positioned her hands carefully under his shoulders. "Deep breath on three. One, two, three—"

She lifted with smooth efficiency, and Lauren slid the pillow into place. Jake's exhale came out shaky, but he nodded when Robin lowered him back down.

"Better or worse?" Robin asked.

"Actually better. Takes some pressure off my lower back."

"Good. We'll fine-tune your positioning over the next few days as we figure out what works best." Robin turned to the lead EMT. "Anything else I need to know before you head out?"

"The hospital sent along a copy of his complete chart and medication schedule. Everything should be in the packet." The EMT gestured toward the dresser, where several folders lay stacked. "Physical therapy is scheduled in a week, and the home health aide should arrive around nine tomorrow morning."

"Perfect. I'll coordinate with both services." Robin shook the EMT's hand. "Thanks for the smooth transport."

"He's a good patient. Didn't complain nearly as much as some we've dealt with." The EMT grinned at Jake. "You take care, man. Listen to your nurse."

"Yes, sir."

The EMTs filed out, their footsteps echoing through the house, and then it was just the four of them—Wyatt, Lauren, Robin, and Jake.

Robin cleared her throat and reached for her stethoscope. "Okay, Jake. Let's do a quick assessment so I know exactly what we're dealing with." She glanced at Lauren and then briefly at Wyatt. "You're both welcome to stay, but I'll need to ask some potentially uncomfortable questions and examine his surgical sites. If you'd prefer privacy—"

"I'm good with them staying," Jake said quickly. "Lauren's already seen me at my worst in the hospital, and Wyatt needs to know what's involved in case there's an emergency when you're not here."

Robin nodded. "Fair enough. But if you change your mind at any point, speak up."

She moved through the examination thoroughly, explaining each step as she went. Listening to Jake's lungs and heart, checking the surgical incisions on his abdomen and the external fixation devices stabilizing his pelvis, and assessing his pain levels and range of motion in his upper body. Her questions were gentle but direct, covering everything she needed to know.

Wyatt found himself learning more about his brother's injuries in fifteen minutes than he'd absorbed from all the hospital consultations combined. Robin had a gift for translating medical jargon into plain language, for making the complex understandable without being condescending.

"The spinal injuries are healing well according to the hospital reports," Robin said, making notes on her tablet. "But nerve regeneration is slow, and we won't know the full extent of your motor function recovery for several months. Right now, the priority is preventing complications—infections, blood clots, pressure sores—while we give your body time to heal."

"So basically just take it day by day to see if I'll ever walk again," Jake said.

"Well, basically yes. Though I'd phrase it more positively as optimize healing conditions to maximize recovery potential."

Lauren moved closer to the bed, her hand finding Jake's. "What can we do to help? Wyatt and I—we want to make sure we're supporting his recovery properly."

"The best thing you can do is follow the care plan that's been established and communicate with me about any changes or concerns." Robin pulled a chair closer to the bed and sat. "Jake's going to need a lot of help with basic activities for the next few months. Bathing, getting dressed, and moving from bed to wheelchair. The home health aide will handle most of that during their shift, but you'll need to coordinate care during off-hours."

"I can do that," Wyatt heard himself say. "I'm here full time until Jake's recovered enough to run the farm again."

Robin's gaze met his, and the impact sent electricity down his spine. "Wyatt, I would suggest you and Lauren both take turns caring for Jake. Trying to do everything yourself will wear you down, and then you'd be no good to anyone. Today, we have no home health aides available, so unfortunately you're on your own after I leave. But on the bright side, Jake is still recovering; the ride from the hospital will probably have worn him out. I suspect he'll sleep well for most of the day today."

Her expression gave nothing away—no hint that seeing him again had affected her at all, no acknowledgment of the history that hung between them like smoke from a forest fire. Maybe she'd moved on completely. Maybe twelve years had erased whatever they'd once meant to each other.

The thought should have brought relief. Instead, it felt like a loss.

"I'll be here daily for the first week, arriving around nine in the morning," she continued. "After the first week, we'll transition to Monday, Wednesday, and Friday visits unless complications arise that require more intensive monitoring."

"What about pain management?" Wyatt asked. "He's going to need round-the-clock medication, right?"

"For now, yes. The hospital sent him home with a carefully calibrated schedule that we'll adjust based on his needs." Robin's tone was matter-of-fact, addressing him with the same professional courtesy she'd shown the EMTs. "I'll teach you and Lauren how to administer the medications safely, including what to watch for in terms of side effects or adverse reactions."

"Adverse reactions like what?"

"Respiratory depression is the biggest concern with the opioid doses Jake requires. We'll monitor his breathing carefully, especially during the first week as we adjust to home care." Robin glanced at

Jake, who was listening with obvious effort despite the pain and exhaustion. "Your physical therapy will start in a week. The therapist will be here Monday, Wednesday, and Friday afternoons. They'll work on range-of-motion exercises and eventually progress to more active rehabilitation as your bones heal."

Lauren was nodding, absorbing the information, but Wyatt could see the exhaustion settling deeper into his sister's features. She'd been running on adrenaline and fear for three weeks, and now that Jake was home, the reality of long-term care was beginning to sink in.

"This is a lot," Robin said gently, as if reading Lauren's thoughts. "You don't have to remember everything right now. I'll be here every day for the next week, and we'll go over procedures until they become second nature."

"What about farm operations?" Jake asked. "I need to know what's happening with the Christmas prep. Opening day is less than three weeks away."

"You need to focus on healing," Wyatt said firmly. "I've got the farm handled."

"But the wholesale orders—"

"Are being managed. Tom's been incredible, and I'm learning your systems pretty quickly." Wyatt moved closer to the bed, careful not to crowd Robin but needing Jake to see his certainty. "The farm will be fine. You won't be fine if you don't rest and let your body heal."

Jake's jaw tightened—stubborn, frustrated, and clearly hating his helplessness. Wyatt recognized the expression because he'd seen it in the mirror often enough during his own struggles with situations beyond his control.

"He's right," Robin added. "Stress impedes healing. The more you can relax and trust others to handle business operations, the faster your body can focus on recovery."

"Easy for you to say," Jake muttered. "It's not your family legacy at stake."

"True. But it is my professional reputation at stake if you develop complications because you wouldn't follow medical advice." Robin's tone was light but firm. "So humor me and pretend to be a cooperative patient."

Despite everything, Jake managed a weak smile. "Pretending is about all I can manage right now."

"That's a start." Robin stood and moved to the dresser where the EMTs had left the hospital discharge papers. She flipped through several pages, making notes and occasionally glancing back at Jake. "Your next dose of pain medication is due in about an hour. I'll stay until then to make sure the transition from hospital to home protocols goes smoothly."

"You don't have to babysit me," Jake protested.

"I'm not babysitting. I'm establishing baseline observations during your first hours in a new care environment." Robin's smile softened the professional jargon. "Besides, it gives me time to go over care instructions with Wyatt and Lauren while you fail terribly at pretending you're not miserable."

"I'm not that bad at pretending."

"Jake, you're about as good at hiding pain as I am at pretending to enjoy running," Robin said. "Which is to say, not at all."

Lauren laughed—the first genuine sound of amusement Wyatt had heard from his sister in weeks. "She's got you there."

The next hour passed in a strange mixture of medical routine and uncomfortable awareness. Robin moved through Jake's care with gentle efficiency, explaining each step to Wyatt and Lauren while demonstrating proper techniques for everything from medication administration to safe patient positioning. She answered their questions with infinite patience, never making them feel ignorant despite the complexity of what they were learning.

Wyatt found himself watching her more than he watched the procedures. The way her hands moved with confidence. The soft tone she used when explaining something painful to Jake. The quick intelligence that showed in how she anticipated needs before they became problems.

This was Robin, but also not Robin. The girl he'd known had been smart and kind and occasionally a little shy, but this woman carried an authority and competence that came from years of experience with human suffering. She'd built a life and career he knew nothing about and had become someone capable and confident.

Jake's eyes had started to droop by the time Robin administered his next dose of pain medication, the exhaustion and pharmaceutical relief pulling him toward the sleep he clearly needed.

"Let him rest," Robin said quietly, gesturing to Lauren and Wyatt toward the doorway. "The best things for him right now are sleep and time."

They stepped into the hallway, and Wyatt pulled the bedroom door mostly closed, leaving it open just enough to hear if Jake called out. Lauren sagged against the wall, looking like she might slide to the floor if the house wasn't holding her upright.

"You should rest too," Robin said gently. "The first week is going to be intense, and you'll be more help to Jake if you're not running on fumes."

"I know. I just—" Lauren's voice cracked. "I keep thinking about finding him under that tractor. How still he was."

Robin's hand found Lauren's shoulder, steady and grounding. "He's home now. That's huge. And you saved his life by finding him when you did and getting help there so quickly."

"The doctors said that. But what if—"

"No what-ifs. We deal with what is, not what might have been." Robin's voice was firm but kind. "Jake is alive. He's home. He has excellent medical care and a family who loves him. That's what matters."

Wyatt watched his sister absorb Robin's certainty like rain after a drought, her breathing steadying as she nodded.

"Now go take a nap or at least lie down for an hour," Robin continued.

Lauren hesitated, then squeezed Robin's hand. "Thank you. For everything." She glanced at Wyatt, something complicated in her expression. "I'm going to grab some sleep while I can. Yell if you need me."

She disappeared up the stairs, leaving Wyatt alone with Robin in the narrow hallway.

The silence stretched between them, heavy with twelve years of unspoken words. Robin's professional mask was firmly in place, but Wyatt thought he caught a flicker of something in her eyes—awareness, maybe, or discomfort.

"I need to go; I have other patients to check on today. My contact information is on the business card I attached to Jake's care plan. My direct cell phone number is on that card; don't hesitate to call if you or Lauren have any questions or concerns. I'll be back tomorrow morning around nine."

"Robin—"

"I know this is awkward." She cut him off gently but firmly. "But Jake needs both of us to put aside whatever personal history we have and focus on his recovery. Can you do that?"

The directness left him speechless for a moment.

"Yes," he managed. "Jake's recovery is the priority."

"Good." Robin's expression softened slightly. "He's going to need all of us at our best. This won't be easy."

She headed toward the front door, and Wyatt followed, his mind spinning with questions he had no right to ask. What had her life been like these past twelve years? Was she happy? Had she found someone who appreciated what he'd been too young and too focused on distant dreams to fully value?

She paused on the porch, one hand on the railing, and turned back to face him. The late-morning sun caught the natural highlights in her hair, and for a moment, she looked so much like the girl he remembered that his chest ached.

"Your brother is going to need patience and grace as he adjusts to his limitations," she said. "The psychological impact of this kind of injury can be as challenging as the physical recovery."

"I understand." Wyatt shoved his hands in his pockets to keep from reaching toward her. "I'll do whatever it takes."

Robin studied him for a long moment, her hazel eyes searching his face for something he couldn't name. Then she nodded once, decisively, and descended the porch steps.

Wyatt watched her climb into her SUV and head down the long gravel drive, taillights disappearing around the curve that led toward town. Only when she was completely out of sight did he allow himself to lean against the porch railing and acknowledge what the past few hours had cost him.

Seeing Robin again hadn't just stirred old memories. It had awakened every feeling he'd spent twelve years trying to convince himself he'd outgrown.

He'd thought he'd made peace with the choices that had brought him to this moment. He'd told himself that the ache of first love had faded into nostalgia, that grown men didn't carry torches for relationships that had ended.

But standing on his childhood porch, looking at the empty driveway where Robin's vehicle had been, Wyatt had to acknowledge an uncomfortable truth.

Some feelings didn't fade with time.

Chapter 3

"Your heart rate's good, Jake. Much steadier than yesterday." Robin released his wrist and made a note on her tablet, satisfied with the numbers she was seeing. Two days into home care, and Jake's vitals were holding strong despite the trauma his body had endured.

"Does that mean I get a gold star?" Jake's voice carried more strength this morning, though the tightness around his eyes revealed pain that medication could only dull, not eliminate.

"I'll see what I can do about ordering some stickers." Robin smiled as she adjusted the pillow supporting his lower back. "How did you sleep last night?"

"Better than how I slept in the hospital. Wyatt only had to help me reposition a few times during the night."

Josie, the home health aide who'd arrived promptly at nine that morning, moved to Jake's other side. The woman was in her mid-twenties, with kind eyes and capable hands. "That's good; most people sleep better at home than they do while they're in the hospital. Your body is still adjusting, so be patient."

Robin finished her assessment, checking the surgical sites that were healing as expected and reviewing the medication log Wyatt had meticulously maintained overnight. She also answered Jake's questions about when he might be able to sit up in a wheelchair for longer periods. Throughout the examination, she found herself falling into the comfortable rhythm of her work—the one place where everything made sense and she knew exactly what needed to be done.

"Alright, you're all set for now." Robin capped her pen and tucked it into her pocket. "Josie's going to help you with your daily care routine; she'll be here until five this evening, and I'll be back tomorrow to check on you."

"Lucky me. At least you're better company than the hospital staff."

"I'll take that as a compliment." Robin turned to Josie. "His pain medication is due at noon. The schedule is with his care plan, but call me if you have any questions or concerns."

"Will do." Josie was already gathering supplies for Jake's morning care. "We'll be just fine here."

Robin collected her medical bag and hesitated at the doorway. Through the walls, she could hear the low murmur of voices coming from the kitchen—Wyatt and Lauren discussing something in tones that carried the weight of worry and exhaustion. She'd been hoping to avoid prolonged interaction with Wyatt since that first overwhelming reunion yesterday, but ignoring the strain on Jake's family wasn't good medicine. Stress affected recovery, and both Wyatt and Lauren were showing signs of wearing dangerously thin.

"I'm going to speak with Wyatt and Lauren before I leave," Robin told Josie. "I'll be in the kitchen if Jake needs anything."

She followed the sound of voices down the hallway, her medical bag heavy against her shoulder and her nerves pulled tight. Professional conversations with family members were routine—she'd had hundreds of them over the years. But nothing about this situation felt routine.

The kitchen was exactly as she remembered it from her teenage years spent at this farm—warm oak cabinets, cream-colored countertops, and windows that framed views of the tree groves marching up the hillside. Lauren sat at the large farmhouse table with a coffee mug clutched between her hands, dark circles under her eyes making her look older than twenty-six. Wyatt leaned against the counter, his own mug forgotten beside him while he stared at what appeared to be spreadsheets and order forms scattered across the surface.

They both looked up when she entered.

"How's he doing this morning?" Lauren asked immediately.

"Good. His vitals are stable, and he says he slept better last night than he had been in the hospital, which is normal. May I sit and speak with you both?"

"Of course." Lauren gestured to the seat across from her. "Want some coffee? It's fresh."

"I'd love some, thank you."

Wyatt pushed away from the counter and retrieved a mug from the cabinet—the same blue ceramic mugs the Gibson family had used for as long as Robin could remember. He poured coffee with economical movements, added cream without asking how she took it, and set the mug in front of her.

He remembered. After twelve years, he remembered that she took her coffee with cream but no sugar.

"Thank you," Robin said quietly, wrapping her hands around the warm ceramic and trying not to read too much into the small gesture.

Wyatt returned to his position at the counter as Robin took a sip of coffee, gathering her thoughts. She'd learned over years of home health care that the direct approach usually worked best—dancing around difficult topics only prolonged discomfort.

"I want to talk with you both about Jake's care," she began, "but first, I think we need to acknowledge that this is a rather unique situation." She looked directly at Wyatt, then at Lauren. "I'm quite aware that my history with Wyatt makes this potentially awkward for everyone involved."

Lauren's eyes widened slightly, as if she hadn't expected Robin to address it so plainly. Wyatt's expression remained carefully neutral.

"Robin, you don't have to—" Lauren started.

"Actually, I do." Robin kept her voice gentle but firm. "Jake needs the best possible care, and you both need to feel comfortable asking me questions and expressing concerns. That won't happen if we're all tiptoeing around the fact that Wyatt and I have a history."

Wyatt finally spoke, his voice low. "It was a long time ago."

"It was." Robin met his gaze directly, refusing to let him see how much it cost her to maintain this composure. "We were kids, and we made what seemed like the right decisions at the time. Our breakup was mutual. But that doesn't change the fact that it might make things complicated now."

"Does it?" Lauren asked as she looked between them. "Make things complicated, I mean?"

Robin considered the question carefully. "It makes things different from a typical nurse-patient family relationship. But different doesn't have to mean complicated if we're all honest about prioritizing Jake's recovery above any personal discomfort."

"Jake's recovery is the priority," Wyatt said, and Robin heard the echo of his words from yesterday—steady, certain, and somehow sad. "Nothing else matters."

"Good." Robin took another sip of coffee, using the moment to steady herself. "Then let's talk about what you're both dealing with, because I can see the strain, and stress affects everyone in this house—including Jake."

Lauren sagged in her chair as if Robin had given her permission to finally show how tired she was. "Is it that obvious?"

"To someone trained to observe patients and their families? Yes. You've been running on adrenaline and fear for three weeks. Now that Jake's home, reality is settling in, and you're both trying to manage his care while keeping a major agricultural operation running during your busiest season."

"That about sums it up," Wyatt said. He moved to the table and sat down, his long legs stretched out in front of him. "I'm learning Jake's systems, but there's a steep curve between understanding how things work and actually making good decisions."

"And I'm terrified every time I walk into Jake's room," Lauren admitted. "What if something happens and I don't recognize the signs? What if I give him the wrong medication or do something that makes his recovery harder?"

Robin reached across the table and covered Lauren's hand with her own. They'd known each other through church and community connections for years, a friendship that had weathered the awkwardness of Robin's history with her brother through mutual respect and genuine affection. "That's why I'm here. To teach you what to watch for, to answer questions, and to be available when you're uncertain."

"But you won't be here all the time," Lauren said. "After this first week, it's just Monday, Wednesday, and Friday visits."

"True, but you'll have Josie or Cora or one of our other home health aides here daily, the physical therapist three times a week starting next week, and access to me by phone anytime if you need guidance." Robin squeezed Lauren's hand before releasing it. "Plus, you're more capable than you think. You kept Jake alive by finding him quickly and getting help. You coordinated with doctors, made medical decisions, and got this house prepared for home care. Not only that, but you're stronger than your fear."

Lauren's eyes filled with tears; she blinked them back quickly. "I just keep thinking about how still he was under that tractor. What if I'd been five minutes later? What if—"

"No what-ifs," Robin said firmly, echoing her words from yesterday. "What-ifs will drive you crazy and serve no purpose. Jake is alive. He's home. He's getting excellent care. That's what you focus on."

Wyatt had been watching this exchange with an expression Robin couldn't quite read. When he spoke, his voice carried a roughness that suggested emotion carefully controlled. "What about Jake's prognosis? Off the record, as a friend of the family, what do you really think his chances are for complete recovery?"

Robin took another sip of coffee, choosing her words carefully. "Honestly? I cannot even begin to imagine the outcome for Jake in the future. Spinal injuries are unpredictable, and nerve regeneration happens on its own timeline. Some patients regain full function. Some don't. Jake's young, strong, and otherwise healthy, which are all factors in his favor. But there are no guarantees."

"That's what the doctors said," Lauren murmured. "We were hoping maybe you'd seen enough cases to have a better sense—"

"I've seen patients with similar injuries achieve remarkable recoveries, and I've seen others who face permanent limitations." Robin's tone was gentle but honest. "All we can do right now is follow his recommended care plan, pray about it, and work to keep Jake's spirits high while his body heals."

"How do we do that?" Wyatt asked. "Keep his spirits high when he's facing months of pain and uncertainty?"

"Include him in conversations. Let him be part of farm decisions—the non-stressful ones that don't require physical work. Be with him." Robin ticked off suggestions on her fingers. "Maybe watch a movie together in the evening. Eat meals with him as often as possible. Anything you can do to make him feel less alone, keep his mind engaged, and lessen his worries about his future."

"So basically treat him like Jake instead of a patient," Lauren said.

"Exactly. He needs to feel like himself, not like an invalid. Though you'll have to balance that with making sure he follows medical advice and doesn't push too hard too fast."

"That's going to be the challenge," Wyatt said. "Jake's not exactly known for patience."

"None of you Gibsons are," Robin said before she could stop herself, then felt heat rise in her cheeks at the too-familiar comment.

But Lauren laughed—a genuine sound of amusement that broke some of the tension in the room. "She's got you there, Wyatt. Remember when you broke your arm in tenth grade and tried to go back to farm work after three days?"

"That was different. The cast was fine."

"Mom nearly had a heart attack when she found you trying to operate the chainsaw one-handed."

Despite everything, Wyatt's lips curved into something approaching a smile. "I was young and stupid."

"Some things never change," Lauren teased, and for a moment, the exhaustion lifted from her features.

Robin watched the sibling interaction. This was good—this was what Jake needed from them. Not just medical competence, but the love and normalcy that made recovery feel possible rather than like a prison sentence.

"Speaking of decisions," Wyatt said, his attention shifting back to Robin. "Jake's been asking about getting a laptop set up in his room so he can review business records and keep track of orders. Is that okay from a medical standpoint?"

"Mental engagement is good for recovery, as long as it doesn't cause excessive stress. I'd say start with an hour or two a day and see how he handles it. If he's losing sleep or showing increased pain from tension, we'll need to scale back."

"That's fair." Wyatt made a note on one of the papers in front of him. "What about visitors? Church members and his friends have been calling and asking when they can stop by."

"Short visits are fine—fifteen to twenty minutes for this first week. But stagger them so Jake's not exhausted by too many people in one day." Robin pulled out her phone and opened her notes app. "I'll send you both a list of general guidelines for visitors and activity levels. The key is balance—enough engagement to keep his spirits up, but enough rest for his body to heal."

They spent the next twenty minutes going through questions and concerns, everything from medication side effects to how to handle Jake's frustration when things became difficult. Robin answered each question with the patience and thoroughness that had become second nature after years of this work. She explained positioning techniques to prevent pressure sores, reviewed signs of potential complications that required immediate medical attention, and provided resources for family support groups.

Throughout the conversation, she was acutely aware of Wyatt's presence across the table—the way he listened with complete focus, asked intelligent questions, and took notes with the same meticulous attention to detail she remembered from when they'd studied together as teenagers. He'd always been like this, she realized. Intense and thorough when something mattered to him, unwilling to accept surface answers when a more in-depth understanding was possible.

The realization unsettled her. She'd spent twelve years telling herself that Wyatt had changed, that the boy she'd loved had become someone else entirely. But sitting here watching him absorb information about his brother's care with fierce dedication, she recognized the core of who he'd always been.

Some things, apparently, time didn't change.

"I think that covers everything," Robin said finally, glancing at her phone. She'd been here for two hours and forty-five minutes—longer than she'd intended, but the conversation had been necessary. "Do either of you have any other questions?"

Lauren shook her head. "Just thank you. For everything. For being patient with our questions and for being here for Jake."

"It's my job," Robin said automatically, then softened the words with a smile. "But it's also my pleasure. All of you are like family to me. Jake's a good patient, and remember, you're both doing better than you think you are."

"That's generous," Wyatt said quietly. "I feel like I'm barely holding things together."

"Welcome to crisis management. Nobody feels competent during the crisis itself—that realization comes later." Robin stood, gathering her medical bag. "But for what it's worth, you're handling this well. Jake's lucky to have you both. I'm going to check on Jake before I leave for the day."

She headed toward the doorway, needing to put some distance between herself and this too-comfortable conversation before she said something that crossed the professional boundaries she'd been so careful to maintain.

"Robin?" Wyatt's voice stopped her at the threshold.

She turned back, and the expression on his face made her breath catch—something raw and unguarded that disappeared almost as quickly as it had appeared.

"Thank you," he said simply. "For everything you're doing for Jake. And for being honest about the awkwardness of this situation."

"You're welcome." Robin's throat felt tight. "I'll see you both tomorrow."

She walked down the hallway toward Jake's room, her footsteps echoing on the hardwood floors. Through the partially open door, she could hear Josie's gentle voice guiding Jake through morning stretches, the routine sounds of medical care that had become the soundtrack of her professional life.

Robin took a moment to gather herself in the hallway before entering the room, one hand pressed against the wall as she tried to steady her breathing.

Seeing Wyatt again was affecting her far more deeply than she wanted to admit. Not just the shock of his presence or the memories his face triggered, but something more immediate and unbalancing. The way her pulse jumped when he spoke. The awareness that prickled across her skin when he was in the same room. The traitorous part of her heart that wanted to know if his hands were as strong as they looked or if his voice still dropped to that particular timbre when he was trying not to show emotion.

She'd thought twelve years should have been enough. Enough distance, enough other relationships, and enough life lived separately to have erased the imprint he'd left on her heart.

But standing in the hallway of his family's farmhouse, Robin had to acknowledge an uncomfortable truth.

Some connections didn't sever cleanly. They just learned to hide.

<h1 style="text-align:center">Chapter 4</h1>

"**S**o the poinsettia orders are locked in through December fifteenth?" Wyatt scrolled through the spreadsheet on Jake's computer, squinting at the numbers that represented thousands of plants in various stages of bloom. "After that, we're just filling walk-in purchases?"

"Right." Lauren didn't look up from her own screen across the office, her fingers flying over the keyboard as she updated wholesale customer accounts. "The big box stores placed their orders back in August, and the garden centers finalized theirs in September. We're actually ahead of projections this year."

Wyatt made a note on the pad beside him, adding it to the growing list of details that defined Gibson's Tree Farm operations during their most critical season. Three weeks of managing the farm had given him a crash course in agricultural business complexity—the delicate timing of tree harvesting, the coordination of seasonal employees, and the logistics of delivering fresh product to customers across three states. The work itself felt familiar, rooted in childhood memories of helping his parents. But the business side carried a weight he hadn't fully appreciated when he'd left for forestry school twelve years ago.

"What about the wholesale tree deliveries?" He clicked to another tab, reviewing the schedule Tom had created for coordinating harvest crews with delivery trucks. "The schedule shows we're starting Monday with the Charleston accounts."

"Tom's got that handled. He's been running the tree operation for years now, and he knows it better than any of us." Lauren finally glanced up, pushing a strand of dark hair behind her ear. The afternoon light through the office windows highlighted the exhaustion still evident in her features despite this morning's conversation with Robin. "You can trust him to manage the crews and handle quality control."

"I do trust him. I just want to make sure I understand how everything fits together in case he needs backup." Wyatt saved the file and leaned back in Jake's desk chair, the leather creaking under his weight. The office felt strange—half familiar from childhood memories, half foreign with its updated technology and business systems that had strengthened far beyond the simple operation their parents had run.

The converted office still held traces of the cozy family room it had once been. Built-in bookshelves lined one wall, though agricultural reference materials and business binders had replaced the novels and photo albums their mother had displayed. Two office desks—Lauren's neat workspace faced the windows overlooking the greenhouses, while Jake's more cluttered station commanded a view of the main tree groves. A third chair sat empty near the door, the spot where their father used to sit during evening planning sessions, reviewing the day's work and mapping tomorrow's priorities.

Wyatt's gaze drifted to that empty chair more often than he wanted to admit.

"You're doing great, you know." Lauren's voice pulled him back to the present. "Jake couldn't have asked for better support during all this."

"I'm just trying to keep things running until he's back on his feet," he said as he rubbed his eyes, fatigue settling into his bones. He'd been up several times during the night helping Jake reposition. Plus, he woke up every time Jake made the slightest sound in his sleep. He'd finally risen at dawn and gotten ready for his day, then coordinated with Tom out in the fields before Robin's morning visit.

"Robin seems optimistic about his progress."

"She does. She seems professional and competent."

"She's the best." Lauren saved her work and swiveled her chair to face him directly. "I've known Robin for years, and she's not just skilled—she genuinely cares about her patients. Jake's lucky to have her."

"Good to know." Wyatt met his sister's gaze. "This morning's conversation helped. Clearing the air about the obvious elephant in the room... the awkwardness."

"Is it awkward?"

Wyatt considered lying, then decided Lauren deserved honesty. "Yes, and no. The professional discussion was fine—she knows her stuff, and she made everything clear and manageable. But having her here, in this house." He trailed off, unsure how to articulate the strange displacement he felt. "It's like stepping into a memory that's been edited. Everything's the same but different."

"She's different from what you remember?"

"That's the problem." Wyatt stood and moved to the window, staring out at the tree groves where crews were working. "She's exactly who she always was—kind, competent, and funny when she relaxes.

But she's also this accomplished professional with years of experience I know nothing about. It's disorienting."

Lauren was quiet for a moment, and when she spoke, her voice carried gentle understanding. "Can I ask you something? And I want your honest answer, not polite deflection."

"That depends on the question."

"What do you feel when you see her?"

The directness caught him off guard. Wyatt pressed his forehead against the cool glass, watching his breath fog the window. "Everything I thought I'd put away. Regret. Curiosity. This uncomfortable awareness that she's the standard I've been measuring everyone I've dated against."

"Have you dated many others?"

"A few. Nothing serious." Wyatt turned back to face his sister. "I told myself it was because of the job—too much travel, too many deployments, and the isolation that comes with wildfire work. But standing in that kitchen this morning, watching her explain Jake's care with such patience and expertise, I have to admit I've been comparing everyone to a memory of who she was at eighteen."

"And?"

"And nobody measured up to that memory. Which is ridiculous, because I was the one who left for college, and initially I was the one who suggested we break up. I was the one who chose forestry school four hours away upstate. We agreed that trying to maintain a relationship across that distance wasn't fair to either of us."

"But?"

"But I've spent twelve years questioning that decision." Wyatt returned to Jake's desk and sank into the chair, suddenly exhausted by more than just sleepless nights. "What if we'd tried to make it work? What if I'd selected a school closer to home, or come back every weekend, or—" He shook his head. "What if is a dangerous game."

"Sometimes it's a necessary one." Lauren stood and moved to perch on the edge of his desk, her expression serious. "Wyatt, I've noticed over the years that you come home for holidays, short vacations here and there, and family events; you call regularly, and you're involved in all the major business decisions. But you've kept yourself separate somehow. Like you're visiting your old life instead of living in it."

The observation stung because it was accurate. "I built a career away from here. A good one."

"You built a solitary one. And before you say that's what forestry and wildfire work requires, allow me to point out that most of your colleagues have families. Tom knows three guys at your station who have wives and kids. They make it work."

"That's different—"

"Is it? Or did you structure your life around avoiding the kind of connection that requires your involvement and caring deeply for someone?" Lauren reached over and squeezed his shoulder. "I'm not criticizing. I'm observing. And I wonder if maybe God's timing in bringing Robin back into your life right now is worth considering."

Wyatt wanted to argue, but the words stuck in his throat. How many times had he volunteered for the most isolated assignments? How many relationships had he sabotaged with his unwillingness to discuss anything deeper than surface pleasantries? How many years had he told himself that independence equaled strength?

"What's she like now? Really like, I mean."

Lauren's expression softened. "She's wonderful. Still that girl you knew—warm, funny, genuinely kind—but with this quiet confidence that comes from years of helping people through their worst moments. She volunteers at church, coordinates community fundraisers, and visits elderly patients even when she's off the clock." She paused, choosing her words carefully. "She was engaged a few years ago. To a pharmaceutical sales rep named Liam."

The information hit harder than Wyatt expected. "Engaged?"

"He ended it. Got a promotion that required relocating to Chicago and apparently decided Robin wasn't worth taking with him." Lauren's voice carried an edge of protective anger. "She didn't talk about it much, but I could tell it devastated her. Made her question her worth, I think."

Wyatt's hands clenched into fists. "What kind of man—"

"The kind who doesn't recognize what he has until it's gone," Lauren said pointedly. "Sound familiar?"

The parallel wasn't subtle. Wyatt stood and paced to the window again, needing movement to process the surge of emotions. Anger at this Liam person who'd hurt Robin. Regret over his own choices. Fear that twelve years had created a gap too wide to bridge. And underneath it all, a dangerous hope he would rather not acknowledge.

"I can't do this right now," he said finally. "Jake needs me focused on his recovery and keeping the farm running. I don't have the emotional bandwidth for—" He gestured vaguely. "Whatever this is."

"I'm not suggesting you start anything. I'm recommending you be open to friendship. Robin's going to be here every day this week, then three times a week after that. You will see each other regularly. It would be easier for everyone if you could find a way to be comfortable around each other."

"I thought that's what this morning's conversation accomplished."

"Professional comfort, maybe. But I'm talking about genuine friendship. The kind where you don't look like someone punched you in the chest every time she walks into a room."

"I don't—" Wyatt stopped, recognizing the futility of denial. "Is it that obvious?"

"To someone who knows you? Yes." Lauren's smile was sympathetic. "You don't have to figure everything out right now. Just... don't shut the door completely. Be kind. Be present. See where God leads."

"And if He leads nowhere? If Robin has no interest in reconnecting beyond professional necessity?"

"Then at least you'll know. And you can move forward instead of carrying this question mark for another twelve years." Lauren stood and stretched, joints popping audibly. "Speaking of moving forward, are you coming to church tomorrow? It would do you some good to get out of this house for a few hours."

"I should stay here with Jake—"

"Jake will be fine for two hours. Josie or another home health aide will be here, and you can keep your phone on." Lauren fixed him with a look that brooked no argument. "You need community right now. And honestly, people are starting to ask why you're avoiding services since you've been home."

"I haven't been avoiding—"

"You've been here three weeks and haven't attended once." Lauren crossed her arms. "That's avoiding. Come tomorrow. You might be surprised how good it feels to be part of something bigger than crisis management and farm operations."

Wyatt wanted to refuse, but his sister's expression told him the discussion was over. Besides, she was right. He'd been using Jake's care and farm responsibilities as justification for isolation, the same pattern he'd established in his Forest Service life.

"Robin still goes to Laurel Ridge Community Church," Lauren added, her tone deliberately casual. "Has for years. She usually sits with her parents if they come or sometimes with me and Jake."

The implication was clear. Attending church meant seeing Robin outside the context of medical care, in the community setting where she'd built her life during the twelve years he'd been gone. The prospect filled him with equal parts anticipation and dread.

"Not tomorrow, sis. I'd rather stay here in case Jake needs me. Maybe next Sunday."

"Okay." Lauren headed toward the office door. "I'm going to check on Jake and see how his afternoon is going. You should probably review the employee schedule for next week—Tom sent it over this morning, and there are a few shifts that need approval."

She disappeared into the hallway, leaving Wyatt alone with his thoughts.

He returned to Jake's desk and pulled up the schedule Lauren had mentioned, but the names blurred together. His mind kept circling back to this morning's kitchen conversation—the way Robin had addressed their history with such direct honesty, establishing boundaries while simultaneously acknowledging the discomfort. She'd been kind and firm, yet professional and genuine.

She'd also been careful not to show whether seeing him again affected her at all.

Maybe it didn't. Maybe she'd moved on completely, built a full life that had no room for memories of teenage romance. Possibly the only person struggling with unresolved feelings was himself.

Through the window, the afternoon sun cast long shadows across the tree groves that represented three generations of the Gibson family legacy. Everything that mattered was right here. Family, legacy, community, and purpose.

So why did he feel like the most important thing was still somehow just out of reach?

Three weeks ago, he'd been fighting a prescribed burn in the Monongahela Forest, living the life he'd carefully constructed around independence and professional achievement. Now he sat in his childhood home, managing family crises and rediscovering connections he'd spent twelve years avoiding.

And at the center of it all stood a hazel-eyed woman who represented everything he'd convinced himself he didn't need.

Chapter 5

"Easy now. Just let me know if anything hurts worse." Wyatt slid one arm carefully beneath Jake's shoulders while supporting his brother's head with his other hand, moving with the deliberate slowness Robin had shown yesterday. Early morning sunlight pressed against the bedroom windows, and upstairs, Lauren was still sleeping. Wyatt wasn't about to wake her for something he could handle alone.

"Little to the left," Jake said through gritted teeth, his face pallid. "The pressure on my lower back is killing me."

Wyatt adjusted his grip and lifted, mindful of the surgical sites and the complex arrangement of braces that kept Jake's spine and pelvis immobilized. The pillow repositioning that looked simple when Robin did it felt terrifyingly complicated when you were the one responsible for not causing additional damage.

"Better or worse?"

"Give me a second." Jake's breathing came shallow and quick, the way it did when pain spiked beyond manageable levels. After a moment, some of the tension left his jaw. "Actually better. Thanks."

"Don't thank me yet. I still need to adjust the pillow under your knees." Wyatt moved to the foot of the bed, exhaustion making his movements clumsy. He'd been awake since two-thirty, when Jake's restless sounds had pulled him from the fitful sleep the recliner chair allowed. Three medication doses administered throughout the night, four repositioning attempts, and countless moments of lying awake listening to make sure Jake was still breathing steadily.

His back ached from the chair's awkward angle, his neck had a crick, and his eyes felt like someone had rubbed them with sandpaper. But Jake was home, which was what mattered.

"I bet you never imagined yourself helping me like this," Jake said as Wyatt positioned the pillow to take pressure off his brother's legs.

"Yeah, well, I never imagined a lot of things about the past three weeks." Wyatt returned to the recliner and sank into it, rubbing his face with both hands. "But you're my brother. Where else would I be?"

"Back in your real life." Jake's voice carried an edge of guilt that made Wyatt look up. "You shouldn't have to put everything on hold because I was stupid enough to try moving a tree alone."

"You weren't stupid. You were doing what needed to be done." Wyatt leaned forward, resting his elbows on his knees. "And this is my real life too, Jake. I haven't lived here in years, but this farm, this family—it's still home. Still matters."

"Does it? Or are you just doing what you think you should do?"

Wyatt studied his brother, seeing past the pain and frustration to the fear underneath. Jake had built something extraordinary here, taking their parents' modest operation and expanding it into a thriving agricultural business. And now he lay helpless, dependent on others for basic care, uncertain whether he'd ever run the farm again.

"You want the honest answer?" Wyatt asked.

"Always."

"Coming back scared me. Not just because of what happened to you, but because I'd spent years convincing myself I'd outgrown this place." Wyatt gestured vaguely at the room, the farm beyond the windows. "I told myself I'd built something better, something that mattered more than this farm. But standing in that kitchen yesterday watching Lauren barely hold herself together, realizing you might never walk again, and working with Tom to keep operations running—" He paused, searching for the right words. "This matters. You matter. And I'm doing my best to honor what you've built here."

"You're doing more than that." Jake's voice was rough. "You've stepped into systems you barely understand and kept everything running smoothly. Tom says you're a natural at delegation and problem-solving. Lauren told me that you've been incredible with the stress you're under. I know if the situation were reversed, I'd do the same for you. But that doesn't make me any less grateful you came home."

The Gibson family had never been particularly demonstrative with emotions—their parents had shown love through actions rather than words, through shared work and support rather than verbal affirmation. But lying in that hospital bed, Jake had come too close to permanent loss for either of them to pretend words didn't matter.

"You're going to be okay," Wyatt said finally. "However long it takes, whatever adjustments we need to make—we'll figure it out."

"And if I'm not? If I never walk again, never run the farm the way I planned—"

"Then we'll adapt. Lauren's brilliant with the business side, I can handle agricultural operations for however long you need, and Tom's more than capable of managing day-to-day operations." Wyatt held his brother's gaze.

The sound of a vehicle in the driveway interrupted their conversation. Through the window, Wyatt caught a glimpse of Robin's SUV pulling up to the house. He glanced at the clock—five minutes before nine.

Footsteps sounded in the hallway moments later, and then Robin appeared in the doorway, medical bag over her shoulder and her hair pulled back in a ponytail.

"Good morning," she said. "How's everyone doing?"

"Tired," Jake admitted. "But upright. Sort of."

Robin's smile was sympathetic as she moved into the room and set her bag down. "I wanted to let you both know that Josie's running late this morning. She had a flat tire on the way here, but she should arrive within the next thirty minutes or so."

"That's fine," Wyatt said, standing to move around and stretch.

Robin pulled out her tablet and began making notes, her movements efficient and practiced. "How did you sleep last night, Jake?"

"Honestly? Not great." Jake shifted slightly, wincing. "I couldn't seem to get comfortable. Kept waking up with pain in my lower back and hips."

"And medications? Any issues with the schedule?"

"No issues." Wyatt said. "Everything was administered on time. Pain levels stayed mostly around six or seven, spiking to nine during repositioning."

Robin nodded, making notes. "That's actually pretty typical for this stage of recovery. Your body's still adjusting to being out of the hospital environment." She glanced at Wyatt. "How did you sleep?"

The question caught him off guard. "I didn't, really. Every sound Jake made woke me up. I kept thinking maybe something was wrong, or he needed help, or—" He rubbed the back of his neck. "It was a rough night."

"That's completely normal for family caregivers," Robin said gently. "But we need to make sure you're getting adequate rest, or you'll burn out fast." She turned back to Jake. "Let's do your assessment and morning medications, then we'll talk about adjusting the care plan to give Wyatt more sustainable sleep."

Wyatt watched as Robin moved through Jake's morning care routine. She checked vitals, examined surgical sites, and assessed pain levels and range of motion—all while maintaining a running conversation that kept Jake engaged.

"Your incision sites are healing beautifully," she said, carefully cleaning one of the surgical wounds on Jake's abdomen. "No signs of infection and minimal inflammation. You're doing everything right."

"That's all Wyatt and Lauren," Jake said. "They've been following your instructions to the letter."

"Good caregiving makes a huge difference in recovery outcomes." Robin prepared Jake's morning medications, checking each dose against the schedule before administering them. "How's your breathing? Any tightness or difficulty?"

"A little tight."

Robin pulled out her stethoscope and listened to Jake's lungs, her face a mask of concentration. Wyatt found himself studying her profile—the way her brow furrowed slightly as she focused, the competent set of her shoulders, and the gentle way she touched Jake's back while positioning the stethoscope.

She was beautiful. More beautiful than she'd been as a teenager, though he hadn't thought that possible. The girl he'd known had been pretty in an uncomplicated way, all fresh-faced youth and natural charm. But the woman she'd become carried a depth that went beyond physical appearance—confidence earned through years of helping people through their worst moments, compassion refined by experience, and a quiet strength that made her presence feel like safety.

"Wyatt?"

He blinked, realizing both Robin and Jake were looking at him expectantly.

"Sorry, what?"

"I asked if you could hand me the blood pressure cuff on the table next to you," Robin said, and was that amusement in her eyes?

"Right, yeah." Heat crept up his neck as he retrieved the device, feeling like an idiot for zoning out. "Here."

"Thanks." Robin wrapped the cuff around Jake's arm and started the reading. "You should probably grab some coffee, Wyatt. You look like you're about to fall asleep standing up."

"I'm fine."

"You're exhausted," she corrected gently. "And that's not criticism—it's observation from someone who sees sleep-deprived caregivers regularly. If you don't take care of yourself, you can't take care of Jake."

Before Wyatt could respond, Lauren appeared in the doorway, still in her pajamas and robe, her dark hair tousled from sleep. "Morning, everyone." She took one look at Wyatt and frowned. "You look terrible."

"Good morning to you too, sis."

"I'm serious. You look like you haven't slept in days." Lauren moved into the room, studying him with the same concern Robin had shown. "Have you changed your mind about coming to church? Or would you rather stay home and try to get some actual rest?"

The thought of church—seeing people, making conversation, pretending to be more functional than he felt—made exhaustion settle deeper into his bones. "I'm staying home. I need sleep."

"That's probably wise," Robin agreed, recording Jake's blood pressure reading. "You need a solid block of uninterrupted rest, or you're going to make yourself sick."

Lauren crossed her arms, her gaze moving between Wyatt and the recliner chair. "We really should look into buying a rollaway cot or something. Wyatt cannot continue sleeping in that chair, and I'd rather not either when it's my turn."

"That chair is miserable," Wyatt admitted. "I think I've developed a permanent spinal curve that matches its shape."

"I'll shop online today and order something decent," Jake offered. "A rollaway cot or maybe one of those camping beds that's actually comfortable."

"That would be helpful," Lauren said.

Robin began packing up her supplies. "I'm going to leave the morning care in Josie's hands when she arrives. Wyatt, can you help me position Jake so he can have breakfast?" She glanced at Wyatt. "And make sure you actually sleep today. That's medical advice, not a suggestion."

"Yes, ma'am." The response came automatically, echoing years of taking orders from supervisors and incident commanders. Robin's lips curved into a small smile that made something warm unfold in his chest.

"Alright, I need to head upstairs and get ready for church," Lauren said. "I'll check on you both before I leave." She disappeared into the hallway, her footsteps echoing up the stairs.

Robin and Wyatt worked together to position Jake for breakfast, adjusting pillows and raising the bed to an angle that would make eating easier. Their movements synchronized easily—Wyatt following Robin's lead as she directed where to place support and how much elevation Jake needed. Her hands brushed his once as they both reached to adjust the same pillow, and Wyatt found himself acutely aware of how close she was.

"That should work until Josie arrives," Robin said, stepping back to assess their work. "Jake, are you good?"

"I'm good. Thanks."

Robin gathered her medical bag and jacket, preparing to leave. At the doorway, she paused and turned back toward Wyatt, her hazel eyes serious in the morning light. "I'll have my cell phone on silent while I'm in church, but you can text me if you need anything. Even if it's just a question about Jake's care."

"I appreciate that."

"And Wyatt?" She held his gaze. "You really need to rest. Not just lie down—actually sleep. If Jake needs help, that's what Josie is here for; let her handle it. That's what she's trained to do."

"I'll try."

"Don't try. Do it. Jake needs you functional, not running on fumes and adrenaline."

She left before he could respond, her footsteps fading down the hallway followed by the sound of the front door closing. Through the window, Wyatt watched her SUV pull down the gravel drive, taillights disappearing around the curve.

"She's right, you know," Jake said from the bed. "You look like death warmed over."

"Thanks for the vote of confidence."

"I'm serious. Go lie down in a real bed and actually sleep. I'll be fine until Josie gets here. Lauren can bring me breakfast later."

Wyatt wanted to argue, but exhaustion made his eyes feel heavy and his thoughts sluggish. "I'll sleep with my cell phone near me; if you need me, just text or send Josie up to wake me."

As Wyatt walked out of the room and climbed the stairs to his room, Robin's face kept appearing in his mind—the gentle way she'd examined Jake, the professional competence that made complex medical care look effortless, and the concern in her eyes when she'd told Wyatt to rest.

She'd grown into someone extraordinary. Not just competent and skilled, but genuinely caring in a way that went beyond professional duty.

Twelve years ago, he'd loved a girl who was kind and sweet and made him believe in futures built on more than solitary ambition. Now he found himself drawn to the woman she'd become—capable and confident, yet still carrying that essential warmth that had first caught his attention when they were teenagers discovering what it meant to care about someone beyond yourself.

The realization was dangerous. He was here for Jake, for the farm, and for a family crisis that required his complete focus. He didn't have room for the complicated feelings Robin's presence awakened—the attraction that went beyond memory into genuine admiration for who she was now and the uncomfortable awareness that seeing her again had cracked open doors he'd spent years keeping tucked away.

As Wyatt lay down and drifted to sleep, all he saw was a certain set of hazel eyes that still mesmerized him to this day.

Chapter 6

"You've been quiet today, sweetheart." Dottie Fitch said as she snapped green beans into a bowl.

Robin, who'd been peeling carrots, paused and looked up.

The Sunday afternoon light slanted through the kitchen windows of her parents' homestead. Robin had been grateful for the task when her mother handed her the peeler—grateful for something to do with her hands, something to focus on besides the turmoil that had been churning through her thoughts since Friday morning when she'd walked into the Gibson farmhouse and found Wyatt there.

"Just tired from the week." Robin resumed peeling, watching orange curls fall into the bowl. "New patient cases always take extra energy while I'm learning their routines."

It wasn't a lie. Jake Gibson's care required significant attention, coordination, and patience. But it wasn't the whole truth either.

"How is Jake doing? I heard about the accident from Martha at the diner. Terrible things, tractors, and hills."

"He's doing well, considering. The surgical repairs were extensive, but he's young and otherwise healthy. That makes a significant difference in recovery outcomes."

"It does. And his siblings, how are they doing? Must be hard on them, worrying about both the farm and Jake's recovery."

"They're managing." She kept her voice steady. "Lauren's handling a lot more than she normally does, and Jake's worried about the farm, but they've got excellent employees. Tom Hartwell's been with them for years and knows the operations inside and out."

"That's Tom who grew up off Route 9, right? His mother was in my quilting circle before we moved out here." Dottie dumped the green beans into a colander, rinsing them under the tap. "Always thought that boy would end up working with plants. Had a gift for growing things even as a child."

The surrounding kitchen reflected five years of her parents' retirement, the life they'd built after leaving behind Chuck's decades of underground work pulling coal from West Virginia's mountains and Dottie's years of hospital nursing. The space felt both smaller and somehow more generous than the house Robin had grown up in.

Copper pots hung from a rack Chuck had installed above the island, their bottoms gleaming despite years of use. The countertops showed wear patterns from hundreds of meals prepared; the butcher block scarred from years of chopping. A wooden cross hung beside the kitchen window, hand-carved by Chuck during his first winter of retirement when his hands had needed something to do.

This life they'd created here—simpler, quieter, deeply rooted in land and seasons and each other—represented everything Robin had always assumed her future would hold. A partner to build something lasting with. Work that mattered but didn't consume. Time for gardens and Sunday dinners and the kind of peace that came from knowing exactly where you belonged.

"Robin." Her mother's hand covered hers, stilling the peeler that had been working the same carrot for too long. "What's going on, honey?"

The gentleness in Dottie's voice nearly undid her. Robin set down the peeler, staring at the half-naked carrot in her hand. Her mother had always possessed the uncanny ability to see past whatever front Robin presented. Years of nursing had honed Dottie's instincts for reading people, but motherhood had given her something deeper—the capacity to feel her children's pain as if it were her own.

"It's complicated." Robin's throat felt tight.

Dottie squeezed her hand once before releasing it, returning to her own work with that characteristic patience that never demanded more than someone was ready to give. The beans went into a pot with water and a sprinkle of salt. The bread came out of the oven, its crust golden and crackling as it cooled on the rack.

The front door opened and closed, Chuck's footsteps crossing the living room toward the kitchen. He appeared in the doorway wearing his usual flannel shirt and jeans.

"Firewood's all stacked for the week." He kissed Dottie's cheek, then Robin's, his beard tickling her temple the way it had since she was small enough to ride on his shoulders. "Smells like heaven in here. When do we eat?"

"Twenty minutes." Dottie moved to the oven, checking the pot roast. "Why don't you two set the table?"

The dining room opened off the kitchen through a wide doorway that had once held a door before Chuck removed it, preferring the way the spaces flowed together. The table—oak, handmade by Chuck's father, and refinished by Chuck himself—could seat eight, but today would hold a setting for three.

The dining room walls held photographs spanning decades—Robin and her siblings at various ages, school pictures and graduation photos, and Chuck and Dottie's wedding portrait from over forty years ago.

On the mantle above the stone fireplace sat their family Bible, its leather cover cracked with age and use. Her parents had spent this morning studying it together. Their own private church service. Every so often they needed quiet time with the Word and each other, without distractions, and preferred to stay home instead of attending church.

"Your mother tells me you've got a new patient." Chuck arranged napkins with the same precision he'd once used to set charges in mine shafts. "Jake Gibson, right?"

"Yes, he's doing well, all things considered."

"Good family, the Gibsons. I've known them since before you were born. Dan and Mary did things right, raising those kids. They're hard workers and honest." Chuck paused, his weathered hands resting on the table's edge. "Heard Wyatt came back to help out on the farm. How's he doing?"

The name landed like a stone dropped into still water, ripples spreading outward in concentric circles of implication.

"He seems to be doing okay given the circumstances." She managed to keep her voice even. "He took family medical leave from his position with the Forest Service, is what Lauren told me."

"That right?" Her father's tone stayed casual, but his blue eyes, sharp despite sixty-eight years of living, watched her with the same attention he'd once given to roof bolts and gas detectors. "Seems like I remember him being important to you, once upon a time."

Once upon a time. Such a gentle way to describe the relationship that had consumed her entire junior and senior years of high school, the boy who'd made her believe in forever before reality taught them both that some forevers could end.

"That was years ago, Dad." Robin filled the glasses with more care than the task required. "We were kids."

"Kids who loved each other." Chuck's statement held no judgment, just fact. "Your mother and I, we always thought you two made sense together. Similar values, both good hearts, and both stubborn enough to make the other one better."

"Dinner's ready." Dottie appeared in the doorway carrying the pot roast on a platter that had belonged to Chuck's mother, saving Robin from having to respond.

They settled into their usual seats after bringing the rest of the food to the table. Chuck sat at the head of the table with Robin and Dottie flanking him. The pot roast sat center stage, surrounded by carrots and potatoes that had cooked in its juices, the green beans glistening with butter, and the bread releasing its yeasty perfume.

"Shall we?" Chuck extended his hands to each of them, waiting until their fingers linked before bowing his head. "Lord, we thank You for this food, for the hands that prepared it, and for the day You've given us to share it together. We ask Your blessing on this meal and on our conversation, that we might speak truth in love and listen with open hearts. Guide our Robin as she serves Your children through her work and give her wisdom for every decision she faces. In Jesus' name, Amen."

"Amen," Robin and Dottie echoed.

The food made its way around the table, plates filling with generous portions of Dottie's cooking. The pot roast fell apart at the touch of a fork, tender and rich. The vegetables carried the perfect balance of salt and butter.

For several minutes, they ate without speaking. This was another thing Robin had always loved about her parents' home—the way quiet felt peaceful rather than awkward, the way they could simply be together without needing to fill every moment with words.

"So," Dottie said eventually, her tone deceptively casual as she buttered her bread. "Tell us about the Gibson farm. I've heard it's quite an operation these days. I remember when it was just Christmas trees, but Martha mentioned they've expanded significantly."

Robin swallowed her bite of pot roast, buying time. "They have. Nut trees—walnuts, pecans, and some chestnuts. The poinsettia operation is substantial. Jake and Lauren have really done an outstanding job with their farm."

"Wyatt must have his hands full trying to help out while Jake is down." Her father's observation came with a pointed look.

Robin set down her fork, the metal clicking against the china. "He's managing, as far as I can tell."

"How's it going working around him after all these years?" Dottie asked.

Robin picked up her water glass, taking a slow sip while she considered her answer.

"It's not easy... it's complicated."

"Complicated how?" Chuck's question held no pressure, just gentle interest.

Robin looked between her parents—her father's weathered face reflecting decades of hard labor and harder choices, her mother's softer features showing the marks of years spent caring for people in their most vulnerable moments. They'd built a life together that had weathered financial stress, raising three children, Chuck's dangerous work underground, and Dottie's night shifts at the hospital. They somehow emerged with their love not just intact but deeper, richer, and more beautiful for having been tested.

What did they know about navigating the space between what was wise and what your heart wanted? What wisdom had they earned through forty-plus years of choosing each other, day after day, in seasons of plenty and seasons of struggle?

"I thought I was past it." The admission came out quieter than she'd intended. "Past him, past us, past whatever we had that felt so important at eighteen. For years I've told myself that Wyatt had been puppy love, that what I felt then was just hormones and proximity and the romance of first love."

"But?" Dottie prompted when Robin fell silent.

"But seeing him for the first time in twelve years..." Robin's fingers traced the condensation on her water glass. "It didn't feel past. It felt immediate and terrifying and like no time had passed at all. And now we've had to work together the past few days coordinating Jake's care, managing his pain, and handling his anxiety about the farm—and it was..."

"Natural?" Her father supplied.

Robin nodded, not trusting her voice.

"Like breathing," Dottie added.

"Yes." Robin looked up, meeting her mother's eyes. "Like breathing. Like we'd been doing it together for years instead of living completely separate lives. And that scares me, because I don't know if it's real or if I'm just romanticizing what we had because crisis situations make everything feel more intense."

Chuck set down his fork, leaning back in his chair. "Can I tell you what I see when I look at you today?"

Robin waited.

"I see my daughter, who's spent the past three years convinced she's not enough. Not enough for Liam, not enough for any man to fight for, not enough to deserve the kind of love that actually shows up when life gets hard. Liam was never right for you, and when he broke your engagement off and left for good... well, it was a blessing in disguise."

The accuracy stole Robin's breath.

"And I see," he continued, his voice rougher now, "that Wyatt has shaken that lie you've been telling yourself. Because maybe—just maybe—the reason nothing's worked since him is because you've been comparing every man to a standard they couldn't meet. You already knew what right felt like, and settling for anything less was always going to leave you empty."

"Chuck." Dottie's hand found her husband's, squeezing gently, though her eyes stayed on Robin. "What your father's saying, perhaps less delicately than necessary, is that we've watched you these past three years since Liam. Building a good life, serving people who need you, and being faithful in your work and your walk with the Lord. All important things. But, honey, we've also watched you convince yourself that wanting more—wanting partnership, wanting love that doesn't quit when things get complicated—somehow makes you weak or naïve."

"It doesn't," her father said firmly. "It makes you human. It makes you someone created for relationship, for partnership, and for the kind of love that sharpens both people into better versions of themselves."

Robin blinked against the sudden burning in her eyes. "But what if I'm wrong? What if I'm just vulnerable because Liam hurt me and Wyatt represents some kind of safe nostalgia? What if working together feels natural because we're both competent people, not because there's anything real between us?"

"What if the Lord brought you back into each other's paths because His timing is finally right for what couldn't work when you were younger? What if this situation—Jake's injury, Wyatt's return, and your nursing skills being undoubtedly what they need—isn't coincidence but providence?" Dottie said.

Providence. The idea that God ordered steps, that He placed people in each other's paths for purposes beyond human understanding, and that sometimes what looked like crisis was actually opportunity.

"I'm supposed to maintain professional boundaries." Robin's protest sounded weak even to her own ears. "Jake's my patient. I can't let personal feelings compromise his care."

"No one's suggesting you compromise anything," Chuck said. "But there's a difference between maintaining boundaries and building walls around your heart. One protects the appropriate space. The other prevents any connection from forming at all."

Dottie rose to clear their plates, waving Robin back down when she moved to help. "Dessert in a minute. I made your favorite—blackberry cobbler with the berries I froze last summer."

While her mother worked in the kitchen, Robin sat with her father. Through the window, the late afternoon sun gilded the dormant garden beds and painted long shadows across the grass. A cardinal called from the oak tree near the house, its whistle sharp and clear in the November air.

"Your mother and I," Chuck said eventually, "we almost didn't make it, you know. The early years of our marriage..."

Robin looked at him in surprise. Her parents' love story had always seemed inevitable and unshakable.

"I was working long shifts underground; she was doing nights at the hospital. We'd go days barely seeing each other, and when we did, we were both too tired to be good company. Started telling myself that maybe we'd married too young, that maybe we wanted different things from life."

He paused, his weathered hands folded on the table.

"Then one day—you were maybe two years old—I came home from a particularly brutal shift. Explosion at the coal mine; three men didn't make it out. And I walked into the house covered in coal dust and fear, and your mother took one look at me and said, 'You need to talk about it.'"

"And I said, 'I'm fine.' Because that's what you do, right? You protect the people you love from the hard parts. But she said—and I remember this like it happened this morning—she said, 'Chuck Fitch, I didn't marry you to be protected from your life. I married you to share it. All of it. The good, the hard, and the terrifying. You need to trust me with the truth of what you're feeling and start realizing this is a marriage and not just two people living in the same house.'"

Robin had never heard this story. Never imagined her parents' relationship as anything other than solid, certain, and complete.

"Changed everything," Chuck continued. "Realizing that real partnership—the kind that lasts, that grows deeper instead of just older—requires letting someone see you at your worst and trusting they'll still choose you. Requires risking your heart every single day, not just at the beginning when it feels easy."

Dottie returned with three bowls of cobbler, the blackberries dark and sweet beneath golden, sugared crust, vanilla ice cream melting into purple rivers along the edges.

"What your father's trying to say," Dottie settled back into her chair, "is that sometimes the Lord gives us second chances not because we failed the first time, but because we weren't ready, then for what He wanted to build through us. You and Wyatt at eighteen—you made the choice that was right for that moment. You both needed to grow into yourselves and to understand who you were individually before you could build something lasting together."

"But now?" Robin's question came out barely above a whisper.

"Now," her mother smiled, "you're both thirty years old. You've built careers that matter to you. You've experienced heartbreak and learned what you don't want. You've developed faith that's been tested instead of just inherited. And the Lord has placed you back in each other's paths at a moment when Jake needs exactly your skills and Wyatt needs exactly your presence."

"So you're saying I should..." Robin trailed off, unsure how to finish the sentence.

"We're saying," Chuck interjected, "that you should stop trying to protect yourself from possibilities and start trusting that the God who created you knows what He's doing. Stay professional with Jake's care—absolutely. But don't use professionalism as an excuse to keep your heart locked away from opportunities the Lord might be offering."

They ate their cobbler in thoughtful silence, the sweetness of the berries and the richness of the ice cream grounding Robin in this moment.

"Whatever happens," Dottie said as Robin helped clear the dessert bowls, "whatever you discover about your feelings for Wyatt or his feelings for you, remember that you are not almost enough for anyone. You are exactly enough, perfectly made for purposes we can't always see but can trust are good."

Robin hugged her mother in the kitchen doorway, breathing in the familiar scent of her that had meant safety her entire life. "Thank you."

"That's what we're here for." Dottie pulled back, cupping Robin's face in her weathered hands. "Walk with the Lord on this one, sweetheart. He'll show you which path to take."

Chapter 7

The scent of fresh coffee hit Robin as soon as she opened the door to the Gibson home. Wyatt was in the kitchen, his flannel shirt untucked and his dark hair still disheveled.

Something warm and unwelcome fluttered in Robin's chest at the sight. This was exactly the kind of domestic normalcy that made maintaining professional distance feel increasingly complicated.

"Morning."

Wyatt turned, his green eyes still carrying traces of sleep. "Robin. You're early."

"Ten minutes." She set her bag on the kitchen table.

"Coffee?" He gestured toward the pot. "Fair warning though—I make it stronger than most people prefer."

"Strong works for me. Cream, no sugar."

"I remember. I mean—Lauren takes hers the same... so it's easy to remember how you take yours as well. I'll grab the cream from the fridge."

Robin bit back a smile at his awkwardness.

"How was yesterday? Were you able to sleep some in the afternoon?" She asked.

"I did. Then I caught up on paperwork while Jake and I watched a movie. Did you have a good day yesterday?"

"I did. I had dinner with my parents after church." Robin wrapped both hands around the coffee mug, grateful for something to do with them. "Mom made pot roast."

"Dottie's pot roast." Something wistful crossed Wyatt's expression. "I remember that from youth group dinners back in high school. And her fresh garden vegetables... your mom could make a feast out of whatever was in season and have everyone convinced they'd eaten like royalty."

"She hasn't lost her touch. How's Jake doing this morning? Any changes?"

The shift to professional topics seemed to ground them both. Wyatt straightened from his casual lean against the counter, his expression becoming more focused.

"He had a rough night. Pain woke him up around two; he couldn't get comfortable no matter how many pillows we tried. He finally took another dose of medication around three and managed a few more hours of sleep." Wyatt set down his mug. "He's awake now, though."

Robin nodded, already mentally adjusting her assessment plan. Increased nighttime pain this many days post-hospital could indicate several things—healing progression causing nerve sensitivity, positioning issues, the mattress itself, or potentially something requiring closer monitoring.

"Let me go check on him."

The door stood partially open. Jake lay propped against a fortress of pillows, his tablet in his hands.

"Morning, Jake," Robin said as she entered the room.

Jake's face brightened despite the pallor of discomfort still clear in his features. "Robin. Thank goodness. Wyatt's been hovering like a worried mother hen since dawn. Please tell him I'm fine so he'll go do something productive."

"I'll evaluate your definition of 'fine' and make my own determination." Robin set her coffee on the dresser and retrieved her stethoscope from her bag. "Your brother mentioned you had increased pain last night. Want to tell me about it?"

Behind her, Wyatt had followed into the room, standing near the doorway.

"It wasn't that bad." Jake shot Wyatt a pointed look. "Someone's being dramatic."

"Someone was groaning in pain loud enough to wake me." Wyatt crossed his arms. "That qualifies as 'that bad' in my book."

Robin smiled despite herself as she helped Jake adjust his position for the examination. The brothers' dynamic reminded her of her brother Zane's protective instincts toward her and her sister Ella—that particular blend of exasperation and fierce love that defined sibling relationships.

"Let's see what we're working with," she said as she began checking Jake's surgical sites. The incisions showed appropriate healing progression—no signs of infection, swelling within expected parameters. His vitals remained stable, though his elevated heart rate suggested lingering pain despite his attempts to downplay it.

"Wound healing looks good," Robin said, making notes on her tablet. "But I think we need to adjust your pain management schedule. I'm thinking it's too long between doses, letting the pain build instead of staying ahead of it."

Robin finished her assessment, then pulled up Jake's medication schedule on her tablet. "I'm going to adjust the timing so you're taking your pain medication every four hours. That should help you maintain better comfort levels, especially at night."

"Whatever you think is best." Jake shifted against the pillows, wincing slightly. "You're the expert."

"Speaking of which—" Robin glanced toward the doorway where Wyatt still stood. "I wanted to show you both some exercises that will help with Jake's recovery. Range of motion work that you can do between my visits to help maintain circulation and prevent complications."

Interest sparked in Wyatt's eyes as he moved closer. "What kind of exercises?"

"Simple ones." Robin positioned herself at the foot of the bed where she could access Jake's legs. "Jake, I'm going to demonstrate with your right leg first. Let me know if anything causes more than mild discomfort."

She gently lifted Jake's right leg, supporting it with both hands. "First exercise is ankle pumps and circles. These help maintain circulation and prevent blood clots, which is crucial while mobility is limited."

Robin slowly flexed Jake's foot up toward his shin, then pointed it down again, moving through the motion with careful deliberation. "You want the movement to be smooth and controlled—not forced. Think of it like pumping the pedals on a bicycle—gentle pressure."

"Feels fine," Jake confirmed. "Actually, it feels kind of good to move something that doesn't hurt."

"That's the idea." Robin demonstrated the circular motion next, rotating Jake's ankle slowly clockwise and then counterclockwise. "Circles work different muscle groups and keep the joint from getting stiff. You'll want to do about ten pumps and ten circles in each direction. Do this several times a day." She glanced at Wyatt. "Want to try the left ankle so you get the feel for it?"

Wyatt positioned his hands the way Robin had demonstrated, supporting Jake's ankle and lower calf.

"Like this?" He flexed Jake's foot upward.

"Almost. You want your hand here." She placed her fingers on his wrist, guiding his position slightly lower on Jake's calf. "That gives you better leverage and control. Now, when you flex—"

She demonstrated by moving Wyatt's hand through the motion, acutely aware of the warmth of his skin beneath her fingers and the way his breathing seemed to still slightly at her touch.

Focus, she reminded herself as she released his wrist and stepped back, trying to ignore the way her pulse had kicked up.

"Better?"

"Perfect. Now try the circles."

Wyatt moved through the rotation with more confidence this time, though his angle on the second circle strayed off course. Robin reached out instinctively, her hands covering his to guide the movement back to the proper plane.

"Keep the rotation smooth and even," she instructed. "Not too fast, not too much pressure."

From his position on the bed, Jake made a small sound that might have been a cough or might have been something else entirely. Robin glanced up to find him watching them with unmistakable interest, his gaze flicking between Robin's hands on his brother's and Wyatt's focused expression.

Jake caught his sister's eye as Lauren appeared in the doorway carrying a white bakery box.

Robin quickly released Wyatt's hands and stepped back, heat creeping up her neck. "You've got it now. Just remember—gentle, controlled, and consistent."

"Gentle, controlled, consistent," Wyatt repeated. "Got it."

"What did I miss?" Lauren set the bakery box on the dresser, the scent of fresh pastries immediately filling the room. "I brought muffins from Taste of Heaven. Shirley said to tell you she's praying for you, Jake."

"Tell her thanks the next time you see her." Jake's expression softened at the mention of the bakery owner's name. "And thanks for picking those up; I've been craving Shirley's baked goods."

Lauren distributed paper napkins and muffins. She handed one to Robin with a warm smile. "You need to keep your strength up too."

"I won't argue with fresh muffins." Robin accepted the offering, touched by Lauren's thoughtfulness. The muffin's interior was still slightly warm when she broke it open, studded with plump blueberries and crowned with a sugar-crystal crust.

"So," Lauren perched on the edge of a chair near Jake's bed, her muffin balanced on a napkin. "I spent a few minutes this morning fielding calls from wholesale customers wanting to confirm their Christmas tree orders. Apparently, word got out about Jake's accident, and everyone's worried we won't be able to fulfill contracts."

"What did you tell them?" Jake's question came sharply with concern despite his casual tone.

"The truth—that we have excellent employees, Wyatt's coordinating operations, and Gibson's has never failed to deliver on a commitment. Most of them relaxed once they heard Wyatt was back. Your name still carries weight in the industry, Wyatt."

Robin watched Wyatt's expression shift at his sister's words—pride mixed with something that looked like guilt.

"Tom's doing the heavy lifting," Wyatt deflected. "I'm just making sure nothing falls through the cracks."

"You're being modest." Lauren turned to Robin. "He's usually out the door by seven every morning coordinating crews, checking inventory, and reviewing quality control. The farm's still running smoothly."

"Because I'm not second-guessing Tom's decisions the way Jake does." Wyatt's teasing held affection. "No offense, brother, but you micromanage."

"Someone has to maintain standards." Jake's protest lacked heat. "You'll understand when you see how many customers expect perfection during the Christmas season."

Robin finished her muffin and started demonstrating one more exercise—gentle knee bends that kept Jake's leg muscles from stiffening while respecting his healing limitations. She had to keep her time with Jake focused. "Lauren, Wyatt, this is another exercise you can do for Jake. Bend his knee just to here—" she positioned Jake's leg at the appropriate angle. "Not too far, not forcing anything. The goal is movement, not maximum range."

She guided Wyatt and Lauren through the technique, her professional focus firmly back in place. Jake tolerated the movements well, his earlier humor returning as he teased Lauren about her gentle-but-awkward handling of his leg.

"You look like you're defusing a bomb," Jake said. "I'm not going to explode."

"You might if I accidentally hurt you." Lauren stuck her tongue out at her older brother. "Some of us aren't naturally gifted at medical procedures."

The easy banter among the siblings created an atmosphere of warmth that made her smile. She glanced at her watch, noting that her scheduled visit was right on track. Her next patient wasn't until noon, but she needed to document Jake's assessment and medication adjustments before leaving.

"I should finish my notes and let you all get back to your morning." Robin pulled up the electronic charting system on her tablet, her fingers moving efficiently across the screen. "Jake, remember what I said about the new pain medication schedule. Follow it; don't wait until you're miserable to take the next dose."

"Yes, ma'am."

"And both of you—" Robin glanced between Wyatt and Lauren. "Keep up with those exercises. They seem simple, but they make a real difference in preventing complications and speeding recovery."

"We will." Wyatt's assurance came with a nod.

Robin finished her charting and began gathering her supplies, tucking her stethoscope back into her bag and making sure she had everything she'd brought.

"Same time tomorrow?" Lauren asked from her position near Jake's bed.

"Nine tomorrow." Robin confirmed. "Call if anything changes before then or if Jake's pain isn't better managed with the new schedule."

"Will do." Lauren walked with her toward the bedroom door. "Thanks for everything, Robin. We really appreciate how well you're taking care of him."

Chapter 8

"Perfect, Josie. That's exactly the angle I need." Robin's voice carried quiet encouragement as she and Josie adjusted Jake to be more comfortable.

Wyatt stood near the doorway of Jake's bedroom, watching the careful choreography of medical care that had become part of their daily routine. Tuesday morning sunlight streamed through the windows, catching the concentration on Robin's face as she checked Jake's incisions—the same expression she'd worn in high school when studying for chemistry exams, that slight furrow between her brows that meant she was processing information with absolute focus.

"How's the pain level today?" Robin asked, her fingers gentle as she palpated the healing tissue around Jake's incision.

"Better." Jake's response came without his usual attempt to downplay discomfort. "Slept through most of the night. Whatever you changed with the medication schedule seems to be working."

"Good. That's what I hoped to hear."

Josie helped Jake shift position, providing the physical support that allowed Robin to focus on the incisions and wounds on his back.

"You're doing great work, Josie," Robin said. "The positioning techniques you're using are textbook perfect."

"I learned from the best." Josie's warm smile crinkled the corners of her eyes.

Robin finished her assessment and charting, then spent several minutes reviewing Jake's care plan with Josie, their conversation filled with medical terminology that Wyatt only partially understood. He'd learned enough over the past several days to follow the general concepts—wound healing progression, pain management protocols, mobility goals—but the depth of knowledge both women demonstrated reminded him that nursing required far more expertise than most people realized.

"Alright, Jake." Robin tucked her tablet into her bag. "I'll see you tomorrow morning. Remember what I said about the exercises—consistency matters more than intensity."

"Yes, ma'am."

Josie gathered her supplies, preparing to help Jake with his morning routine after Robin's departure. Wyatt knew he should probably return to the office where Lauren was coordinating wholesale tree deliveries or head out to the greenhouses where Pete was monitoring the poinsettia production. Tom had the field crews well in hand, but there were always a dozen small decisions requiring attention during the farm's busiest season.

Instead, he asked Robin, "Do you have time for coffee?"

Robin paused in organizing her medical bag, surprise flickering across her features.

"I—" She glanced at her watch. "I have some time before I need to be at my next visit."

Relief crashed through him with unexpected force. Robin followed him down the hallway, her footsteps quiet against the hardwood floors.

"Have a seat." Wyatt busied himself at the coffeemaker, grateful for something to do with his hands.

He measured coffee grounds with more concentration than the task required, acutely aware of Robin's presence behind him.

"So," he said as the coffee began its familiar percolation. "Tell me about your work. How did you end up specializing in home health trauma recovery?"

Robin leaned back in her chair, her hazel eyes taking on the distant focus that suggested she was reaching back through years to find the beginning of that story.

"I did hospital nursing first, right after I got my RN degree. Medical-surgical floor at the regional hospital in Beckley. Good experience, learned a lot about acute care." Her fingers traced absent patterns on the table's worn surface. "But I kept noticing that the patients who struggled most weren't the ones with the most severe injuries. They were the ones who were going home without proper support systems. Some had families overwhelmed by medical equipment they didn't understand. I noticed loved one's trying to navigate recovery alone because insurance wouldn't cover enough home health visits."

Wyatt turned to face her, leaning against the counter as the coffeemaker gurgled behind him. "That's what drew you to home health?"

"That's what convinced me I could make more of a difference working with patients in their own environments rather than in a hospital room. When someone's recovering at home, you're not just treating injuries. You're helping them rebuild their entire lives around new limitations. Teaching families how to be caregivers. Prob-

lem-solving everything from bathroom modifications to meal prepa-
ration."

"Sounds complicated."

"It is. But it's also incredibly rewarding when you see someone who couldn't imagine managing at home eventually thriving
there." Robin's smile carried genuine satisfaction. "I had a patient last
year—an elderly gentleman who'd broken his hip in a fall. The hospital
wanted to send him to a nursing facility because he lived alone and
they didn't think he could manage. But he'd lived in the same house
for sixty years, and the idea of leaving it broke his heart."

Wyatt poured coffee into two mugs, adding cream to Robin's. He
carried both mugs to the table and settled into the chair across from
her.

"What happened?"

"His family and I worked with his neighbors, his church community, and a physical therapist to create a support system that let him stay
home safely. We modified his bathroom with grab bars and a shower
chair. We set up a meal delivery service and coordinated with friends
who could check on him daily." Robin wrapped her hands around the
mug, the gesture achingly familiar. "Six months later, he was walking
independently, cooking his own meals, and living exactly the life he
wanted."

"Because of you."

"Because of many people working together. I just helped coordinate
the pieces."

Wyatt took a long sip of coffee, studying the woman across from
him. The shy teenager, who'd needed encouragement to speak up in
youth group, had grown into someone who orchestrated complex care
plans and advocated fearlessly for the elderly and her patients. The
transformation was both surprising and entirely logical—she'd always

possessed that quiet strength, that intuitive understanding of what people needed. She'd just learned to wield those gifts with confidence.

"Lauren mentioned you're involved with a lot of community organizations," Wyatt said. "Church fundraisers, meal trains, that kind of thing?"

Robin's face lit up in a way that made his chest tighten. "The community here has always been special. Everyone shows up for each other when things get hard. I enjoy helping wherever I'm needed."

"What does that look like?"

"Last month, the Thompson family lost their house in a fire. Within forty-eight hours, we had temporary housing arranged, clothing drives organized, and enough meal donations to feed them for weeks." Robin's pride in their small town radiated from her. "Martha Kincaid turned her diner into donation central. Leslie Williams provided flowers for their temporary apartment to make it feel more like home. The whole town just mobilized."

Wyatt thought about his years living away from Laurel Ridge, the way his Forest Service colleagues remained friendly but ultimately separate from each other's lives outside work. "I'd forgotten what that level of community feels like."

"It's easy to forget when you're not immersed in it daily. I imagine your work keeps you pretty isolated?"

Wyatt stared into his coffee mug, watching steam rise in lazy spirals.

"More isolated than I realized until recently." The admission emerged rough and honest. "Fire season means weeks or months deployed to remote locations. Living in crew camps and working twenty-hour days occasionally. The work itself is intense—life-or-death decisions, physical exhaustion, and the kind of adrenaline that doesn't let you sleep even when you're off shift."

"That sounds incredibly demanding."

"It is. But it's also what I thought I wanted." Wyatt glanced up to find Robin watching him. "Conservation work matters. Protecting wilderness areas, managing forest health, responding to fires that threaten communities—all of it feels important and purposeful."

"I sense a 'but' in there somewhere."

"But somewhere along the way, I realized that home meant going back to an empty house ninety minutes from my family here. My colleagues are professionals who do their jobs well, but we're not—" He searched for the right word. "We're not building anything together beyond successful fire suppression and general forestry work. At the end of the day, everyone scatters to their real lives, and I'd gotten good at convincing myself that the work was enough."

"Until Jake's accident?"

"Until Jake's accident forced me to come back here and remember what it feels like to be part of something that extends beyond a career choice." Wyatt ran a hand through his hair. "Being here, working on the farm, watching Jake's recovery, helping Lauren coordinate operations—it's reminded me that I've spent twelve years building a career but not a life."

The kitchen fell quiet except for the ticking of the wall clock and the distant sound of farm equipment somewhere outside. Wyatt wondered if he'd revealed too much, if Robin would see his admission as criticism of the choices he'd made in his life.

Instead, she said, "I think a lot of us spend our twenties figuring out the difference between those two things."

"Tell me about your family. How are your parents doing?"

Robin's smile returned, warm and genuine. "They're wonderful. Retired a little over five years ago—Dad from the mines, Mom from hospital nursing. They bought a place outside town, way up in the mountains, nothing fancy, just enough land for Mom's garden and

Dad's woodworking shop. They're living their best homesteading life."

"Dottie retired from nursing?"

"After forty-two years. Said she'd earned the right to grow vegetables instead of checking blood pressures." Robin's laugh held deep affection. "They're so happy now. They lead a simple life and spend all their time together."

"And your siblings? Zane was—what, five years older than us?"

"Seven years older, actually. He's a doctor now, working at the hospital in Fayetteville. Married to Tabitha, he has twin sons who just turned three." Robin's pride in her brother shone through. "He specializes in emergency medicine, which makes sense. Zane was always the calm one during any family crisis."

Wyatt remembered Zane vaguely—serious, protective of his younger sisters, the kind of older brother who'd made teenage Wyatt nervous. "Sounds like he found his calling."

"He did. And Ella—my little sister—she's doing wonderful too. She owns a marketing company in Charleston. She started it three years ago with just herself and a laptop; now she's got five employees and clients all over the state."

"Ella... drama club and student council, right?"

"That's her. All that energy she used to drive our parents crazy with? She channeled it into building a business. She's married to a great guy, Adam, who keeps her grounded while encouraging her wildest ideas."

"Your whole family sounds like they're thriving."

"We've been blessed. What about Lauren? She seems to be handling incredible pressure with Jake down and the farm's busiest season hitting simultaneously."

Wyatt felt his own pride surge at the mention of his sister. "Lauren's tougher than she looks. When Mom and Dad died, she was still in college. She's had every reason to fall apart back then, but instead she came home, completed her degree online, and threw herself into learning every aspect of the farm business. She's the reason we've been able to expand into wholesale operations. Jake's got the agricultural expertise, but Lauren's business acumen is what transformed us from a local Christmas tree farm into a regional supplier."

"She speaks highly of you too. She says the farm's running smoothly under your direction."

"She's being generous. Tom Hartwell knows these operations better than I do. I'm just trying not to screw up what she and Jake have built here. The first few weeks were tough," he admitted. "When Jake was still in the hospital, I was scrambling to learn how everything worked now. The farm's changed so much since I left. We've got computerized inventory systems, wholesale contracts with specific quality standards, and greenhouse operations I barely understood. I kept thinking I was going to make some catastrophic mistake that would destroy everything."

"But you didn't."

"I didn't because Jake and Lauren hired good people who actually know what they're doing. Tom doesn't need my supervision—he needs someone to coordinate the big picture so he can focus on his expertise. Pete knows more about poinsettia cultivation than I'll ever learn. Emma Kate works wherever she's needed on the farm. She's getting the Christmas Shop ready to open soon. Emma Kate works as if she's running a military operation. My job is mainly staying out of their way while making sure communication flows."

"You're being modest. Lauren says wholesale customers were panicking until they heard you were back."

Wyatt felt heat creep up his neck. "That's because of Dad's legacy, not mine. People trust the Gibson name because of the reputation he established."

"But you're the one honoring that reputation." Robin leaned forward slightly. "That matters, Wyatt. A lot of people would have panicked or delegated everything. You came home, learned systems, and kept a major agricultural operation running smoothly during its most critical season."

The praise settled uncomfortably in his chest, mainly because it came from Robin—whose opinion had always mattered more than anyone else's, even after twelve years of separation.

"It helps that I'm motivated." He tried for lightness. "Jake would haunt me if I let the farm fail."

Robin laughed, the sound filling the kitchen. "Fair point. He does seem like the type to take business failure personally."

"He's obsessive about maintaining standards. Always has been." Wyatt found himself smiling at memories of his brother's perfectionism. "When he was sixteen, he spent an entire summer hand-pruning every tree in the Fraser fir section because he didn't trust the seasonal workers to get the shape exactly right. Dad finally had to order him to delegate before he worked himself into exhaustion."

"Some things don't change. He's questioned every aspect of his care plan, wanting to understand the reasoning behind each decision."

"That must make him a challenging patient."

"Actually, it makes him an excellent patient. People who understand their treatment are more likely to comply with instructions. Jake asks questions because he wants to participate in his own recovery, not because he's trying to be difficult."

Wyatt thought about his brother's personality—the way Jake approached every challenge with fierce determination, refusing to accept limitations. "He's lucky to have you coordinating his care."

"I'm lucky to have a patient who's willing to do the work that recovery requires." Robin glanced at her watch, and Wyatt's stomach dropped at the realization that their time was running out. "Speaking of which, I should probably head out. My next visit is in Fayetteville, and traffic can be unpredictable."

"Right. Of course." Wyatt stood as Robin gathered her medical bag, disappointment settling heavy in his chest. They'd been talking for almost an hour. The time had passed quickly, their conversation flowing with the same natural ease he remembered from high school. Back then, they could talk for hours about everything and nothing, never running out of things to share.

Apparently, twelve years hadn't changed that.

Robin stood, slinging her bag over her shoulder. "Thanks for the coffee. And the conversation."

"Anytime you want coffee, the pot's usually on."

"I'll remember that."

Wyatt walked her to the front door, holding it open as she stepped onto the porch.

"Drive safe," he said.

"I will. See you tomorrow." Robin descended the porch steps with the same quiet grace that characterized all her movements.

Wyatt remained in the doorway as she walked to her car parked in the gravel drive. She set her medical bag in the passenger seat, then glanced back toward the house. Their eyes met across the distance, and something passed between them—recognition, possibility, the acknowledgment of a connection neither seemed ready to name but both felt acutely.

Then she was in her car, the engine starting, gravel crunching under tires as she pulled away. Wyatt watched until her vehicle disappeared around the curve in the drive, the red of her taillights winking out behind the tree line.

Chapter 9

Robin traced the edges of Jake's surgical incision with methodical precision, her brow furrowed in concentration as she examined the healing tissue.

"Any pain when I press here?"

"Barely," Jake said as he shifted against his pillows, his movements noticeably easier than they'd been a week ago. "More like manageable discomfort than actual pain."

"Good. That's exactly what I want to hear." Robin made notes on her tablet, then moved to check his range of motion, guiding his leg through exercises with the same meticulous attention she'd applied to the wound examination.

Josie stood nearby, ready to assist if needed.

Wyatt studied Robin's expression as she worked—the slight furrow between her brows when she was processing information, the competent efficiency of her movements that somehow conveyed both professionalism and genuine care. He'd memorized these details over the past week, cataloging them in his mind.

"Vital signs are excellent." Robin's announcement pulled Wyatt from his thoughts. "Blood pressure stable, heart rate normal, and his temperature perfect. Wound healing is progressing beautifully, Jake—no signs of infection, swelling is minimal, and tissue regeneration is ahead of schedule."

"Ahead of schedule?" Jake's question carried hopeful interest. "Does that mean I can start doing more?"

"It means your body is responding exceptionally well to treatment." Robin said as she set down her tablet. "Your pain tolerance has improved significantly, your mobility is increasing, and you're following all care instructions with excellent compliance."

Pride flickered through Wyatt at the mention of Jake's progress. They'd worked hard this past week—maintaining medication schedules, performing exercises consistently, and ensuring proper rest balanced with appropriate activity. Hearing those efforts validated by Robin felt like a small victory worth celebrating.

"So I'm healing well?" Jake pressed.

"You're healing remarkably well. In fact, your recovery has exceeded my expectations for the first week home from the hospital."

Relief washed through Wyatt with unexpected force. He hadn't fully acknowledged how much worry he'd been carrying about his brother's recovery, the constant low-level anxiety that something might go wrong despite their best efforts. Hearing Robin's confident assessment lifted the weight that had been pressing on his chest ever since Jake had come home.

"That's great news." Wyatt said. "Really great."

"It is great news." Robin pulled up a different screen on her tablet. "Which is why I'm comfortable transitioning Jake's care schedule from daily visits to a Monday-Wednesday-Friday routine, just as we'd hoped for, effective immediately."

The words took a moment to register. When they did, something cold and sharp twisted in Wyatt's gut.

"Monday-Wednesday-Friday?" He heard himself repeat the schedule as if confirming he'd understood correctly. "Starting when?"

"Starting next week. Josie or Cora will still visit daily to assist with daily care, but I'll transition to three times per week for assessment and treatment planning."

Jake whooped from his position on the bed, his enthusiasm immediate and genuine. "No offense, Robin, but I'm getting tired of being poked and prodded every day before breakfast."

"None taken." Robin's laugh held warmth. "Most patients feel that way about daily visits. This is a positive sign that you're healing well."

Wyatt struggled to process the information through the unexpected dismay flooding his system. Less intensive care meant Jake was recovering successfully—which was exactly what they all wanted, what they'd been working toward since his brother's homecoming. The reduction in visits represented medical progress, evidence that their collective efforts were yielding results.

So why did it feel like a loss?

"What about warning signs?" Wyatt asked. "Things we should watch for between your visits?"

Robin glanced up from her tablet, her hazel eyes meeting his. "Excellent question. The main concerns at this stage would be signs of infection—increased redness, swelling, warmth around the surgical site, any drainage that's discolored or foul-smelling, or a fever above 100.4 degrees. Also watch for sudden increases in pain that aren't managed by medication or any changes in mobility that seem like setbacks."

Wyatt nodded, committing the information to memory while simultaneously recognizing that his questions served dual purposes. Yes, he genuinely needed to understand Jake's care requirements. But he was also extending their conversation, creating reasons for Robin to keep talking.

"What about physical therapy?" He grasped at another medical concern. "Should we be coordinating with a specialist or continuing the exercises you've taught us?"

"The exercises I've shown you and Lauren should continue as tolerated." Robin pulled up another screen, her professional focus firmly in place. "And remember, Jake has a physical therapy plan in place already. Regular sessions with a physical therapist begin next Monday in the afternoon."

"And pain management? We stick with the current medication schedule?"

"Yes, though we may start reducing the dosage if Jake's pain continues improving at this rate."

"Remember," Robin continued, addressing both brothers. "Jake's progress shouldn't create overconfidence about his limitations. You're healing well, Jake, but you're still healing. Patience matters as much now as it did the first day home."

"I know, I know." Jake's response carried good-natured exasperation. "No pretending I'm recovered before I actually am."

"Exactly. The Gibson family tendency toward stubborn independence is admirable, but it won't serve you well if it leads to setbacks that could have been prevented."

Josie chuckled. "She's got your number, Jake. I've seen you test your limits when you think no one's paying attention."

"Busted." Jake's grin held zero repentance.

Robin gathered her supplies, tucking her stethoscope into her medical bag.

"You know," Wyatt said, "you're welcome to stop by for coffee even on your off days. Not for medical reasons, just—" He fumbled for casualness he didn't feel. "Just if you're in the area and want to take a break."

Robin's hand stilled on her bag's zipper, her expression shifting to something Wyatt couldn't quite read. Surprise? Uncertainty? Something that looked almost like regret?

"I appreciate the offer, Wyatt. Really. But maybe it's best if we share coffee on my regularly scheduled days. When I'm here for Jake's care."

The gentle refusal landed with more force than it should have. Robin's tone held nothing harsh, no judgment or rejection—just professional boundaries being carefully maintained. She was Jake's nurse. Wyatt was her patient's brother.

She finished organizing her bag, checked that she had all her supplies, and then turned to Jake.

"I'll see you Monday morning, Jake. Keep up with your exercises, follow the medication schedule, and don't push yourself too hard."

"Yes, ma'am."

"Josie, keep up the good work," she said.

"Will do." Josie said with a smile.

Robin glanced toward Wyatt, her hazel eyes meeting his for just a moment. Then she was moving toward the doorway, her footsteps quiet against the hardwood floor.

"Drive safe," Wyatt managed, the words automatic and insufficient.

"Always do." Robin paused at the bedroom door, looking back at Jake rather than Wyatt. "Have a good weekend, Jake. I'll see you on Monday."

Then, she was gone. Wyatt heard the front door open and close, heard the sound of her car door, and then heard her engine starting.

Four days until Monday. Ninety-six hours until she would walk back through that door.

"You okay, big brother?" Jake's voice broke through Wyatt's thoughts. "You look like someone just canceled Christmas."

Wyatt forced his expression into something he hoped resembled normal. "Fine. Just processing the schedule change."

"Right. Because that's obviously why you invited Robin for off-day coffee visits." Jake's knowing grin made Wyatt's face heat. "Nothing to do with the way you've been watching her like a man who can't quite believe she's real."

"Don't you have exercises to do?" Wyatt deflected, his discomfort obvious even to himself.

"Not until after breakfast." Jake's satisfaction at having landed his teasing blow radiated from him. "But I'll let it drop. For now."

Wyatt escaped to the hallway, Jake's laughter following him out of the bedroom.

Chapter 10

"So the key thing to watch for," Robin said to Josie as they stood near Jake's bedside, "is any regression in his mobility. If he seems stiffer or more resistant to the exercises, that could indicate he's overdoing it between sessions."

Josie nodded, making notes on her care pad. "And I should contact you right away if I notice any changes, correct?"

"Exactly. Better to catch potential problems early than wait until they become setbacks." Robin pulled up Jake's updated care plan on her tablet. "His pain management is working well, wound healing continues to progress beautifully, and his overall recovery trajectory exceeds expectations."

"Music to my ears," Jake said from his position propped against pillows. Four days had made a noticeable difference—his color looked better, his movements carried less hesitation, and his characteristic humor had returned full force. "Does this mean I get to graduate from invalid status soon?"

"You were never an invalid." Robin's correction came with a smile. "You're a patient recovering from significant trauma. There's a difference."

"Tell that to my brother, who still hovers like I might spontaneously combust if left unsupervised." Jake shot a pointed look toward the doorway where Wyatt leaned against the frame, coffee mug in hand.

"I don't hover. I monitor. Responsibly."

"Whatever."

Robin bit back a laugh at their banter. "Remember that Jake's physical therapy program starts today. The physical therapist should arrive around one this afternoon. She'll evaluate his current range of motion and create a progressive exercise plan tailored to his specific injuries."

"More exercises." Jake's dramatic sigh made Josie chuckle. "Just what I've always wanted."

"These will be different from what I've shown you—more intensive, more targeted. The physical therapist specializes in post-surgical recovery and will push you harder than I do." Robin tucked her tablet into her bag. "Which is exactly what you need at this stage."

She reviewed a few more care coordination details with Josie, then gathered her things, preparing to leave.

"Do you have time to see something before you go?" Wyatt's question caught her off guard.

She glanced at her watch. Her next appointment wasn't until one. "What did you have in mind?"

"Lauren and Emma Kate have been working like crazy getting the Christmas Shop ready for the season. I thought you might like to see what they've created so far. The displays are pretty impressive this year."

Robin grinned. "I'd love that. I actually visit the Christmas Shop every year—it's one of my favorite traditions during the holiday season. I collect ornaments, and I always find the most beautiful and unique pieces here."

"I didn't know that."

"I have ever since the Christmas Shop opened nine years ago. Every year the displays and selection get better. I can't wait to see what Lauren and Emma Kate have planned this season."

"Then you're in for a treat." Wyatt said as he set his coffee mug on the dresser.

Robin followed Wyatt outside the house, and down the gravel drive that curved gently from the house.

They walked side by side, their footsteps crunching on the gravel. The farm spread around them in all directions—orderly rows of Christmas trees stood as far as the eye could see in geometric precision, the greenhouse complex gleamed, and the nut orchards stood bare-branched and dormant in their winter rest in the far distance.

"Lauren had this vision ten years ago," Wyatt explained as they descended the drive. "She'd just gotten her business degree and was convinced she could transform our old barn into something special. I was skeptical—worried about the investment and the risk of expanding beyond what we knew. But Lauren created projections, vendor lists, and marketing plans. She had answers for every concern Jake and I both had."

"She's remarkable. The business acumen combined with creative vision—that's a rare combination."

"It is. Jake handles the agricultural side brilliantly, but Lauren's retail operation is what transformed us from a seasonal Christmas tree farm into a year-round enterprise." Pride filled Wyatt's voice. "The poinsettia wholesale business, the expanded nut orchards, the gift shop revenue—all her innovations."

They reached the gravel parking area beside the Christmas Shop. The building itself rose before them—a beautifully restored barn that somehow maintained its rustic charm while radiating commercial polish. Wide porches wrapped the front, decorated even now with seasonal greenery and empty planters that would soon overflow with winter arrangements. Large windows reflected the morning sunlight, offering glimpses of the magic contained within.

"It's even more beautiful than I remembered from last year," Robin said, pausing to take in the full effect.

"Wait until you see inside." Wyatt climbed the porch steps and held the door open for her.

The scent hit first—cinnamon and vanilla and pine and something sweetly spiced that made Robin think of cookies baking and candles burning and every Christmas memory she'd ever cherished. Then her eyes adjusted to the interior lighting, and she found herself standing in what could only be described as a winter wonderland.

Everywhere she looked, Christmas magic demanded attention. The space was a series of connected rooms, each flowing naturally into the next while maintaining distinct themes and atmospheres. To her right, a traditional Victorian Christmas display featured deep reds and forest greens, with vintage ornaments and classic decorations that could have graced homes a century ago. To her left, a modern metallic section sparkled with silver and gold, geometric shapes, and contemporary designs that spoke to current trends.

"Oh my word," Robin breathed, turning slowly to take in the full scope. "This is incredible. Lauren's expanded even more."

"She has. Emma Kate deserves most of the credit for the displays," Wyatt said, watching her reaction with obvious pleasure. "She has an eye for creating little vignettes that tell stories. See that corner over there?"

He gestured toward a display featuring a miniature Christmas village—tiny buildings with lights glowing in windows, miniature people ice skating on a mirror pond, and evergreen trees dusted with artificial snow. The attention to detail was extraordinary, each element carefully positioned to create a scene that invited viewers to step into its magical world.

"It's like something from a storybook." Robin moved closer, enchanted by the craftsmanship. "Look at the little church with the stained-glass windows. And the train station with actual tiny luggage on the platform."

"Emma Kate and Lauren both source these pieces from all over—some are antiques, some are new handcrafted items from local artisans. Emma Kate creates different scenes each year, and according to what Lauren has told me, people come back specifically to see what she's imagined." Wyatt moved to stand beside her, close enough that Robin could feel the warmth of his presence. "This year's theme is 'Homecoming.' All the little details suggest people traveling back to their mountain roots for the holidays."

The nearness of him made Robin acutely aware of how alone they were in this vast space. Just the two of them, surrounded by Christmas magic.

Robin forced herself to step toward another display, putting space between them that felt simultaneously wise and disappointing. "What's this section?"

"Handcrafted ornaments from West Virginia artisans. Lauren's built relationships with craft guilds and individual artists throughout the region. She provides them with a venue and promotion, and they provide unique pieces you won't find anywhere else."

Robin examined the ornaments with genuine interest—blown glass in jewel tones, hand-painted wooden designs featuring mountain landscapes, and intricate wire sculptures shaped into snowflakes and stars. Each piece bore a small tag identifying the artist and their hometown, personal touches that transformed commercial transactions into connections with real people creating beautiful things.

"I need to come back when you're open," Robin said, already mentally cataloging which ornaments she wanted for her collection. "My tree is going to be overloaded this year."

"How many ornaments do you have?"

"Honestly? I stopped counting around three hundred." Robin's admission came with a self-deprecating laugh. "I have a problem. Every year I tell myself I'm only buying two or three new ones, and then I see something beautiful and unique, and suddenly I'm walking out with a dozen."

"Three hundred ornaments? That must be quite a tree."

"I actually have two trees. One in my living room with my special ornaments, the handcrafted pieces, and the ones with stories behind them. And one in my dining room with themed ornaments that coordinate with my holiday décor. I know it's over the top, but I love it."

"It's not over the top. It's joy. Pure, unfiltered joy in something that matters to you. That's not something to apologize for."

Their eyes met across a display of rustic wooden signs bearing Christmas messages in elegant script.

Robin broke eye contact first, moving toward another section where shelves overflowed with holiday décor in every imaginable style. Contemporary minimalist arrangements sat beside elaborate traditional displays. Sleek silver and blue designs contrasted with warm copper and burgundy themes. Everywhere she looked, thoughtful curation invited shoppers to imagine how these pieces might transform their own spaces.

"Lauren and Emma Kate's color coordination is brilliant," Robin observed, running her fingers along a display of coordinating ribbon and garland. "Everything in each section works together, but there's enough variety that people can mix and match according to their preferences."

"They both spent months planning the layout."

They moved through the shop at a leisurely pace, Wyatt explaining the various vendor relationships Lauren had cultivated. He pointed out items created by church members—quilted table runners, knitted stockings, and carved wooden nativity scenes. He showed her work from local craft guilds—pottery, metalwork, and woven baskets. Not only that, but he identified pieces from regional artists who appreciated having their creations featured in such a well-respected venue.

Pride filled his voice with every explanation, revealing the deep respect he held for his sister's contributions to their family enterprise. Robin was drawn not just to the beautiful displays but to Wyatt's obvious love for his family and appreciation for the work that sustained their legacy.

"What's your favorite part?" Robin asked as they paused near a display of vintage-inspired ornaments. "Of all this Christmas magic, what speaks to you most?"

Wyatt considered the question with the same thoughtfulness he brought to everything. "Honestly? The families. When we're open and customers are browsing, there's this energy—kids pressing their noses against displays, parents debating color schemes, and grandparents sharing memories of Christmases past. Lauren and Emma Kate created a space here that's not just about selling decorations. It's about giving people a place to dream about how they want Christmas to feel in their homes. I was here for a week last year right after the season opened to help out some on the farm, and I'll never forget it. I truly enjoyed watching the customers shop here."

The insight surprised Robin. She'd expected Wyatt to choose something related to the business side of the operation. Instead, he'd identified the human element, the way commerce and connection intertwined during this magical season.

"That's beautiful," she said.

Their tour concluded near a corner display that caught Robin's breath. Photographs covered an entire wall—families selecting trees over the years, children posed beside towering evergreens, and parents carrying fresh-cut Fraser firs toward waiting vehicles. The images spanned decades, creating a visual history of Gibson's Tree Farm's place in community Christmas traditions.

Robin studied the photographs, with emotion tightening her throat. She recognized faces—neighbors, church members, and families she'd known since childhood. And there, in one faded photograph that must have been taken twenty years ago, she saw her family. Her mother and father, impossibly young. Zane as a teenager, helping their dad carry a tree. Ella as a small child, bundled in a winter coat and mittens. And Robin herself, maybe ten years old, grinning at the camera while holding a candy cane.

"That's us," she whispered, pointing to the image. "I remember that day. It was snowing, and your dad—he gave all the kids candy canes and hot chocolate. We must have spent three hours walking through the groves before we found the perfect tree."

Wyatt moved closer to examine the photograph. "I remember the candy canes. Dad did that every year—said it made the tree selection process easier when kids had something sweet to keep them patient."

"It worked." Robin smiled at the memory. "I remember my parents spent more time speaking with your mom and dad than actually looking at trees."

"They were close friends back in the day. When Mom and Dad died, your parents were at the funeral, at the house afterward, and they checked on us for months afterward. Small-town connections—they matter more than people realize."

Robin nodded, unable to speak past the emotion in her throat. This farm, this family, these traditions—they were woven into her life in ways she hadn't fully acknowledged until this moment.

"We open to the public the day after Thanksgiving," Wyatt said, breaking the reflective silence. "That's when everything gets really crazy for about four weeks. Customers come from all over the state, tour buses from surrounding towns, and local families... the farm is an annual tradition for many."

"I usually come the first weekend in December. Beat the last-minute rush, but still get the full experience."

"You know—" Wyatt seemed to choose his words carefully. "If you wanted to help during some of the busiest weekends, we could always use extra hands. Customer service, gift wrapping, and directing traffic in the parking lot. Lauren coordinates all the community volunteers, and I know she'd welcome your help if you're interested."

The offer surprised Robin with its appeal. She should probably decline—maintain boundaries, keep her involvement limited to Jake's medical care, and avoid further entanglement with this family and their operations. The wise thing to do would be to smile politely and change the subject.

Instead, she heard herself saying, "I'd love that. Really. Just let me know which weekends would be most helpful, and I'll make sure I'm available."

"Yeah?" Wyatt's face lit up in a way that made Robin's breath catch. "That would be great. Lauren will be thrilled."

They stood smiling at each other in the middle of the Christmas Shop, surrounded by magic and memories and possibilities. The moment stretched—too long to be casual, too charged to be comfortable, and too perfect to break without regret.

"I should probably get going," Robin finally managed. "My next appointment is in Fayetteville."

"Right. Of course." Wyatt led her back through the shop toward the entrance, both of them moving slowly.

They stepped onto the porch, where the November sunshine painted everything golden and the scent of evergreens perfumed the air. Robin descended the steps, acutely aware of Wyatt following close behind, both of them walking toward her car with the same reluctance to end their time together.

"I meant what I said about helping," Robin said as she reached her vehicle.

"I'll tell Lauren." Wyatt's hands were shoved in his pockets, his stance casual but his eyes intent. "And Robin? Thanks. For everything you're doing for Jake, obviously, but also for—" He seemed to struggle for the right words. "For caring. It means more than you probably realize."

Robin unlocked her car, needing the action to give her hands something to do. "Your family makes it easy to care."

She settled behind the wheel, started the engine, then lifted her hand in a small wave, and forced herself to put the car in gear and pull away. In her rearview mirror, she watched Wyatt remain motionless, watching her go until she turned onto the drive and trees blocked her view.

Throughout the entire drive toward Fayetteville, Robin couldn't stop thinking about the photographs on the shop wall, about Christmas traditions that connected past to present, and about how she had offered to help during their busiest weekends. She volunteered to be part of their Christmas chaos, to immerse herself in the Gibson family enterprise beyond her obligations to care for Jake. The offer had felt natural, right, like the logical extension of everything she'd been feeling since you had walked into the Gibson home just over a week ago.

Natural and right and terrifying.

Wyatt had a life ninety minutes away—a Forestry Service career and work that gave his life meaning and purpose. Once Jake recovered fully, Wyatt would return to that life, and she would be left here in Laurel Ridge with an aching space where these daily interactions used to be.

Getting used to his presence and their conversations was just setting herself up for heartbreak she'd already experienced once and had sworn never to repeat.

The smart thing would be to pull back now. Maintain distance. Let their interactions remain bounded by Jake's medical needs and nothing more.

Except when had her heart ever chosen the smart thing over the thing that made her feel most alive?

Chapter 11

"Thank you again for the tour of the Christmas Shop on Monday," Robin said, turning back toward where Wyatt stood on the porch steps. He had walked her to her car after her Wednesday morning care visit with Jake. "I'm still thinking about all those beautiful displays. Lauren and Emma Kate have really outdone themselves this year."

"They've worked practically nonstop since September." Wyatt descended the steps, his boots crunching against the gravel as he closed the distance between them.

"How are the preparations going for opening day? You must be in the final push now."

"We are. The seasonal staff starts training next week, and Lauren's working through vendor orders to make sure we have everything covered." He paused, studying her with an expression she couldn't quite decipher. "What's your day look like? Do you have time for a tour of the farm?"

Robin glanced at her watch. "I have about an hour and a half before I have to leave for my next appointment."

"Perfect. That's plenty of time for a quick tour." His grin transformed his face, revealing the boy she'd known alongside the man he'd become.

They walked toward one of the large barns that flanked the main drive. The double doors stood open, revealing the organized chaos of farm equipment—tractors, pruning tools, and a row of side-by-sides parked along the back wall.

Wyatt headed for a dark green utility vehicle, its cargo bed equipped with wooden side panels. He climbed into the driver's seat while Robin settled beside him, the vinyl bench seat cracking slightly under her weight.

The engine turned over with a mechanical rumble that vibrated through the floorboards. Wyatt guided them out of the barn and onto the gravel road that curved away from the main buildings, following the natural contours of the land as it wound between sections of perfectly aligned evergreens.

"We'll start with the Fraser firs," Wyatt said, gesturing toward the nearest grove. "They're our bread and butter—premium trees that command the highest prices because of their needle retention and branch strength. See how they're planted in rows that follow the hillside? That's not just for aesthetics. It allows for proper drainage and makes harvesting more efficient."

Robin studied the trees as they passed, their silvery-green needles catching the sunlight. She'd walked these groves as a child and had purchased her Christmas trees here for years, but she'd never considered the strategy behind their placement.

"How long does it take to grow a six-foot tree?"

"Seven to eight years from seedling to marketable size." Wyatt slowed the vehicle, pointing toward a section of younger trees barely reaching waist height. "Those were planted three years ago. They'll be ready for harvest in another four or five seasons."

"That's remarkable patience."

"Farming requires it. You plant knowing you won't see the results for years, trusting that the work you do today will eventually bear fruit—or in this case, the perfect Christmas tree."

They continued along the gravel track, passing section after section of trees in various stages of growth. Wyatt explained the differences between Fraser firs, Noble firs, and Nordmann firs with an enthusiasm that reminded Robin of the passion he once demonstrated describing wilderness conservation projects when he'd been a teenager.

When they reached a section where trees stood about five feet tall, Wyatt pulled the side-by-side to a stop and cut the engine.

"Come on. I wanna show you something."

Robin followed him into the grove, her shoes sinking slightly into the carpet of fallen needles beneath the trees. Wyatt stopped beside a particularly well-shaped Fraser fir and gestured toward its branches.

"See the shaping of the tree? That doesn't happen naturally. Every tree gets hand-pruned multiple times during its growth cycle." He reached out, his fingers tracing the branch structure. "You're shaping not just the tree but the customer experience—creating that perfect pyramid form families envision when they think of Christmas."

"I never realized how much work goes into each one."

"Most people don't. They see the finished product—the beautiful tree in their living room. But behind that are years of cultivation, daily monitoring, and constant maintenance. It's not glamorous work, but there's something deeply satisfying about it."

Robin studied his profile as he examined the tree, noting the lines around his eyes that spoke of years spent squinting against the wilderness sun and wildfire smoke. The contrast between this moment and his Forest Service career struck her suddenly—both involved conservation and careful stewardship, but one was solitary and itinerant while the other was rooted in family and community.

"Do you miss it? Your work with the Forest Service? You've been here for over a month now."

Wyatt's hand dropped from the tree branch. He turned to face her, his expression thoughtful. "Sometimes. There's an intensity to wildfire suppression—the adrenaline, the clear objective, the immediate impact of your decisions. It's addictive in its way. I do miss the normal days too, wandering the forests, checking for signs of tree disease or storm damage. I miss the physical fieldwork of hiking into dense woods, marking trees, and testing soil."

"So... you're looking forward to a full recovery for Jake and returning to your job?"

"I'm not really sure. I mean, I want Jake to recover, sure... but... well, let's just say I'm taking it day by day and enjoying the time I have here."

They returned to the side-by-side and continued their journey through the farm. The gravel track climbed a gentle slope, revealing vista after vista of Christmas trees marching across hillsides in geometric precision. At the crest of the hill, Wyatt stopped again, this time beside a grove that stood apart from the others—larger trees, some reaching fifteen or sixteen feet, their branches full and perfectly shaped.

"This is the special grove," Wyatt said, pride evident in his voice. "These are the trees we grow for community events, town celebrations, large businesses—anywhere that needs something more substantial than a typical home Christmas tree."

The trees towered above them, magnificent specimens that must have taken a decade or more to reach their current size. Robin walked among them, craning her neck to see their tops reaching toward the blue November sky.

"Laurel Ridge's Christmas tree for the town square will come from this grove," Wyatt continued.

"I remember when your dad cut down the town tree one year." The memory surfaced unbidden, sharp with childhood clarity. "I must have been ten or eleven, maybe. Your mom and dad invited all the church members to come out and watch. I remember there was this massive crowd gathered around while your dad and a few employees worked for what seemed like hours. When the tree finally fell, everyone cheered."

Wyatt's expression softened. "I remember that day too. I think I was ten, and Jake was eight. Dad let us help with some of the smaller tasks—clearing branches, securing ropes. He was so meticulous about everything, making sure the tree fell exactly where he wanted it, that no other trees were damaged in the process." He paused, his gaze distant. "I remember delivering that tree to town too. The whole drive, he kept talking about the responsibility—how this tree would become part of hundreds of people's Christmas memories. He took that seriously."

"He should have. The town tree is tradition."

"It is." Wyatt turned to face her fully. "I'm going to be part of the crew that cuts and delivers it this year. Lauren's handling the logistics. This year will be my first year ever to lead the crew and transport on my own. It feels important somehow—carrying on what Dad started."

"I'm on the decorating committee this year. We're scheduled to start working on it the day after it's delivered."

"You should come watch the delivery... it's amazing to see."

"Maybe I will."

They returned to the side-by-side, resuming their tour. They descended from the special grove and drove past section after section of nut trees—black walnuts with their broad canopies, pecans in orderly rows, and younger chestnut trees that represented investment in future harvests.

"The nut operation is what keeps the farm profitable year-round," Wyatt explained. "Christmas trees bring in seasonal income, but the walnuts and pecans give us steady wholesale revenue during the slower months. We sell saplings and two- and three-year-old trees to nurseries around the state, and the nuts go wholesale to a mix of local and other businesses throughout the state."

"That's smart diversification."

"It's survival. A single bad season could devastate a farm that depends entirely on Christmas tree sales. But when you have multiple revenue streams, you can weather the inevitable ups and downs."

Robin listened as Wyatt described the harvest schedules, the processing facilities, and the wholesale relationships that Lauren had cultivated with specialty food retailers across the region. His knowledge was comprehensive, his explanations clear, but beneath the practical information she detected something else—a genuine connection to this land, this work, and these trees that had shaped his childhood.

"When I left for college," Wyatt said suddenly, "I was so certain that staying here would be settling for less. I wanted adventure, wilderness, the kind of work that felt important on a grand scale." He gestured toward the farmland surrounding them. "But coming back, managing the operation these past weeks—I've been remembering satisfactions I'd convinced myself didn't matter. The rhythm of seasonal work.

The tangible result of patient cultivation. The way community and commerce and tradition all intertwine during the Christmas season."

Robin's heart hammered against her ribs. "So you are reconsidering your plans about going back to the Forest Service?"

"I'm saying I'm not as certain about anything as I used to be."

The gravel road curved toward the greenhouse complex—four large structures gleaming in the late morning sun. Wyatt parked near the closest building and led Robin through the entrance.

The temperature shift was immediate and dramatic. Warm, humid air wrapped around them, carrying the earthy scent of things growing and rich potting soil. Row upon row of tables stretched the length of the structure, each laden with poinsettias in various stages of bloom—traditional red, pristine white, delicate pink, and elegant variegated varieties.

"Wow," Robin breathed, turning in a slow circle to take in the sheer volume of plants.

"Pete Norton manages the greenhouse operation. He's been with us six years, and he's expanded production every season." Wyatt walked between the tables, gesturing toward different sections. "These are the wholesale orders—grocery stores, garden centers, and florists throughout the state. And over there are the retail plants we'll sell directly from the Christmas Shop."

Robin moved closer to examine a particularly stunning red poinsettia, its bracts perfectly formed and vibrant against dark green foliage. "The church always has a gigantic display from your farm. Every year in December, the sanctuary is filled with them."

"Lauren coordinates that donation every year. Says it's good for business and good for the soul."

"Your family has created something remarkable here. Not just a business, but a whole network of traditions and memories for so many people."

"We have. Though I'm only now fully appreciating the scope of it."

They stood surrounded by thousands of poinsettias, the warm greenhouse air making Robin's cheeks flush. Or perhaps it wasn't the temperature at all but rather Wyatt's nearness.

"I should probably get you back," Wyatt said finally, his tone reluctant. "You need to leave soon."

"Right, yes." Robin checked her watch, surprised to discover that time had passed so quickly.

They returned to the side-by-side, and Wyatt started the engine and navigated back through the farm, taking a different route that offered new perspectives on the operation's scope.

When they reached the barn where they'd started, Wyatt parked the vehicle but didn't immediately move to exit. He sat with both hands on the steering wheel, staring through the windshield at the Christmas tree groves visible in the distance.

Robin waited, sensing he wanted to say something but couldn't quite find the words.

"I'm glad you're here," he said finally. "Not just because Jake needs care but because getting to know you again means a lot to me."

Wyatt climbed out of the vehicle and circled around to her side. He offered his hand to help her down, his grip warm and steady.

They walked back toward her car in silence; the gravel crunching beneath their feet. Robin's mind raced with everything she should say, everything she wanted to ask, but the words tangled themselves into knots that refused to untangle.

She reached her car and opened the door, then turned back toward Wyatt. He stood a few feet away, hands in his jacket pockets, his expression unreadable in the midday light.

"Thanks for the tour," Robin managed.

"Anytime. I like spending time with you."

Chapter 12

Robin slid into the red vinyl booth near the front windows of Martha's Diner, her fingers drumming against the checkered tablecloth. Through the glass, the town square stretched out across Main Street; trees full of autumn color stood sentinel around the white gazebo. Beyond, she could just glimpse the pewter shimmer of the New River catching morning sunlight.

The bell above the door jingled, and Megan Harlan breezed in, her blonde hair escaping from its ponytail as usual, bright-green eyes sparkling with their characteristic mischief. She spotted Robin immediately and waved, her animated gestures drawing smiles from the other patrons as she wove between tables.

"Sorry I'm late!" Megan dropped into the booth across from Robin, unwinding her scarf with theatrical flair. "Mrs. Harvey needed an extra few minutes this morning explaining—in excruciating detail—why she thinks her new medication is giving her prophetic dreams about her neighbor's cat."

Robin laughed despite her nerves. "Prophetic dreams?"

"According to her, the cat is planning to run for mayor." Megan's grin widened. "I suggested she might want to discuss the medication side effects with her doctor, but she's convinced the cat has political aspirations."

"Only in Laurel Ridge."

"Only with Mrs. Harvey." Megan settled into her seat, then paused, her expression shifting from playful to penetrating. "Okay, what's wrong?"

"Nothing's wrong."

"Robin Elizabeth Fitch, I've known you since we were six years old. You're vibrating like a tuning fork, and you've already shredded your napkin." Megan gestured toward the pile of paper scraps. "Spill."

Before Robin could deflect, Martha Kincaid materialized beside their booth, coffeepot in hand and her signature smile firmly in place. The diner's owner looked exactly as she had for the past decade—silver hair pulled into a neat bun, a blue apron tied over a simple dress, and her gold cross necklace catching the light.

"Well, if it isn't my two favorite nurses." Martha filled their cups without asking. "How're you girls doing this beautiful Saturday morning?"

"Wonderful," Megan said. "Robin's having some kind of crisis, but she won't tell me what it is yet."

"I am not having a crisis."

"You've murdered that napkin, honey." Martha's twinkling brown eyes missed nothing. "That's definitely crisis behavior."

Robin opened her mouth to protest, but Martha was already pulling out her order pad. "You girls want your usual? Blueberry pancakes, extra butter?"

"Yes, please," they answered in unison.

Martha scribbled on her pad, then looked directly at Robin. "How's Jake Gibson doing? I heard he's making good progress."

"He is. The recovery's going well—better than expected, actually."

"That's wonderful news." Martha's smile widened. "And how's Wyatt? Must be nice having him back in town, even under such difficult circumstances."

The world tilted slightly. Robin felt Megan's attention snap toward her like a rubber band pulled taut.

"Wyatt's... fine. He's managing the farm operations and coordinating Jake's care. Very hands-on." Robin heard her voice climbing toward overly bright territory and couldn't seem to stop it. "Well-organized about everything. Very... present."

Martha's knowing look could have illuminated the entire diner. "I'm sure he is, dear. I'll get these pancakes started for you."

The moment Martha disappeared toward the kitchen, Megan leaned across the table, her voice dropping to an urgent whisper that somehow managed to convey both excitement and accusation.

"Wyatt Gibson is back in town? Your Wyatt? High school sweetheart Wyatt?"

"He's not my Wyatt."

"The Wyatt you dated for two years and then cried over for an entire semester after you broke up?"

"We decided mutually to end things before college. It was practical and mature."

"The Wyatt whose name you still won't say without getting that look on your face?"

"I don't have a look."

"You absolutely have a look." Megan's eyes were dancing now.

Robin's cheeks heated. "I don't—"

"Robin. Focus. Wyatt Gibson is back in Laurel Ridge, you're Jake's nurse, and you didn't tell me?" Megan's expression shifted from teasing to genuinely hurt. "We tell each other everything."

"I was going to tell you."

"How long has he been back?"

"Since Jake's accident. A little over a month."

"A month?" Megan's voice climbed high enough to draw glances from nearby tables. She lowered it immediately, leaning even closer. "You've been working with him for a month and didn't mention it once?"

"I wasn't working with him. I've been working with Jake for two weeks now. Wyatt's just... there. Managing things. Being supportive..."

Megan sat back, her expression transforming into something between sympathy and satisfaction. "Oh, honey. You've got it bad, don't you?"

"I don't have anything. We're just... it's professional. I'm Jake's nurse. Wyatt's his brother. We're being cordial and—"

"Cordial?"

Robin's throat tightened.

"You're blushing like a teenager, and you just confirmed everything I suspected." Megan's grin was absolutely triumphant. "Now stop deflecting and tell me everything."

The floodgates opened. Robin found herself describing the past two weeks in detail—the shock of walking into Jake's room and finding Wyatt there, the way they'd fallen into easy conversation despite twelve years apart, how natural it felt to share coffee and discuss medical updates and farm operations. She mentioned the Christmas Shop tour, the farm tour on Wednesday, how Wyatt made her laugh and challenged her thinking, and listened to her observations with genuine interest.

"He showed me the special grove where they grow taller trees for large businesses and such," Robin said. "And he mentioned his dad, about carrying on traditions, about how coming back to the farm has reminded him of things he'd forgotten. And then he just... he looked at me and said, getting to know me again means a lot to him."

Megan's hand found Robin's across the table, squeezing gently. "That doesn't sound like a cordial interaction to me."

"But that's exactly what it has to be because Wyatt lives ninety minutes away. He has a career with the Forestry Service—important work that he loves. Once Jake recovers enough to manage the farm again, Wyatt's going back to his real life."

"Are you certain about that?"

"What else would he do? His entire career is built on wilderness conservation. He can't just abandon that."

"People change careers all the time, especially when they find something—or someone—more important."

Robin shook her head, the familiar fear rising in her chest. "I can't do this again, Megan. I can't fall for someone whose life is somewhere else. I tried that with Liam. I tried making a relationship work when we lived an hour apart, when his job kept him traveling, and when I was always the one adjusting my schedule and driving to see him. And look how that ended—with him taking a job in the Midwest and admitting he didn't love me enough to make it work."

"Wyatt isn't Liam."

"How do you know?"

"Because Liam never looked at you the way I'm willing to bet Wyatt does." Megan's voice gentled. "And because you never talked about Liam, the way you're talking about Wyatt right now. You never shredded a napkin over Liam."

"That's not—"

"Robin, listen to me. You can't protect yourself from heartbreak by refusing to feel anything. That's not living. That's just... existing." Megan leaned forward, her usual playfulness replaced by earnest intensity. "You're a nurse. You know that healing requires risk—that patients have to trust their bodies to do what seems impossible, to take steps that hurt, and to believe in recovery even when they're terrified. Why won't you apply that same faith to your heart?"

"Because patients' hearts don't get broken by physical therapy."

"No, but they get stronger. They learn what they're capable of. They discover that fear doesn't have to win." Megan's green eyes held Robin's without wavering. "You deserve someone who chooses you, not as a convenient option but as their clear priority. And from everything you've just told me, Wyatt is showing you through his actions that you matter to him. Maybe it's time to trust that."

Martha arrived with their pancakes, the aroma of blueberries and butter momentarily derailing the conversation. She set the plates down, refilled their coffee, and departed with a wink.

They ate without speaking for several minutes, Robin finding comfort in the familiar sweetness while her mind wrestled with everything Megan had said. Her friend was right—she did spend her professional life encouraging patients to trust the healing process, to take risks that felt impossible, and to believe in outcomes they couldn't yet see. Why was she so unwilling to extend that same courage to her own emotional life?

"I'm scared," Robin admitted finally, the words barely above a whisper. "I'm terrified that I'm reading too much into casual conversation and friendly gestures. That I'm projecting my feelings onto someone who's just being kind to his brother's nurse. And even if I'm not—even if Wyatt does have feelings for me—what happens when Jake's better? When Wyatt has to choose between a career he's built for twelve years and... what? The possibility of something with me? That's not fair to ask of anyone."

"You're right. It's not." Megan took a bite of pancake, chewing thoughtfully. "But here's the thing—you're not asking. If Wyatt makes a choice, it's his to make. And if he chooses you, it won't be because you forced him or manipulated him or somehow trapped him in Laurel Ridge. It'll be because you're worth choosing."

"I don't—"

"You are worth choosing, Robin. You are worth fighting for, worth changing plans for, and worth building a life around. When are you going to believe that?"

The bell above the diner's door jingled again. She glanced up automatically and felt her heart execute a complicated maneuver somewhere between a skip and a complete stop.

Wyatt walked through the entrance, Tom Hartwell beside him. Both men wore work clothes—flannel shirts and worn jeans that spoke of early morning farm tasks. Wyatt's hair showed evidence of wind and possibly a backward baseball cap recently removed. His face lit up the moment he spotted her.

"Well," Megan murmured, her voice rich with satisfaction. "This just got interesting."

Wyatt approached their booth, Tom trailing slightly behind, and Robin became acutely aware of how she must look—Saturday casual instead of professional nurse attire, her hair down instead of pulled back.

"Robin, hey." Wyatt's smile reached his eyes, genuine and warm. "Megan Harlan? Is that really you?"

Megan stood, pulling Wyatt into a friendly hug that he returned with obvious surprise and pleasure. "Wyatt Gibson! Welcome home! When did you get back?"

"About a month ago. When Jake had his accident."

"I heard about that. Robin told me he's making excellent progress."

"He is, thanks to Robin's care." Wyatt's gaze shifted to Robin, holding for just a beat longer than necessary. "She's been incredible."

"She always is," Megan agreed, her tone absolutely dripping with barely contained delight that made Robin want to kick her under the table.

Tom stepped forward, offering polite greetings that Robin returned while trying to steady her suddenly unreliable pulse.

"We've been checking the irrigation systems in the greenhouses this morning," Wyatt explained. "Making sure everything's ready for the temperature drop they're forecasting this week."

"Exciting Saturday morning stuff right there," Megan said brightly.

"Could be worse." Wyatt's attention remained focused on Robin. "Robin... are you up for an adventure?"

Robin's coffee cup paused halfway to her lips. "What?"

"My afternoon's wide open now. The weather's perfect today, and the autumn foliage is at its peak in the mountains. You wanna go exploring one of the hiking trails around Laurel Ridge? Nothing too strenuous, just... I thought you might enjoy seeing the fall colors from the ridgeline."

The question landed with the force of a physical impact. Robin's mind went completely blank, every practiced response and carefully constructed boundary evaporating in the face of Wyatt's nervous grin.

Megan kicked her gently under the table.

"I... yes. I'd like that." The words emerged before Robin's rational brain could intervene with all the very logical reasons why spending her afternoon alone with Wyatt in the mountains was probably a terrible idea.

"Yeah?. How about we hit the River's Edge Trailhead?"

"River's Edge sounds perfect."

"Should we meet there in, say, three hours... around noon?"

"Noon works."

They smiled at each other like teenagers making their first date plans.

"Well," Tom said finally, his voice holding barely suppressed amusement. "We should probably order our breakfast before Martha thinks we're just here to block the aisle."

"Right. Sure." Wyatt seemed to shake himself back to awareness of their surroundings. "I'll see you at noon, Robin."

"See you then."

Wyatt and Tom headed toward a booth near the back, leaving Robin to sink back into her seat with the distinct feeling that something significant had just occurred, but her processing capabilities remained stubbornly offline.

Megan was grinning like she'd just won the lottery. "So. Just friends, huh? That was... cordial."

"Shut up."

"That man just invited you on a date, Robin. An actual, let's-spend-time-together-because-I-enjoy-your-company date."

"It's a hike. People hike with friends all the time."

"Do they?" Megan's eyebrows climbed toward her hairline. "Because from where I'm sitting, that looked like a man who's been working up the courage to ask you out and finally found his opening."

"It's just hiking."

"Keep telling yourself that." Megan attacked her pancakes with renewed enthusiasm. "Wear something cute too."

They finished their meal while Megan alternated between teasing and offering fashionable clothing advice for hiking. Across the diner,

Robin could feel Wyatt's presence like a magnetic pull, her awareness of him making it difficult to focus on Megan's cheerful commentary.

When Martha brought their check, she leaned close to Robin's ear. "That Gibson boy hasn't taken his eyes off you since he sat down, honey."

Robin paid for their breakfast in a daze, following Megan out to the parking lot where the November sun warmed her face despite the crisp air.

"You're going to have a wonderful time," Megan said, pulling her into a fierce hug. "And you will let yourself enjoy it without analyzing every word and gesture to death. Promise me."

"I can't promise that."

"Then promise me you'll try. Wyatt obviously cares about you, Robin. Let yourself care back. Let yourself hope." Megan pulled back, holding Robin by the shoulders. "You deserve this. You deserve someone who makes you feel the way you obviously feel when you talk about him. Don't let fear steal that from you."

They said their goodbyes, and Robin drove home with Megan's words echoing in her head.

Just friends, she told herself firmly. Nothing more.

Chapter 13

Wyatt's truck rolled into the gravel parking area at River's Edge Trailhead a few minutes before noon. He cut the engine and sat for a moment, hands still gripping the steering wheel, trying to identify the peculiar combination of anticipation and nerves coursing through his system.

He'd changed from his morning work clothes into hiking boots, cargo pants, and a flannel shirt layered over a thermal under-shirt—practical choices for a November afternoon hike. Yet he'd spent an embarrassing amount of time in front of his bathroom mirror, debating whether the flannel looked too deliberately casual or not casual enough, before finally deciding that overthinking his wardrobe for a simple hike was ridiculous.

A silver SUV turned into the parking area, and Wyatt's pulse kicked up several notches.

She climbed out wearing black leggings, hiking boots, and an over-sized gray sweatshirt that somehow made her look younger and more approachable than her normal nursing scrubs. Her chestnut hair fell in loose waves past her shoulders, catching the filtered sunlight that broke through the canopy of nearly bare trees overhead.

"Hey," she said, shouldering a small backpack. "I brought water and trail mix. Hope that's okay."

"Perfect." Wyatt gestured toward the trailhead marker. "Ready?"

They started up the path, fallen leaves crunching beneath their boots. The November air carried a distinctive crisp edge that promised snow wasn't far off, though the afternoon sun provided enough warmth to make the temperature comfortable for hiking. Through the thinning foliage as they climbed higher, Wyatt caught glimpses of the valley below, where Laurel Ridge nestled among the rolling Appalachian foothills.

"I forgot how beautiful autumn can be," Robin said. "I drive through these mountains every day and sometimes forget to just enjoy the view."

"It's easy to take for granted what you see every day." Wyatt pointed toward a rocky outcropping visible through the trees. "That's Eagle's Perch... I haven't seen it in years. If I remember right, we should pass below it in about half a mile, and there's a decent overlook where we can stop and catch our breath."

They settled into a simple rhythm, their strides naturally matching as they navigated the moderate trail. When they reached a section where exposed tree roots created natural obstacles, Wyatt offered his hand without thinking. Robin accepted it just as naturally, her grip warm and steady as she stepped over the gnarled roots.

The trail steepened, and their conversation paused while they focused on the climb. Wyatt was hyperaware of Robin beside him—the sound of her breathing, the efficient way she moved over uneven terrain, and the occasional brush of her shoulder against his arm when the path narrowed.

They crested a small rise, and the trees opened up to reveal the valley spread below them like a patchwork quilt of autumn colors punctuated by the silver thread of the New River winding through the landscape.

"Wow," Robin breathed, stopping to take in the view. "I definitely don't appreciate this area enough."

"It's something special, that's for sure." Wyatt leaned against a boulder, giving them both a moment to catch their breath. "Different from the wilderness areas I usually work in—more settled, more human. But beautiful in its own way."

Robin turned to face him, her hazel eyes curious. "Tell me about your work. The wildfire suppression—what's that actually like?"

"It's intense," he admitted. "Physically demanding in ways that are hard to explain unless you've experienced it. You're working twelve, fourteen, sometimes twenty-four-hour shifts in extreme conditions—heat, smoke, terrain that would be challenging even without a fire bearing down on you."

"That sounds terrifying."

"It is. It's exhausting at times, terrifying during certain moments, and it can be exhilarating.... But the last fire I worked..." Wyatt paused, memories of those three weeks rising unbidden. "It was on the West Virginia and Virginia border. We spent three weeks living in a makeshift camp, fighting a fire that kept shifting and changing based on wind patterns and fuel sources. By the time we finally contained it, I felt like I'd aged years."

Robin listened without interrupting, her focus absolute in a way that made him want to keep talking.

"When I got back to base after that deployment, I looked in the mirror and barely recognized myself. Exhausted doesn't even begin to cover it. And I found myself wondering..." He trailed off, unsure how much to reveal.

"Wondering what?"

"How many more years can I keep up at this pace? Whether the physical and emotional toll is sustainable long-term, or if I'm just running myself into the ground because it's easier than figuring out what I actually want my life to look like."

They resumed walking, the trail leveling out as it followed the ridgeline. Robin walked beside him in silence for several minutes.

"You're brave," she said finally. "Fighting wildfires that can shift direction in minutes, putting yourself in danger to protect forests and communities—that takes real courage."

"Sometimes it feels less like courage and more like a convenient way to avoid dealing with other things."

Robin glanced at him sharply. "Have you thought about stepping away from it? Maybe focus more on the forestry work instead of the firefighting?"

"After that last fire, yeah. I've given it serious thought. The forestry work—the surveying, the conservation planning, the education—I enjoy that aspect of the job. But the firefighting..." He shook his head. "The toll it takes on a person became really clear on that last deployment."

They walked in comfortable silence for a while, the trail winding through stands of oak and maple trees that had dropped most of their leaves, creating a carpet of gold and russet beneath their feet. Wyatt pointed out native plants as they passed—mountain laurel that would bloom gorgeously in spring, wild ginger hiding in the leaf litter, and the distinctive bark of black birch trees.

Robin mentioned her small vegetable garden and her attempts at growing medicinal herbs. Their conversation flowed with an ease that felt both familiar and entirely new, as if they were discovering each other fresh while building on foundations laid years ago.

The trail climbed one final rise before reaching the highest point, where a massive fallen log provided natural seating overlooking the valley. They settled side by side, close enough that Wyatt caught the faint scent of her perfume—something floral and clean that brought back memories of teenage hikes, back when the world had seemed full of possibility.

Robin pulled water bottles from her backpack, handing one to Wyatt before opening her own. She took a long drink, then pulled out bags of trail mix and offered him one.

"This is gorgeous," she said, gazing out over the valley where Laurel Ridge was barely visible among the rolling hills. "I am so glad I get to wake up every morning surrounded by this beauty."

"There's something special about this area. I didn't fully appreciate it until I'd been away for a while. Now every time I come back, I see it with fresh eyes."

Robin turned to face him abruptly, her expression shifting to something more intense. "What are we doing here, Wyatt?"

He blinked and grinned. "Well, it looks like we're sitting on a log enjoying the day."

She gave him a look that suggested his attempt at humor had completely missed the mark. "No, Wyatt. What is going on between us?"

His heart hammered against his ribs. The moment of truth, and he had no prepared response, no carefully constructed answer.

"I..." He set down his water bottle, turning to face her fully. "I've been trying to figure out how to tell you that everything I thought I'd resolved years ago—all the feelings I convinced myself were just nostalgia or teenage intensity—none of it went away."

Robin's expression remained unreadable, but she didn't interrupt.

"Since you walked into Jake's room two weeks ago, my entire world has been off-kilter. Every conversation we have, every moment we spend together, just confirms what I've been trying to deny." He ran a hand through his hair, frustration and vulnerability warring for dominance. "I never stopped caring about you, Robin. Not really. Not in any way that matters."

The silence stretched between them, filled only by the rustle of wind through bare branches and the distant call of a crow.

"Say something," Wyatt finally managed. "Please."

Robin took another drink of water, her movements deliberate and controlled. When she looked at him again, her hazel eyes held a mixture of emotions he couldn't quite parse.

"Being friends might be the best thing for both of us," she said quietly. "Because I'm not sure if I can offer more than that with everything still up in the air."

The words landed like a physical blow, but Wyatt forced himself to listen rather than react.

"Jake is still recovering," Robin continued. "Not one person on this earth can honestly say whether he'll make a full recovery or not. Your life is ninety minutes away—your career, your home. And I can't..." She paused, her voice catching slightly. "I'm not willing to risk my heart on anything more than friendship. I can't go through that again, Wyatt. I can't be in a relationship that involves traveling long distances to see each other, adjusting my schedule around someone else's unpredictable work, and always wondering if this time I'll be enough."

The fear in her voice cut deeper than the rejection. This wasn't about not having feelings for him—it was about being too afraid to trust those feelings.

"If that's all we can be…" Wyatt forced the words past the tightness in his throat. "Friends. Then I'm grateful for that. For you being in my life at all, in whatever way you're comfortable with."

"Honestly?"

"Honestly." He meant it, even as disappointment settled in his chest like a stone. "I'd rather have your friendship than nothing at all."

Robin's expression softened slightly.

They sat in awkward silence for several minutes, the easy camaraderie from earlier in the hike fractured.

"We should probably head back," Robin said finally.

"Right. Sure." Wyatt stood, then held out his hand to help her up.

Robin accepted it, and when she was standing, Wyatt was unable to let go immediately. Their eyes met, and acknowledgment passed between them of what they were choosing not to pursue, mourning for possibilities being set aside.

He released her hand and gestured toward the trail. "After you."

They started the descent in silence, both processing what had been said and left unsaid. Wyatt walked slower than necessary, as if extending their time together might somehow change the outcome of their conversation.

Halfway down the trail, Robin stumbled slightly over a hidden root. Wyatt's hand shot out automatically, steadying her until she regained her balance.

"Thanks," she said with a small smile.

"That's what friends do, right?"

Robin's smile widened slightly. "Friends do lots of things together."

"They do." Wyatt felt a spark of something—not quite hope, but not complete resignation either. "Friends go out to dinner, right?"

"Sure."

"Friends can watch movies together. With their recovering brothers, of course."

"Of course." Robin's eyes were dancing now, the tension from earlier beginning to ease. "Friends can definitely do that."

"Friends sit together in church, right?"

"Absolutely."

Wyatt stopped walking, turning to face her. "Are you going tomorrow?"

"I am."

"Then I'll be there too." His smile felt more genuine now, even if it couldn't quite reach the depth of what he was actually feeling.

Chapter 14

Robin pulled into the gravel parking lot of Laurel Ridge Community Church as the bell in the white steeple began its melodic call to worship.

She'd changed three times this morning before settling on a navy dress and her favorite cardigan.

Robin grabbed her purse and Bible from the passenger seat and headed toward the entrance, joining the stream of familiar faces making their way up the steps. The scent of vanilla candles greeted her as she stepped into the sanctuary, where polished wooden pews stretched toward a modest altar adorned with fresh fall flowers.

"Robin! Over here!" Lauren's enthusiastic voice drew her attention as she gestured toward a spot she'd saved in a pew about halfway up the center aisle.

Robin slid in beside her, and Lauren leaned close immediately, her blue eyes sparkling. "So? How was the hike yesterday? Tell me everything."

Heat crept up Robin's neck. "It was nice. Beautiful views, good conversation—"

"Just nice?" Lauren's eyebrows climbed toward her hairline.

"What do you want me to say?"

"I want details! Did he—"

"Good morning, ladies." Wyatt's voice came from the end of the pew, and Robin's pulse executed an impressive series of acrobatics.

He slid into the pew beside Robin, bringing with him the clean scent of soap and the subtle spice of aftershave. He wore dark slacks and a white dress shirt with the sleeves rolled to his forearms, his hair still slightly damp from a recent shower. When he smiled at her, Robin felt a flush of heat rise up her neck.

"Morning," she managed, hyperaware of how close he sat.

Lauren shot Robin a look that clearly communicated, We'll talk later, before turning her attention to the front as Pastor Andrew Whitman approached the pulpit.

Andrew looked as approachable as always in dress slacks and a button-down shirt with rolled sleeves, his warm brown eyes scanning the congregation with genuine affection. Lily, his wife, sat in the front row, her hand resting on the small swell of her pregnancy, radiating the kind of contented joy that Robin found both beautiful and achingly enviable.

"Good morning, church family," Andrew said, his voice carrying easily through the sanctuary. "Before we begin, I want to thank everyone who brought food to the Gibson family these past few weeks. Lauren tells me their refrigerator has been overflowing with kindness."

"Today's message is called 'The Strength of a Gentle Heart,'" Andrew continued. "We'll be focusing on Matthew 5:5 this morning, and I want to start with a question: What does real strength look like?"

Robin tried to focus on the sermon as Andrew opened his Bible to Matthew 5:5. *Blessed are the meek, for they shall inherit the earth.* But her attention kept fracturing, pulled toward Wyatt beside her like a compass finding true north.

She could feel the warmth of him. Could hear the slight rustle when he shifted position. Could sense when he glanced in her direction, though she kept her eyes determinedly forward.

"Real strength isn't control," Andrew said, his voice carrying conviction. "It's compassion under restraint. It's choosing kindness when pride would rather pull away. It's the quiet power of gentleness—the strength it takes to remain tender in a world that often demands hardness."

The words hit Robin with uncomfortable accuracy. Wasn't that exactly what she'd done yesterday? Pulled away when Wyatt had been vulnerable? Chosen self-protection over the risk of tenderness?

She stole a glance at Wyatt and found him already looking at her.

He reached into his shirt pocket and pulled out several wrapped butterscotch candies. He offered one to Lauren with a grin, then held one out to Robin.

She accepted it automatically, unwrapping the cellophane as quietly as possible. The sweet butterscotch flavor burst across her tongue, bringing with it a rush of memories—high school study sessions, teenage walks through town, and Wyatt always carrying butterscotch candy in his jacket pocket because he knew they were her favorite.

Robin leaned toward him and whispered. "These are my favorite."

Wyatt's smile transformed his face as he leaned closer, his breath warm against her ear. "I remembered. That's why I stopped on the way to church this morning and bought some. Gotta take care of my friend."

The world tilted slightly. First, he remembered she liked her coffee with just cream. Now butterscotch candy. Simple things, perhaps, but they represented something larger—that Wyatt had carried memories of her through twelve years of separation and had held onto details that mattered to her even when they'd chosen to walk different paths.

Dear Lord, help me here, Robin prayed silently, her heart hammering so hard she worried Wyatt might actually hear it.

Soon, the congregation rose for a hymn, and Wyatt shifted his hymnal so they could both see the words. His baritone voice blended with her soprano as they sang "Great Is Thy Faithfulness," creating a harmony that sounded natural and right, as if their voices had been designed to complement each other.

Lauren glanced over, noticed their synchronized singing, and shot Robin a smile that held entirely too much satisfaction and hope.

Robin focused on the words of the hymn, letting their truth anchor her scattered thoughts. *Morning by morning new mercies I see. All I have needed, Thy hand hath provided.* God's faithfulness remained constant even when her emotions felt like a ship in a storm.

When they sat back down, Robin was acutely conscious of Wyatt's presence beside her during the rest of the sermon. The way he listened to Andrew's words with complete attention. The occasional nod when a point particularly resonated. The slight smile when Andrew used humor to illustrate a spiritual truth.

"Gentleness requires tremendous strength," Andrew said, his voice earnest. "It takes courage to remain soft when you've been hurt. It takes faith to believe that vulnerability isn't weakness. And it takes wisdom to understand that the strongest hearts are often the gentlest ones."

The service moved into the prayer request portion, and several church members asked for continued healing for Jake Gibson. Lauren stood, her voice steady despite the emotion Robin could hear beneath it.

"I just want to thank everyone for the incredible support," Lauren said, one hand gripping the pew in front of her. "The food, the visits, the prayers—they've meant more to our family than I can express. Jake is making progress thanks to God and exceptional medical care." She gestured toward Robin. "Robin's nursing has been nothing short of miraculous. I ask for continued prayers for Jake's recovery."

Wyatt nodded in agreement, and Robin felt her cheeks flush as multiple heads turned in her direction with warm smiles.

Andrew bowed his head. "Heavenly Father, we lift up Jake Gibson and his entire family. We thank You for the skilled hands and compassionate heart You've given Robin as she cares for Jake. We ask for continued healing, for strength during this recovery process, and for Your peace that surpasses understanding to fill the Gibson home. Guide the doctors, strengthen Jake's body, and remind this family that You are present in both the mountains and the valleys. In Jesus' name, Amen."

"Amen," the congregation echoed.

Andrew concluded the service with a blessing, his words washing over the sanctuary like a benediction. "May the Lord bless you and keep you. May He make His face shine upon you and be gracious to you. May He turn His face toward you and give you peace. Go in grace, and may gentleness be your strength this week."

As the final notes of the closing hymn faded, the congregation began the familiar shuffle of gathering Bibles and purses, greeting neighbors, and making their way toward the exits. Robin, Wyatt, and Lauren joined the flow moving down the center aisle toward the back of the church, where Pastor Andrew and Lily stood ready to greet everyone.

Martha intercepted them halfway down the aisle, her eyes twinkling with the particular brand of knowing mischief that made her both beloved and slightly intimidating to those who preferred keeping their personal lives private.

"Wyatt Gibson," Martha said, her voice carrying enough volume to turn several nearby heads. "How wonderful to see you in church this morning. It's been too long."

"It's good to be back, Martha."

"And sitting with Robin, I see." Martha's knowing look could have melted steel. "Isn't that nice? You two always did look perfect together."

"Martha," Robin said, her tone holding a gentle warning.

"What? I'm just making an observation." Martha's innocent expression fooled absolutely no one. "I must say... The Lord sure does work in mysterious ways."

Before Robin could formulate a response that wouldn't encourage Martha even more, they reached the doorway where Andrew and Lily waited.

"Incredible sermon, Pastor," Lauren said, shaking Andrew's hand.

"Thank you, Lauren. How's Jake doing today?"

"Better. Restless, which Robin says is actually a good sign."

Andrew turned to Robin with a warm smile. "We're grateful for the care you're providing. The whole church has been praying."

"I appreciate that," Robin said.

Lily stepped forward, her pregnancy giving her an extra glow of happiness. "Robin, you look lovely. That color is perfect on you."

"Thank you, Lily."

They moved out into the bright November morning, and Robin paused on the church steps, breathing in the crisp air. The parking lot was full of families clustering in small groups, conversation and laughter filling the air.

Lauren excused herself to speak with someone from the women's Bible study, leaving Robin and Wyatt standing together on the steps.

"So," Wyatt said, his hands in his pockets. "What are your plans for the rest of the day?"

"Nothing special. Lunch at home, probably some reading, maybe a walk if the weather holds."

"Want to join us for Sunday dinner instead? Nothing fancy. Lauren put a crock-pot of chicken and dumplings on this morning. We were just planning to eat in Jake's room and then maybe watch a movie or play cards."

Dinner with the Gibson family.

An afternoon at their home.

More time with Wyatt would make it increasingly difficult to maintain the boundaries she'd established yesterday.

But the alternative was going home alone to an empty house, and somehow that felt like the wrong choice.

"I'd like that," Robin said. "As friends, of course."

Wyatt's grin was immediate and genuine. "Absolutely."

Lauren rejoined them, catching the tail end of their conversation. "Robin's coming for dinner? Perfect! Jake will be thrilled."

They made plans to meet at the farmhouse in an hour, giving Robin time to change out of her Sunday dress. She said her goodbyes and headed toward her SUV, acutely aware of Wyatt watching her walk away.

Once inside her vehicle with the door closed, Robin gripped the steering wheel and closed her eyes.

"Dinner," she said aloud to the empty car. "Just friends. Nothing more."

She started the engine and pulled out of the parking lot, but the smile tugging at her lips refused to be suppressed. The memory of Wyatt's voice during the hymn, the sweetness of butterscotch candy, and the way he'd looked at her when Andrew talked about gentle strength—all of it swirled together into something that felt dangerously close to letting her guard down.

"Lord, if You're listening," Robin said as she turned onto Main Street, "please protect my heart. Because I'm pretty sure 'just friends' isn't going to be enough for much longer, and I don't know if I'm brave enough to want more."

Chapter 15

The aroma of chicken and dumplings filled Jake's bedroom, rich and comforting. Robin sat in a chair pulled close to Jake's hospital bed, a bowl balanced on her lap, while Wyatt occupied the chair beside her and Lauren sat opposite them on the other side of the bed. Jake's bed had been raised to a sitting position, and his bed table held his own bowl within easy reach.

"Lauren, this is incredible," Robin said, savoring another bite. "I've never heard of chicken and dumplings being made in a crock-pot."

Lauren's laugh was warm. "Grandma would probably give me a good tongue-lashing if she were still alive today. She used to make the best chicken and dumplings I ever tasted. I remember being a little girl and watching her spend forever in the kitchen preparing them—making the dough, simmering a whole chicken for the broth, then picking the meat from the bones—it always seemed to take her all afternoon."

"I remember that too," Jake said. "The kitchen would steam up like a sauna, and she'd shoo us out every five minutes because we were underfoot."

"But she'd always sneak us tastes before we sat down as a family for dinner," Wyatt added, his smile softening his features.

Lauren grinned. "I don't always have the time to make them the way she used to, and this recipe is almost as good, plus it's quick and easy. Just gather the ingredients and dump it all in a crock-pot." She gestured with her fork. "I'll share the recipe with you, Robin."

"I'd love that."

Jake shifted slightly, trying to adjust his position, and his face tightened with discomfort. Robin started to set down her bowl, but Wyatt was already on his feet, moving to help his brother.

"Easy," Wyatt said, his hands gentle as he supported Jake's shoulder. "Where do you need to be?"

"Just a little more to the left. My back's cramping."

Wyatt made the adjustment, and Robin noticed how much more confident he'd become with Jake's care over the past two weeks. The initial hesitation and worry had transformed into competence.

Robin stood as well, reaching to help, but Wyatt caught her eye and shook his head with a smile. "You're off duty today. Just relax and enjoy the afternoon. I've got this."

She sank back into her chair, watching as he ensured Jake was comfortable.

"Better?" Wyatt asked.

"Yeah, thanks." Jake took another bite of his meal, then set down his spoon with a sigh. "I keep thinking about Friday."

"Opening day," Lauren said.

"Opening day," Jake confirmed. "This is the farm's busiest time of year, and I'm stuck in this bed watching you two shoulder everything.

Tom and the seasonal staff can only do so much. The customer service, the quality control, making sure families find the perfect tree..."

The guilt in his voice was unmistakable, and Robin recognized the emotional spiral before it could gain momentum. She'd seen it in countless patients—the helplessness that came from watching loved ones carry burdens that should be shared.

"Jake," Robin said gently, "your value to this farm has never depended solely on your physical capability."

He looked at her, skepticism clear in his expression.

"I'm serious. What makes Gibson Tree Farm successful? Is it just the physical work of cutting trees and managing inventory?"

"That's a big part of it."

"But not all of it," Robin pressed. "You've built relationships with customers over the years. You know which families come back annually, what trees they prefer, and how to match people with exactly what they're looking for. That expertise doesn't disappear because you can't walk through the groves right now."

"She's right," Wyatt said.

"I can't exactly greet customers from a hospital bed."

"Maybe not in person," Robin said, "but you could coordinate through phone and computer. Answer customer service questions, manage the scheduling, send thank-you notes to returning customers that you have contact information for, and oversee quality control through photos or videos and reports. Your business planning skills don't require you to be mobile."

Jake was quiet for a moment, considering.

"I know it's hard, Jake, but your body needs time to heal," Robin continued. "Your mind is sharp, your expertise is valuable, and there are meaningful ways you can contribute that won't compromise your recovery. Actually, staying mentally engaged with the farm operations will probably help your healing process."

"Doc Morrison said something similar," Jake admitted. "About staying mentally active being good for recovery."

"Because it is," Robin confirmed. "Depression and isolation slow healing. Purpose and engagement speed it up."

Lauren had been listening to this exchange. "We could set up a laptop on your bed table. You could video chat with Tom or any of the other employees, review the day's schedule, and even handle customer calls if families have specific questions. In fact, I'll let the entire staff know you may FaceTime with them periodically throughout the day so that you can see everything that is going on... that may work better than video chat, actually."

"Sounds like a good plan to me," Jake said, and Robin could see the weight lifting from his shoulders as he began to envision modified roles that would let him participate in farm activities.

"How about we watch a movie? Get your mind off work for a while?" Wyatt asked.

Jake's face lit up. "I vote for 'It's a Wonderful Life'."

"Yes! I almost forgot," Lauren said.

"It's our opening season tradition," Jake explained to Robin. "We always watch it on the Sunday before opening day. It started with Mom and Dad, and we've kept it going."

Robin helped Lauren clear the dinner dishes while Wyatt set up the television and DVD player mounted on the wall opposite Jake's bed. They worked with easy coordination of people comfortable in each other's space, Lauren washing while Robin dried, their conversation drifting from the upcoming week's schedule to church announcements to the annual Christmas tree lighting ceremony.

When they returned to Jake's room, Wyatt had dimmed the lights and queued up the movie. Lauren claimed the chair on the opposite side of Jake's bed again, curling up under a quilt. Robin settled back into her chair beside Jake, and Wyatt sat next to her.

The opening credits rolled, and Robin found herself drawn into the familiar story. She'd seen this movie countless times growing up but still enjoyed watching it every year before Christmas.

About thirty minutes into the film, during a scene where George Bailey realized the weight of his responsibilities, Jake spoke quietly. "This was Dad's favorite movie. He said it reminded him that the work we do matters, even when it feels small. That providing families with Christmas trees wasn't just about commerce—it was about creating memories."

Lauren reached across the bed to squeeze her brother's hand.

"Mom used to cry during the end," Jake continued, his voice thick with emotion. "Every single time. And Dad would always have tissues ready because he knew exactly when she'd need them."

"Twenty-six years of marriage," Wyatt said softly. "And he never forgot."

Robin felt tears prick her eyes. The grief in the room was palpable but not overwhelming—more like a gentle ache for what had been lost and gratitude for what remained.

As the movie progressed, Robin noticed Jake's energy beginning to flag. His eyelids grew heavy, his responses to the on-screen action slower. She glanced around and realized both Wyatt and Lauren had dozed off—Wyatt's head tilted back against his chair, Lauren curled under her quilt with her eyes closed.

Robin smiled, shaking her head at the sight. They were exhausted, both of them worn thin from weeks of caring for Jake while managing the farm's demands.

Moving quietly, Robin stood and adjusted Jake's position slightly, shifting pillows to support his back better.

"Your pain medication," Robin whispered.

"Yeah. Thanks."

She administered his medication and then adjusted his blanket. "Comfortable?"

"Mm-hmm." His eyes were already closing.

Robin returned to her chair and pulled an afghan from the back of it over her lap. On screen, George Bailey was discovering what Bedford Falls would have looked like without him, but Robin's attention had shifted to the people around her.

Jake was sleeping peacefully, his face relaxed.

Lauren, curled up like a child, the worry lines smoothed from her forehead.

Wyatt, his breathing deep and even, looked younger in sleep than he did when bearing the weight of responsibility while awake.

The Gibson family, whole despite being broken, finding moments of peace despite the crisis that had upended their world.

Robin pulled the afghan closer and looked upward.

Thank You for precious moments like this, Lord.

The gratitude swelled in her chest, not just for this afternoon but for the privilege of being here, of being trusted with Jake's care, and of being welcomed into the sacred space of family grief and healing.

On screen, the movie reached its climactic moment—George Bailey surrounded by friends and family, discovering his wonderful life. But Robin wasn't watching anymore. She was living something equally precious and equally sacred.

She let her own eyes close, the movie's familiar dialogue washing over her, and allowed herself to simply be present in this moment of grace. The farm was quiet around them, the November afternoon fading toward evening, and for the first time since walking back into the Gibson family's life, Robin felt something she'd been afraid to acknowledge.

She felt like she'd come home.

Chapter 16

"Just a little more to the left—there, perfect." Robin adjusted the laptop on Jake's bedside table while home health aide Cora Dixon gathered his notepad, pens, and Post-it notes to allow Jake to have a mini office at hand.

The screen on the laptop displayed four camera feeds in a grid layout, showing different angles of Gibson's Tree Farm in full opening day operation. Families wandered through rows of Fraser firs in the upper-left quadrant. The Christmas Shop entrance dominated the upper right, where a steady stream of customers flowed in and out carrying wreaths and garland. The bottom feeds showed the main parking area packed with vehicles and the wagon loading zone where Tom Hartwell coordinated groups heading out to cut their own trees.

Jake shifted in his partially reclined position, his jaw tight as he watched a father and son examining a seven-foot tree in the closest grove. "That family's looking at section twelve. The Nordmann firs we planted eight years ago."

"The ones with the softer needles?" Robin asked, remembering details from Wyatt's tour last week.

"Yeah." Jake's hands gripped the edge of his blanket. "Dad always said Nordmanns would diversify our premium offerings. I thought he was crazy—who needs Fraser firs and Nordmanns? But he was right. Some customers prefer the softer needles for homes with small kids."

Cora finished checking Jake's vitals and recorded them on her tablet. The home health aide had started working with Jake two weeks ago, rotating workdays with Josie. She was in her mid-thirties with highlighted brown hair pulled back in a clip and had the kind of steady, unflappable demeanor that made her excellent at her job.

"Your dad sounds like he was a smart man," Cora said.

"He was." Jake's attention remained fixed on the screen where the family had moved deeper into the grove. "He'd have loved seeing this. Opening day was always his favorite."

Robin noticed the way Jake's shoulders tensed, the slight tremor in his hands that had nothing to do with pain medication and everything to do with frustration. She'd seen this pattern in patients before—the emotional crash that came from watching life continue without being able to participate in the ways that mattered most.

"The cameras are helpful, right?" Cora asked.

"They're great. Wyatt and a couple of the guys installed them this past week." Jake gestured toward the screen. "I can see what's happening; coordinate with Tom if there are issues and answer questions when Lauren or Wyatt call. It's just—"

He stopped, shaking his head.

Robin exchanged a glance with Cora. They both knew what he wasn't saying.

"It's not the same as being out there," Robin finished for him.

"No." The single word held months of pent-up frustration. "It's not."

On screen, Wyatt appeared in the Christmas Shop feed, carrying a cut Christmas tree wrapped in netting. Even from the grainy camera angle, Robin could see the easy way he interacted with customers, pointing toward different sizes. He disappeared into the shop after that.

"Jake, I have the rest of the day off. You're my only patient today," Robin said.

"Lucky me... does that mean you're going to stay and hover over me since Wyatt isn't here?" Jake said with a hint of his usual humor, though it didn't quite reach his eyes.

"I have an idea, but you're going to have to promise not to argue with me about being a burden."

That got his attention. Jake's gaze shifted from the laptop to her face. "What kind of idea?"

"What if I spent the afternoon going to different locations around the farm and FaceTiming with you? You could see everything up close—the customers choosing trees, families loading wagons, and kids running around having fun. Real-time, not just camera feeds."

Jake's expression transformed—hope, longing, and immediate resistance all flickering across his features in rapid succession. "Robin, I can't ask you to spend your day off—"

"You're not asking. I'm offering."

"I love it," Cora said, her voice firm with encouragement. "Jake, you need this. The cameras are wonderful, but Robin's right—this would give you a much better sense of what's happening. You could tell her where to go and what you want to see."

Jake looked between them, and Robin watched him war with his pride. His need to be independent battled against his desperate desire to be part of opening day, even if only virtually.

"I would really appreciate it if you would," he said finally, his voice rough. "Thank you."

"You're welcome." Robin pulled her phone from her scrub pocket. "Let me call Wyatt."

She stepped into the hallway and found Wyatt's contact. He answered on the third ring, slightly breathless.

"Hey, Robin. Everything okay with Jake?"

"Everything's fine. Quick question—what are you doing right now?"

"Stocking more cut trees near the Christmas Shop. We've been going through inventory faster than expected, which is a good problem to have." The sound of rustling branches came through the phone. "Why?"

Robin explained her idea, finishing with, "Would it be okay if I borrowed one of the side-by-sides to drive around? I thought I could take Jake on a virtual tour."

Wyatt was quiet for a moment. "I have a better idea. I'll drive, and we can do this together."

Robin's pulse kicked up. An entire afternoon with Wyatt, just the two of them driving around the farm, sharing this experience with Jake. The professional part of her brain recognized this as excellent patient care—giving Jake connection to the work he loved. The personal part of her brain recognized this as hours of proximity with a man she was supposed to be keeping at friendship distance.

"That would be great," she said, and meant it despite her reservations. "When—"

"Give me thirty minutes to finish up here and coordinate with Tom. I'll pick you up at the house."

"Perfect. See you then."

Robin ended the call and returned to Jake's room, where Cora was adjusting his bed position.

"Wyatt's going to drive me around," Robin said. "He'll be here in thirty minutes."

Jake's grin was the first genuine one she'd seen all morning. "This will be amazing. Thank you, Robin. Really."

"While we wait," Robin said, moving to the foot of Jake's bed, "what do you say we do some exercises? Cora, do you want to help me with some ankle rotations and leg stretches?"

"Absolutely." Cora moved to the opposite side of the bed.

They pulled back Jake's blanket, exposing his legs. Robin had seen significant improvement in Jake's muscle tone over the past weeks, evidence that the daily exercises were preventing atrophy even though he couldn't yet support his own weight. She placed her hands on his left ankle, feeling the warmth of his skin, the structure of bones and tendons that might someday carry him through these groves again.

"Please let me know if anything hurts," Robin said, beginning the gentle rotation she'd taught Wyatt and Lauren weeks ago.

"Will do," Jake said, his attention already drifting back to the laptop screen.

As Robin worked through the familiar motions—rotate left, rotate right, flex the foot, point the toes—her mind wandered to the man who would arrive in less than thirty minutes. Wyatt would pull up in the side-by-side, probably wearing his work jacket and boots, his hair slightly mussed from the wind. They'd spend hours together, just the two of them, ostensibly for Jake's benefit but really—

Robin caught herself. Really what? Really so she could torture herself with being near a man whose real life was ninety minutes away? So she could pretend that "friendship" was enough when every conversation, every shared glance, and every moment of easy partnership made her chest ache with wanting more?

"How's that feel?" Robin asked Jake.

"Good. Better than good, actually."

Robin smiled, but her thoughts had already drifted again. Thirty minutes. Less now, actually. Wyatt would arrive, and she'd climb into that side-by-side beside him, and they'd spend the afternoon pretending that friendship was a sustainable boundary when her heart seemed determined to breach it with every passing day.

She'd told him on that hiking trail that she couldn't risk her heart on anything more than friendship. That his life was in a different place. She'd meant every word.

But that was before this past Sunday afternoon, having dinner and watching a movie with his family. Before realizing how naturally she fit into the rhythms of this household again and wanted to be a part of their lives. Before understanding that what she felt for Wyatt as a teenager hadn't faded.

"Robin?" Cora's voice pulled her back to the present. "Want to switch sides?"

"Right. Yes." Robin moved to work on Jake's right leg while Cora transitioned to the left.

Through the window, she could hear the sounds of the farm in full operation—children's laughter, the rumble of tractors, and voices calling to each other across open spaces. Opening day at Gibson's Tree Farm. The beginning of their busiest season, the culmination of a year's worth of work, and Jake was stuck in this room watching it happen on a laptop screen.

She finished the last rotation on Jake's ankle and straightened, pulling the blanket back over his legs.

"All done," she said. "How do you feel?"

"Like I might actually walk again someday." Jake's optimism had returned; his earlier frustration temporarily shelved. "Thanks, both of you."

Robin glanced at the clock on the bedside table. Twenty-five minutes had passed. Wyatt would arrive any moment.

Her phone buzzed with a text moments later.

Wyatt: *Heading to the house now. Meet you out front?*

Robin's throat tightened. She typed a quick response.

Robin: *Be right there.*

"He's on his way," she told Jake and Cora. "I'll call as soon as we're in position."

She grabbed her coat, scarf, and gloves from the chair and started toward the door, then paused and turned back.

Jake was watching her with a grin on his face. "Have fun," he said.

"I will. Wish me luck."

Chapter 17

The side-by-side rolled to a stop near the Christmas Shop. It bustled with energy—families streamed through the entrance, children pointed at window displays, and the parking area was packed with vehicles.

"Ready?" Wyatt grinned.

"Let's do this." Robin climbed out, tucking her phone securely in her jacket pocket.

Inside, Christmas music played softly beneath the hum of conversation. Every corner of the space held customers—a young couple debating wreath sizes near the front display, an older woman examining handcrafted ornaments, and children clustered around the model train setup that chugged through a miniature winter village.

Robin spotted Lauren behind the counter, her fingers flying across her laptop keyboard, her expression focused. She wore a festive red sweater with a Christmas tree design and had pulled her hair back in a ponytail.

Wyatt led the way through the crowded shop, navigating around displays with ease. When they reached the counter, Lauren glanced up, and her eyes widened.

"Wyatt? Robin?" Alarm flashed across her face. "Is Jake—"

"Jake's fine," Wyatt said quickly, raising both hands in a calming gesture. "Everything's okay. Robin had an idea we wanted to run by you."

Relief flooded Lauren's expression, and she sagged slightly against the counter. "You just scared ten years off my life. What's the idea?"

Robin explained the plan—driving around the farm, FaceTiming with Jake from different locations, and giving him a real-time experience of opening day beyond the camera feeds.

Lauren's face transformed, her smile growing with each detail. "That's brilliant. Jake must be so excited."

"He was pretty happy when I left," Robin said. "Ready to be part of the action."

"Let's call him." Wyatt pulled out his own phone, then paused. "Actually, Robin should make the first call. This was her idea."

Robin retrieved her phone and found Jake's contact. He answered on the first ring, his face filling the screen, his expression eager.

"Where are you?" Jake asked immediately. "What am I looking at?"

"We're in the Christmas Shop."

Wyatt and Lauren immediately moved to flank Robin, positioning themselves so Jake could see them both. Wyatt leaned in close enough that his shoulder pressed against Robin's, and she felt the warmth of him through her jacket.

"Hey, brother," Wyatt said. "Your shop looks pretty good today."

"Your shop, you mean," Jake corrected. "You're the one managing it this season."

"Lauren and Emma Kate are managing it. I'm just trying not to break anything." Wyatt's modesty earned an eye roll from his sister.

"The shop sounds packed," Jake said.

"It is; this is the strongest opening day I've seen in three years," Lauren confirmed. "We're already running low on some inventory. Emma Kate's restocking as fast as she can."

Robin flipped the camera to rear-facing mode and slowly panned the camera, giving Jake a sweeping view of the shop's interior. Families browsed the aisles, children pointed at decorations, and the cash register chimed regularly as a seasonal employee processed sales.

"Look who's here," Lauren said suddenly, waving toward the entrance.

Pastor Andrew and his wife, Lily, had just walked in, and they began examining a display of handcrafted nativity sets near the front window.

"Oh, I love this," Robin said, already moving toward them with the phone held steady. "Jake, you're about to have visitors."

Lauren hurried ahead, her face bright with excitement. Robin watched as she approached the pastor and his wife, gesturing animatedly, clearly explaining the FaceTime situation. Andrew's expression shifted from surprise to delight, and he was already walking toward Robin before Lauren finished talking.

"Jake Gibson!" Andrew's voice boomed across the shop, drawing curious glances. "How are you doing, my friend?"

Robin angled the phone so Jake had a clear view of the pastor's face.

"Pastor Andrew. Hey, Lily." Jake's voice carried through the phone's speaker. "I'm doing better. Getting stronger every day."

"We've been praying for you constantly," Lily said, moving into the camera's frame beside her husband. "The whole church has. How's your pain doing? I've heard it gets pretty tense at times."

"Manageable today. Robin's got me on a medication schedule that's working pretty well."

"Robin's taking excellent care of you, I'm sure." Andrew smiled directly at the camera. "We saw her at church on Sunday. She and Wyatt sat together."

Heat crept up Robin's neck. She was aware of Wyatt standing close behind her, probably grinning at the pastor's pointed observation.

Before Jake could respond, Martha Kincaid appeared at Andrew's elbow, her silvered hair perfectly styled, her expression curious. "What's all the excitement?"

"We're FaceTiming with Jake," Lily explained. "Robin's giving him a virtual tour of opening day."

"Jake Gibson!" Martha moved into view, her face filling the screen. "You must be going stir-crazy in that bed."

"You have no idea, Miss Martha."

"I sent an apple pie home with Wyatt a few days ago; did you enjoy it?" Martha asked.

"It was delicious. Thank you."

More people began drifting toward their growing group. Robin recognized Sarah Thompkins from church—a woman in her mid-thirties with kind eyes and practical clothing suited for farm exploring. Her two children flanked her, both wearing winter jackets.

"What's happening?" Sarah asked, curiosity evident.

"Jake's on FaceTime," Lauren explained again.

"Jake!" Sarah moved closer, her children pressing against her sides. "The kids were just saying how much they miss seeing you at church."

Robin crouched slightly, angling the camera to capture the children at their eye level. Damian gave an awkward wave. But Willow—eight years old with dark braids and missing front teeth—bounced on her toes with unconstrained enthusiasm.

"Hi, Mr. Jake! We made you a card at Sunday school, and Miss Lauren said she'd bring it to you. Did you get it?"

"I did get it," Jake said, his voice warm. "It's hanging on my wall right now. You drew an excellent tractor."

Willow beamed. "Mama says you got hurt by a tractor, so I wanted to draw you a nice tractor to make you feel better."

Robin's throat tightened. She glanced up to find Wyatt watching her, his expression soft.

"This is wonderful," Lily said. "All of us together like this."

"We should sing something," Willow announced suddenly. "We should sing for Mr. Jake to make him feel extra better!"

"That's a lovely idea," Sarah said.

Andrew laughed, the sound rich and genuine. "I think that's a perfect idea. What should we sing?"

"'Joy to the World'!" Willow said immediately. "That's my favorite."

"'Joy to the World,' it is." Andrew glanced around at the gathered group. "Everyone ready?"

Robin held the phone steady. Around them, other shoppers had noticed the commotion and were drifting closer, curious about the impromptu gathering. She stepped back a few paces, widening the camera angle to capture more people.

"Jake, you've got about twenty people here ready to serenade you," Robin said.

"I see that."

Andrew raised his hand like a conductor. "On three. One, two, three—"

"Joy to the world, the Lord is come..."

The voices weren't perfect—some people sang off-key, others came in late on the first line—but the sincerity was unmistakable. Shoppers who'd been browsing set down merchandise and joined in. The young woman at the cash register sang while processing a sale. Emma Kate emerged from the back room, wiping her hands on her apron, and added her voice to the chorus.

Robin's vision blurred. She blinked rapidly, trying to keep the camera steady as tears threatened to spill. This was a community wrapping its arms around one of its own, refusing to let injury and distance diminish his place among them.

The children sang with particular enthusiasm, Willow's voice rising above the others on the high notes. Lily's hand rested on her rounded belly as she sang, and Martha's weathered face glowed with contentment.

When they reached the final verse—"And heaven and nature sing"—the volume swelled. At least thirty people now crowded into the camera frame, their voices blending into something beautiful.

The last note faded into spontaneous applause.

"God bless you, Jake," Andrew said, his voice carrying across the shop. "We hope this brightened your day and reminded you that you're not alone. You're surrounded by love."

"Thank you." Jake's voice was rough. "All of you. This means more than I can say."

Robin managed to flip the camera back to selfie mode, revealing her face—flushed and tear-streaked, yet smiling despite the emotions overwhelming her system.

"Hi," she said to Jake, attempting levity and failing completely.

"Hey." Jake studied her through the screen. "You okay? You look like you're about to cry."

"I am crying." Robin laughed wetly, swiping at her cheeks with her free hand. "I'm just incredibly touched by what I witnessed. This community, your church family—" Her voice broke again.

Warmth settled across her shoulders. She glanced sideways to find Wyatt standing beside her, his arm draped around her. The weight of his arm, the solid presence of him anchored against her side, sent shivers cascading down her spine.

She should step away and maintain the friendship boundary they'd established. She shouldn't lean into his touch like she was starving for it.

Robin did none of those things.

Jake grinned at them through the screen. "So, brother, where should you two head next?"

Wyatt's arm remained exactly where it was. "Your call. What do you want to see?"

"Can you go out to one of the tree sections? I want to see families having fun and trees being cut down."

"You got it," Wyatt said. "Section eight has the best activity right now. Lots of young families and kids running around. It'll be perfect."

"Sounds good. Thanks again, Robin." Jake's image moved as he apparently shifted position. "This is—this is everything."

"You're welcome. We'll call you in about ten minutes when we're set up in the grove."

She ended the call, and immediately Lauren was there, pulling her into a fierce hug.

"Thank you," Lauren whispered against Robin's ear. "Thank you for thinking of this, for caring about him enough to spend your day off making him feel included. You have no idea how much you mean to me."

Robin hugged her back, unable to speak past the emotion lodged in her chest. When Lauren finally released her, Robin found herself surrounded by well-wishers—Martha squeezing her hand, Sarah thanking her for her kindness, and Andrew offering a blessing over Jake's continued healing.

Wyatt stood slightly apart, watching her with an expression that made her pulse skip erratically. When the crowd finally dispersed, returning to their shopping and conversations, he approached and extended his hand toward her.

"Come on, friend." His tone was light and teasing. "On to our next adventure."

Robin grinned despite her tear-stained face, despite the confusion warring in her chest, and despite knowing that taking his hand was probably a terrible idea.

She took it anyway.

"Let's go."

Chapter 18

Wyatt stood in the middle of section eight's Fraser fir grove, Robin beside him, his phone already positioned for the Face-Time call. Around them, families wandered between rows of perfectly shaped trees—fathers measuring heights with outstretched arms, mothers debating fullness, and children darting through the aisles with boundless energy.

He tapped Jake's contact number, and his brother answered immediately.

"Ready for round two?" Wyatt asked, keeping the phone in selfie mode so Jake could see both him and Robin standing together.

"Absolutely. Show me everything." Jake's eagerness was palpable even through the small screen.

Robin leaned in closer to fit in the frame, her shoulder pressing against Wyatt's arm. "We're in section eight. It's beautiful out here."

"That section has some of our best Fraser firs," Jake said. "Seven to nine feet—perfect for residential homes. Are people cutting their own, or are the guys helping?"

"Both." Wyatt flipped the camera to rear-facing mode and began strolling down the aisle. "Looks like we've got about—" he scanned the visible area, "—maybe fifteen families right here in this general area."

The camera captured a young couple examining a tree about twenty feet ahead. The man shook the trunk gently while the woman circled, inspecting branches from all angles. Their toddler sat on the ground nearby, fascinated by a pinecone he'd discovered.

"That's the Warrens," Jake said. "They come every year and always cut their own tree. Mark's particular about symmetry."

Wyatt continued forward, Robin walking beside him. The sounds of the grove filled the air—saws working through trunks, children's laughter, parents calling instructions, and the occasional whoop of triumph when a tree toppled.

"Move left a bit," Jake directed. "That's Tom with the Smiths."

Wyatt adjusted his path and spotted Tom Hartwell about forty yards away, working a two-person saw with Frank Smith. Frank's wife, Greta, stood nearby, watching two identical little girls in matching purple coats bounce around the tree like overstimulated rabbits.

"The Smith twins," Wyatt said with a grin. "This should be entertaining."

Robin was already jogging ahead, her hair swinging in the breeze. Wyatt watched her approach the group and saw her animated gestures as she explained what they were doing. Tom's weathered face broke into a smile, and Greta immediately turned toward where Wyatt was approaching, her expression delighted.

"Jake Gibson!" Frank's voice boomed across the grove. He was in his late sixties, silver-haired and robust, wearing the kind of practical work clothes that suggested he'd never fully retired from manual labor. "How're you doing, son?"

Wyatt positioned the phone so Jake had a clear view of everyone. The twins—Melanie and Monica, four years old and impossible to tell apart—pressed against their grandmother's legs, suddenly shy.

"Hey, Mr. Frank, Miss Greta." Jake's voice carried warmth and genuine affection. "I'm doing better. Getting stronger."

"We've been praying for you every single day," Greta said. Her silver curls framed a kind face creased with concern. "Frank and I wanted to visit, but we didn't want to overwhelm you with too many visitors at once."

"I appreciate the prayers. They're working."

"Why are you in bed?" One twin—Melanie, Wyatt thought, based on the slight difference in their facial features—pointed at the screen. "It's not nighttime. It's tree time."

Jake laughed. "You're absolutely right. I hurt my back, so I have to stay in bed for a while. But I'm getting better."

"Does it hurt a lot?" Monica's question held the kind of blunt curiosity only four-year-olds could manage.

"Sometimes. But my nurse gives me medicine that helps."

"Our nurse is really nice when we go to see her at the doctor's office," Melanie declared. "She gave me a sticker with a puppy on it."

"That sounds like a good nurse."

Frank and Tom had resumed sawing while this conversation unfolded, working the blade back and forth through the trunk in perfect rhythm. Wood chips scattered across the ground, and the tree began to creak ominously.

"It's falling!" Monica shrieked with delight.

Wyatt zoomed out slightly, capturing the moment when the Fraser fir surrendered to gravity. It descended in slow motion, branches shuddering, before landing with a soft whoosh in the bed of needles carpeting the ground.

The twins erupted into jumping, their purple coats flashing as they bounced up and down like they'd just witnessed the most exciting thing in their young lives.

"That was our tree!" Melanie shouted. "We picked the bestest one!"

Robin moved into action immediately, joining Tom and Frank as they positioned themselves around the fallen tree. She grabbed the middle section while the men took the top and base, and together they lifted it—seven feet of Fraser fir weighing probably fifty pounds—and began carrying it down the aisle toward the netting station.

Wyatt followed with the phone, trying to keep everyone in frame. The twins chased after the tree, shrieking instructions that made no sense but conveyed maximum enthusiasm. Greta followed at a more sedate pace, calling reminders about watching where they were going and not running too far ahead.

"Girls, stay where Grandma can see you!" Greta's voice carried exasperation and affection in equal measure.

Melanie veered left to investigate a particularly interesting branch on a nearby tree. Monica, not to be outdone, darted right toward a family group who looked startled by the purple-coated whirlwind suddenly in their midst.

"Monica Grace Smith, you come back here right now!" Greta moved with surprising speed for a woman in her mid-sixties, corralling one twin while keeping visual track of the other.

Jake's laughter came through the phone speaker, rich and genuine. Wyatt grinned, holding the phone steady as Robin and the men reached the netting station at the grove's edge. They fed the tree through the machine that wrapped it in orange plastic mesh, then loaded it onto a wagon hitched to one of the farm's ATVs.

"Jake?" Wyatt said as he shifted the camera back to selfie mode, keeping just his own face in frame for now. "What do you want to see next?"

He stepped away from the activity, finding a quieter spot beside a particularly full tree. The sounds of the grove faded slightly—still present, but muted enough for conversation.

"That was great," Jake said. "The twins are hilarious. Monica's going to be a handful when she gets older."

"She's already a handful. Did you see Greta trying to keep track of both of them?"

"Like herding cats." Jake's smile dimmed slightly. "Man, I miss this. Being out there, seeing customers enjoy the trees, and watching families make memories. There's something about opening day that never gets old."

"We're doing our best to bring it to you."

"I know. And I appreciate it." Jake shifted position, and Wyatt heard the faint rustle of sheets. "Can you do something for me?"

"Name it."

"Go out to the special grove next. The big trees." Jake's tone grew more serious. "I want you and Robin to help pick the tree for the town square. Walk through it, show me the options, and let's select it together. You get to cut it tomorrow, and I want to be part of the decision-making."

Pride swelled in Wyatt's chest. Their father had always involved both sons in choosing the town tree, treating it as a sacred responsibility rather than a routine task. Jake was continuing the tradition, refusing to let injury steal this moment from him.

"We'll do it," Wyatt said. "Anything else?"

"Yeah, actually." Jake's expression shifted to something between mischievous and earnest. "I want you to give Robin a big bear hug for me. Let her know how much this all means to me and how much I appreciate her. I'd do it myself, but—" He gestured vaguely at his surroundings. "Obviously, I'm not there right now."

Wyatt felt his grin widen. "I can do that, brother."

"Good. Now let's go find the town's tree."

The call ended. Wyatt pocketed his phone and jogged back down the aisle toward where Robin was standing. Tom had already climbed into his farm truck, heading off to coordinate another section. The Smiths were loading into their SUV, the twins still chattering about their tree adventure, when Wyatt reached Robin.

She turned as he approached, her cheeks flushed from exertion and cold air, her eyes bright. "Where to next?"

Wyatt didn't answer immediately. He simply stepped forward and wrapped his arms around her in the bear hug Jake had requested—except somewhere between intention and execution, the gesture transformed into something more. He lifted her off her feet, spinning her around once, twice, three times, her startled laughter ringing across the grove.

When he set her down, his arms moved to her waist. Robin looked up at him, still grinning and slightly dizzy from the spinning.

"What brought that on?" Her voice held breathless amusement.

"Jake wanted me to give you a bear hug and tell you how much he appreciates what you've done for him." Wyatt's arms remained exactly where they were, his hands resting against the small of her back. "And I appreciate you too."

Robin's smile softened, her eyes searching his face. She was close enough that he could see the exact pattern of gold and green in her hazel irises, close enough that he could feel the warmth of her breath in the cold November air.

Wyatt's gaze dropped to her lips. Just for a second. Long enough for Robin to notice, long enough for the playful atmosphere to shift into something electric and dangerous.

He started to lean down.

Robin pulled back, her hands coming up to press gently against his chest. "Friends don't kiss, Mr. Gibson."

The words should have been a reprimand. Instead, they sounded like a question—like she was testing him.

Wyatt loosened his hold but didn't release her completely. "Well, this friend really wants to kiss you, Miss Fitch."

Color flooded her cheeks. She glanced away, breaking eye contact, and Wyatt watched emotions flicker across her face—longing, fear, hope, and something that looked like painful indecision.

He released her, taking a deliberate step back, giving her space she clearly needed. But he extended his hand toward her, palm up, offering rather than demanding.

"Come on." His grin felt slightly strained, but he kept his tone light. "Jake has assigned our next adventure. We need to go select the town Christmas tree."

Robin turned back to face him. For a long moment, she simply looked at his outstretched hand like it represented something far more significant than assistance walking across uneven ground.

Then she placed her hand in his, her fingers curling around his palm, and smiled. "Let's go."

Chapter 19

Robin's boots crunched against the gravel as she climbed out of the side-by-side. The special grove stretched before them—a cathedral of evergreens reaching toward the overcast sky, each tree a monument to patience and careful cultivation. These weren't Christmas trees families selected for their homes. These were the giants, fifteen to twenty-five feet tall, grown for town squares, church sanctuaries, and corporate lobbies.

She pulled out her phone and tapped Jake's contact, keeping the camera in selfie mode. Wyatt moved close beside her, close enough that she could feel the warmth radiating through her jacket.

Jake answered immediately, his face filling the screen. "Long time no see, guys."

"Hey, Jake. We're in the special grove," Robin said, angling the phone to capture both her and Wyatt. "Do you have any suggestions about which trees you'd like to see first, or should we just walk up and down between the rows until you see something that you like?"

"I changed my mind. I want you to select it."

Robin blinked. "What?"

"You heard me." Jake's expression was serious. "I want you to choose the town tree."

"Jake, I can't do that." Robin said as she shook her head. "That's something you and Wyatt should decide on. It's a Gibson family tradition, right... you and your siblings pick the tree?"

"It is," Jake agreed. "Which is why I want you to do it."

Beside her, Wyatt was nodding and smiling.

"Jake—"

"Robin, I've made up my mind," Jake's voice gentled. "You've spent weeks caring for me, coordinating my recovery, and teaching my siblings how to help me. You've given up your day off to bring the farm to me when I can't be there myself. The least I can do is let you be part of our tradition."

Her throat tightened. "Okay, I'll do it."

She handed the phone to Wyatt, who immediately switched to rear-facing camera mode. Robin took a breath and started walking down the center aisle, acutely aware that both brothers were watching her.

The trees towered above her, their branches full and symmetrical, each one beautiful enough for Laurel Ridge's town square. How was she supposed to choose?

"I don't know what I'm looking for," Robin admitted, stopping beside a full Norway spruce. "How do you decide?"

"Look for symmetry," Jake said through the phone's speaker. "The tree needs to look good from all angles since it'll be the centerpiece of the square."

"Check the trunk," Wyatt added, moving the camera to follow her as she circled the tree. "Make sure it's straight, with no major bends or curves that'll make it difficult to stand upright."

"And the branches should be strong," Jake continued. "They'll be holding thousands of lights and ornaments."

Robin moved to the next tree, then the next, studying each one with growing confidence. She checked trunks for straightness, examined branch patterns for balance, and walked complete circles around trees to assess symmetry from every angle. Wyatt followed with the phone, his quiet presence somehow making the task feel less daunting.

The overcast sky had darkened slightly, and as Robin approached the fifth tree in the row, she felt something cold and soft land on her cheek. Then another. And another.

Snow.

She tilted her face skyward, watching fat flakes drift down from clouds that seemed to hang just above the treetops.

"It's snowing," she said, wonder coloring her voice.

"Perfect timing," Jake said.

Robin continued down the aisle, snow collecting on her shoulders and dusting the tree branches. She felt like she'd stepped into one of those Christmas movies she loved to watch on television—the kind where snow always fell at exactly the right moment.

She stopped walking.

The tree stood about ten yards ahead, slightly taller than the others surrounding it, its branches spreading in perfect symmetry. Even covered in a light dusting of snow, Robin could see the strength of its structure, the health of its needles, and the way it seemed to command attention without effort.

This was the tree. She knew it the way she sometimes knew a patient was turning a corner toward positive recovery—not through logic or analysis, but through something deeper and more intuitive.

Robin turned to face Wyatt, who immediately adjusted the camera angle so Jake could see her face. Snow had settled in her hair, on her eyelashes, and was melting against her flushed cheeks.

She smiled and clapped her gloved hands together.

"This one." She pointed at the towering evergreen behind her. "This is the tree for Laurel Ridge."

Wyatt lowered the phone slightly, his own smile matching hers. "Why this one?"

"Because—" Robin gestured toward the tree, searching for words to explain what she felt rather than saw. "Look at it. It's strong but graceful. Every branch is perfect, like it's been waiting its whole life for this moment. And when it's lit up in the town square with all those lights and ornaments, it's going to be absolutely magical. Children will remember this tree. Families will take photos in front of it. It'll be the backdrop for proposals and first kisses, and Santa will look perfect sitting next to it the evening all the kids will come and sit on his lap. Just imagine it... all the cute pictures that will be taken." She paused, suddenly self-conscious about her enthusiasm. "Is that a good reason?"

"Those are all perfect reasons," Jake said. "Tag it, brother. That's the tree for Laurel Ridge this year."

Wyatt handed Robin her phone, and she watched through the screen as he pulled a roll of bright orange flagging tape from his jacket pocket. He approached the tree, selected a branch at eye level, and secured the tape in place. The orange stood out brilliantly against the green branches, marking this tree as chosen, claimed, and destined for something beyond growing silently in a grove.

When he finished, Wyatt stepped back and turned toward her. Robin switched the camera back to selfie mode, capturing her face—flushed with cold and excitement, eyes bright, and smile so wide her cheeks ached.

"Jake, thank you." Her voice wavered. "Thank you for letting me be a part of this. I know it's a family tradition, and I know it means something special, and I—" She stopped, blinking against sudden tears. "This meant so much to me."

"Robin." Jake waited until she met his eyes through the screen. "There's no way I could ever repay you for everything you've done for me. For us. This is just a tree. What you've given our family is—" He paused, emotion crossing his features. "It's beyond words."

Tears spilled over again despite Robin's best efforts to contain them. She laughed wetly, swiping at her cheeks with her free hand.

Wyatt moved into the frame, standing close beside her. Snow had collected in his dark hair, melting at the edges where it met his skin.

"Jake, buddy... ya gotta stop making her cry!" Wyatt said with a grin. "What's next, brother?"

"Greenhouse three," Jake said. "I want all three of us to select the poinsettias for the church this year. Pastor Andrew always lets us choose, and I'm not missing it just because I'm stuck in this bed."

"We'll see you in a few minutes," Robin managed, her voice still thick.

"Looking forward to it," Jake said. "And Robin? You picked the perfect tree."

The call ended. Robin lowered her phone, staring at the black screen for a moment before tucking it back in her pocket. Snow continued falling around them, coating the world in white silence.

Wyatt didn't say anything. He simply took her hand—gloved fingers threading through gloved fingers—and started walking back toward the side-by-side.

Robin let him lead her down the aisle between towering evergreens. Her mind whirled with everything that had happened in the past three hours—the singing in the Christmas Shop, the Smith twins' enthusiasm, the near-kiss that had left her pulse racing, and now this moment with the tree, with Jake's trust, with Wyatt's hand warm around hers.

She was falling.

The realization settled over her like the snow—gentle, inevitable, transforming everything it touched. She'd tried so hard to maintain boundaries, to protect her heart, to keep Wyatt safely in the category of friend.

But hearts didn't respect boundaries. They just kept reaching, hoping, and believing that love might be worth the risk.

The question wasn't whether she had feelings for Wyatt. That answer was obvious. The question was whether she was brave enough to admit those feelings, to risk vulnerability again, and to trust that this time might be different.

And beneath that question lurked another, more complicated one: What happened if Jake fully recovered? When the crisis that brought Wyatt home resolved itself, would he return to his Forestry Service life ninety minutes away, leaving her with memories and maybes and a heart broken again?

Wyatt squeezed her hand, pulling her attention back to the present. They'd reached the side-by-side. She climbed in.

He circled around to the driver's side, his expression unreadable. When he settled behind the wheel, he didn't immediately start the engine. Instead, he turned to face her, snow still clinging to his hair, his blue eyes serious.

"Robin—"

"We should go," she interrupted, not ready for whatever he was about to say. "Jake's waiting for us."

Something flickered across Wyatt's face—disappointment, maybe, or understanding—but he nodded and started the engine.

Chapter 20

The humid warmth of greenhouse three enveloped Wyatt the moment he stepped inside, the temperature differential from the snowy afternoon outside making his skin prickle. Row upon row of poinsettias stretched before them in a riot of color—traditional red, pristine white, variegated pink and cream, and even deep burgundy varieties that looked almost black in certain light.

Robin stood beside him near the entrance. Around them, the greenhouse hummed with activity. Three employees worked at the far end, filling wholesale orders and loading plants onto rolling carts. Pete Norton—their poinsettia specialist, who'd been with the farm for over a decade—stood near the center aisle, inspecting a tray of red varieties with the critical eye of someone who knew exactly what perfection looked like.

Wyatt pulled out his phone and called Jake, keeping the camera in selfie mode. His brother answered immediately, his face appearing on screen.

"Greenhouse three... how's it going?" Jake asked.

Wyatt angled the phone to capture both himself and Robin. "It's busy in here. Pete's got the team filling orders, and the poinsettias look incredible this year."

"Pete always delivers," Jake said with obvious pride. "How many plants are we looking at?"

"Enough to supply half the state, probably." Robin leaned closer to fit in the frame, and Wyatt felt the warmth of her proximity. "They're all gorgeous."

Wyatt flipped the camera to rear-facing mode and held it high, giving Jake a sweeping view of the greenhouse interior. The employees glanced up at the movement, and Pete walked closer, his weathered face breaking into a smile when he spotted the phone.

"Jake Gibson!" Pete's voice carried across the space. "How're you feeling, son?"

"Better every day, Pete. The greenhouse looks fantastic."

"We've got some beauties this year. The variegated variety came in especially nice." Pete gestured around the space. "Your brother's been keeping everything running smoothly. He's got a good eye for quality control."

"Everyone, Jake's watching on FaceTime," Wyatt called out to the greenhouse at large. "Come say hello if you'd like."

The three employees immediately abandoned their carts and hurried over, clustered around the phone with greetings and well-wishes. Sophia Patterson, who'd worked seasonal greenhouse duty for five years, told Jake about her daughter's first semester at college. Mark Gallagher updated him on the wholesale orders that had exceeded projections. Young Brendan Wilkes—barely eighteen and new this season—awkwardly waved and mumbled something about hoping Jake felt better soon.

"Robin and I are ready to walk through the greenhouse and select the plants for church, Jake; give us an idea of what you'd like," Wyatt said.

"Twenty plants, right?" Jake's question held a note of consideration. "That's what we usually do?"

"Usually." Wyatt paused, an idea forming. "What if we increased it to thirty this year?"

"I like that. Thirty plants for the church. Mix of colors—mostly traditional red, but throw in some white and maybe a few variegated for variety."

Wyatt started walking slowly down the center aisle, keeping the phone angled so Jake could see the plants they passed. Robin moved beside him, occasionally reaching out to touch a leaf or examine a bloom cluster.

"This one's beautiful." Robin gestured toward a full red poinsettia with deep green foliage. "This color is outstanding."

"That's a good choice," Jake said through the phone. "Classic red, full shape. Grab it."

Robin lifted the pot and carried it to a staging table Pete had cleared near the back of the greenhouse. Wyatt followed with the phone, watching as she set it down before returning to the selection process.

They developed a rhythm—Robin pointing out plants that caught her eye, Jake offering opinions through the phone, and Wyatt providing a third perspective. Some selections were unanimous. Others sparked playful debate about size versus symmetry and color intensity versus overall health.

"Okay, that one's beautiful, but we already have four that size," Jake protested when Robin reached for a tall red variety.

"But it's pretty," Robin countered.

"She's right," Wyatt said, earning a triumphant grin from Robin.

"Fine, fine. I'm outvoted."

They'd selected about twenty plants when Jake's voice took on a slightly strained quality. "Could you guys maybe slow down a bit? All this movement is making me dizzy."

Robin laughed, the sound bright and genuine. "Oh my gosh, Jake, I never even thought about that. I'm so sorry."

"No worries. Just maybe prop the phone up somewhere so I can watch without the constant motion?"

"Good call." Wyatt found a stable spot on a potting bench, angling his phone to capture the main work area. "How's that?"

"Perfect. Now I can watch you two work without feeling like I'm on a roller coaster."

Wyatt and Robin continued selecting plants, while Jake watched. The employees worked around them, and Pete occasionally offered suggestions.

Robin had moved toward a display of variegated poinsettias—stunning plants with cream and pink marbling through their red bracts. She stood examining them with her head tilted, clearly trying to decide between two similar specimens.

"Wyatt?" She glanced back toward him. "Can you help me? I want to choose a few of these variegated ones, but I'm not sure which ones will complement what we've already selected."

He walked over to where she stood. One plant leaned more pink; the other, more cream. Both were beautiful.

"What do you think?" Robin asked, looking up at him.

The question should have been about poinsettias. But standing there in the greenhouse humidity, looking down at Robin's upturned face with flushed cheeks and bright eyes, Wyatt found himself thinking about entirely different things.

Like the way her laugh sounded in the open air of the Christmas tree groves. Like the way she'd clapped her hands together when she found the perfect tree for the town square. Or like how natural it felt to reach for her hand, to have her beside him, and to imagine days and weeks and years of moments like this.

"I think—" His voice came out rougher than intended. "I think you're beautiful."

Robin's smile softened. "I meant, what do you think about the plants?"

"I know what you meant... I couldn't care less about plants right now."

She took a small step closer. Just inches, but enough that Wyatt could count the gold flecks in her beautiful eyes.

His hand lifted without conscious thought, reaching toward her face, and Robin leaned in—

"Guys." Jake's voice cut through the moment like cold water. "Umm, guys? Did you forget I'm here?"

They sprang apart. Robin's hand flew to her mouth, and laughter burst out of her—not embarrassed giggling but full, genuine hilarity. Wyatt joined in, the tension breaking into something lighter but no less significant.

Around them, Pete and the employees were studiously focused on their work with the kind of exaggerated attention that suggested they'd witnessed the almost-kiss and were being polite about pretending they hadn't.

Wyatt walked back to the phone and picked it up, switching to selfie mode. Robin appeared beside him, her face still flushed but grinning widely.

"Sorry, brother," Wyatt said, not feeling sorry at all.

"Maybe save the romantic moments for when you're not on camera with your injured brother?" Jake said with a grin.

"Fair enough," Robin managed through her laughter.

"We'll finish selecting the last few plants and let Pete know they're ready for delivery whenever Pastor Andrew wants them," Wyatt said, trying to regain some semblance of focus.

"Where should we go next?" Robin asked, her voice still bright with residual laughter.

"It's almost four." Jake said. "Several church members are coming to visit and bringing dinner soon. That's enough for today. Why don't you both come up to the house when you're finished and joined us."

Wyatt turned to look at Robin, watching emotions flicker across her face.

"I'd love to," she said.

"See you in a few."

Wyatt ended the call and pocketed his phone. "Go ahead and pick the last few plants. I trust your judgment."

Robin glanced at him quizzically but moved back toward the variegated varieties. She selected plants with care, checking leaf health and bract fullness, occasionally tilting them to examine their structure from different angles.

Wyatt watched her work, his mind churning through everything that had happened today.

He loved her. That was the truth he'd been circling around for weeks but could no longer avoid. His feelings for her had never diminished. He loved her more now than he had in the past. Robin fit into his family, his life, and the rhythms of this farm and this community in a way that felt both startling and completely natural.

The question was whether he could build a life here that would be enough. Whether the work that had driven him for twelve years could be set aside for something that looked more like partnership and permanence. Moving back here and working the farm daily as an equal partner with his siblings instead of a silent partner most of the time.

Would she be willing to try again if he couldn't give her a definite answer about whether he was staying here or not?

Robin set the final poinsettias on the staging table and turned to face him. "All done."

Wyatt closed the distance between them and reached for her hand.

"Will you come tomorrow morning? When we cut down the tree you chose? I want you there."

Robin looked down at their joined hands, her brow furrowing slightly. Wyatt watched her process the invitation, recognizing it for what it truly was—another step toward something that was beginning to feel inevitable.

When she looked back up, her smile reached her eyes. "I'd love to."

Three simple words. But standing in the humid warmth of greenhouse three with Robin's hand in his, those three simple words felt like everything.

Chapter 21

The saw's roar cut through the frosty morning air as Robin pulled her scarf higher against the wind that carried snow across the special grove. From her position about fifteen yards back from where Wyatt and his crew worked, she had a clear view of the massive evergreen she'd chosen yesterday for the town square.

Wyatt and six men stood around the tree, discussing among themselves the enormous job at hand. Wyatt stood at the base of the trunk, examining it from multiple angles, while two others walked a wide circle around the tree's perimeter, pointing toward open spaces in the surrounding grove where the fall needed to land.

Snow drifted down steadily, collecting on Robin's coat shoulders and melting against her cheeks. The scent of winter and pine hung thick in the air. Her breath formed white clouds as she watched the men work, their voices carrying across the grove in fragments of conversation too technical for her to fully understand but fascinating, nonetheless.

Wyatt looked up from his inspection and caught her eye. Even from this distance, she saw his smile—warm and genuine, the kind that made her chest tighten with feelings she was still trying to sort through. He raised one gloved hand in a small wave before turning back to his crew, issuing instructions she couldn't quite hear.

One of the younger crew members climbed a ladder, with a heavy rope coiled over his shoulder. He ascended carefully, testing each rung, until he reached a height of about twelve feet. There, he secured the rope around the trunk, his movements deliberate and sure despite the awkward angle.

Robin held her breath until he descended safely.

"That's the hard part done," someone called out, and the crew laughed—the easy camaraderie of men who'd worked together through multiple seasons.

Wyatt moved to one of the chainsaws, checking something Robin couldn't identify but that seemed important based on his focused expression. He'd explained the process to her this morning over coffee at the farmhouse—something about cuts and angles and controlling the direction of fall—but watching it happen was entirely different from hearing about it.

The lead man with the saw positioned himself at the base of the tree while another crew member stood ready with wedges and a heavy mallet. Robin watched as the first cut began, the saw biting into wood with a high-pitched whine that made her wince.

Sawdust sprayed in golden arcs, scattering across the snow. The smell intensified—fresh pine so strong it was almost overwhelming. The man with the wedges moved in during brief pauses in the cutting, driving the shaped pieces of wood into the growing notch with precise strikes of his mallet.

Wyatt stood slightly back, watching everything with the kind of attention Robin recognized from her own work—the focus of someone who knew that mistakes in this moment could have serious consequences. His hand rested near the radio clipped to his belt, and occasionally he'd call out something to the crew, adjusting positions or confirming measurements.

He glanced her way again, and this time his smile held a question. You okay?

She nodded, even though her fingers had gone numb inside her gloves and her nose felt like ice.

The cutting continued for what felt like hours but was probably only twenty minutes. The crew worked in coordinated silence now, their movements synchronized through what must have been years of shared experience. Two men maintained tension on the ropes attached high on the trunk. Another stood well back, hand signals guiding the sawyer's movements. The man with the wedges drove them deeper with each pause in the cutting.

Robin's mind wandered as she watched, her thoughts spiraling through the past twenty-four hours. Yesterday's almost-kiss in the greenhouse. The way Wyatt's hand felt wrapped around hers. His invitation for her to be here this morning and to witness this tradition.

She wanted this. Wanted to be part of the Gibson family traditions, part of Wyatt's life, part of the quiet morning coffees, and everything in between. The wanting was so fierce it frightened her.

But wanting something didn't make it safe. Didn't guarantee it wouldn't be ripped away when circumstances changed.

When Jake recovered—if Jake recovered fully—what then? Would Wyatt return to his Forest Service life? Would she be left here in Laurel Ridge with another almost-relationship to add to her collection, another person who appreciated her but didn't choose her?

Stop, she told herself firmly. Just stop.

But her heart wouldn't listen. It just kept reaching toward Wyatt and kept hoping that maybe this time could be different.

Robin shook herself back into focus, watching all the activity in front of her. She sensed that the tree would fall soon. She removed her gloves and reached for her phone in her back pocket and began videoing so that she could share this magnificent tree falling with Jake.

The saw's pitch changed. The crew stepped back, everyone moving with urgent purpose. The ropes went taut. Someone shouted a warning she couldn't distinguish over the saw's final roar.

Then—crack.

The sound echoed through the grove, deep and primal. The massive tree shuddered, tilted, and began its descent with the kind of slow-motion inevitability that made Robin's breath catch. Branches rustled and swayed. Needles scattered like green rain. The men controlling the ropes adjusted tension, guiding the fall with steady hands.

The tree landed with a heavy thud that Robin felt through the soles of her boots; the impact sent up a cloud of snow and loose needles. For a moment, everything went silent except for the wind through the remaining trees and the gradually fading echo of that final crack.

"Clean fall!" someone called out, and the crew erupted into cheers and back-slapping.

Wyatt's grin stretched wide as he moved toward the fallen tree, assessing the next steps. A compact tractor rumbled to life somewhere behind Robin, and she turned slightly to video it navigating carefully between trees, approaching the crew with a set of heavy forks extended from its front.

The work continued—trimming excess branches, positioning chains, coordinating the tractor's movements to lift and drag the massive trunk toward the gravel road where a flatbed truck waited.

Robin watched and videoed it all with growing admiration for the skill required, the teamwork, the quiet confidence these men brought to dangerous work.

Wyatt kept glancing her way between tasks. Each time their eyes met.

The crew wrapped the tree in protective canvas, securing it with a thick rope that one man knotted with practiced speed. They loaded it onto the flatbed using a combination of the tractor's strength and manual positioning, everyone calling out warnings and adjustments until the tree rested securely on the truck bed.

Tie-down straps. More checks of security and balance. More coordinated effort that spoke of years of experience and mutual trust.

Robin stopped recording and put her phone back in her pocket. Her fingers were so cold she welcomed the warmth of her gloves again.

Her thoughts wandered again. Could she have a relationship with Wyatt even if he chose not to stay here? Was she willing to at least try? The long-distance relationship part of the equation kept screaming no in her mind, but another part of her kept saying, Put your faith in God and see where he leads you; at least try.

Lord, I don't know what to do; she prayed silently, watching Wyatt secure a final strap. I want to trust You. I want to believe that putting my heart out there again won't end in the same pain. But I'm so scared.

The snow continued to fall as she watched the crew packing up equipment and Wyatt walking toward her.

He pulled off his work gloves as he approached, tucking them in his coat pocket. His cheeks were flushed from exertion and cold, his dark hair dusted with snow, and his eyes bright with the satisfaction of work well done.

"What did you think?" His voice held genuine curiosity, like her opinion mattered more than all the experience and expertise he'd just demonstrated.

"It was incredible. You all make it look easy, but I know it's not."

"Definitely not easy." He gestured toward the loaded flatbed. "Your tree is ready for the town square. We'll deliver it on Monday."

Your tree. Not the tree or our tree, but your tree. Like he'd already given her ownership of this moment, this tradition, this piece of his family's legacy.

Robin's throat tightened. She needed to talk to him. Really talk, not just exchange pleasantries or dance around the feelings growing too large to ignore.

"Wyatt?" She wrapped her arms around herself, partly for warmth and partly because she needed something to hold on to. "Instead of heading back to the house, could we take a walk?"

His expression shifted, growing more serious. "Of course. What's wrong?"

Robin looked up at him, at this man who'd somehow worked his way back into her life and her heart despite every wall she'd tried to build. Snow continued falling around them, coating the world in white silence, and she felt the weight of every choice that had led to this moment pressing down on her shoulders.

"Wrong? Nothing's wrong necessarily. But we need to talk."

Chapter 22

obin and Wyatt walked deeper into the grove of Christmas trees, moving between the towering evergreens that stretched twenty feet or more toward the gray sky.

Snow continued falling steadily, muffling their footsteps. Around them, the massive trees created a cathedral-like space—quiet, reverent, and somehow separate from the busy farm operations visible in the distance.

Robin stopped walking near the center of the grove, turning to face a magnificent Fraser fir that must have been growing for fifteen years or more. Its branches spread in perfect symmetry, and snow collected on each layer like nature's own decoration.

"I need to ask you some things," Robin began, her voice steadier than she felt. She kept her gaze on the tree, finding it easier to speak without looking directly at him. "And I need honest answers, not what you think I want to hear."

Wyatt moved to stand beside her, both of them facing the tree. "Okay. Ask me anything."

Robin took a deep breath, trying to organize thoughts that had been spiraling for days. "What do you think Jake's recovery is going to look like? What's your realistic expectation?"

The question clearly caught him off guard. "I—Robin, you're his nurse. You know better than I do."

"I'm asking what you think. What you're hoping for versus what you're preparing for."

Wyatt was quiet for a long moment, his gaze fixed on the tree branches above them. When he spoke, his voice was careful. "I'm hoping he walks again. That he recovers enough to resume some level of normal activity. But I'm not naive, Robin. I've seen the medical reports, and I've heard the doctors hedge their prognoses. I know the damage was extensive."

"Do you think he'll be able to run the farm the way he did before the accident?"

"I don't know." The admission seemed to cost him something. "Maybe not. Not the physical labor, anyway. He might manage operations from a more administrative role, coordinate crews, and handle the business side. But climbing ladders or hauling trees onto flatbeds?" Wyatt shook his head. "I think those days might be behind him."

Robin nodded, still watching the tree. This was what she'd been afraid he'd say—and exactly what she needed to hear him acknowledge.

She turned to face him then. "Then I need you to answer my next question without factoring Jake into it at all. What do you want, Wyatt? For your life, your future—what does your heart want?"

"Robin—"

"Not based on Jake's recovery timeline. Not based on family obligation or guilt or duty. If you could design your life exactly how you wanted it, what would it look like?"

The wind picked up slightly, sending snow swirling around them. Wyatt studied her face as if he were trying to read something written there in a language he'd forgotten.

"Why are you asking me this?"

"Because I need to know if you're making decisions about us—about your career, about staying here—based on me or based on Jake needing you." Her voice cracked slightly. "I can't be the person you settle for because circumstances trapped you here. I can't be convenient."

Understanding dawned on Wyatt's expression, followed quickly by something that looked like pain. "You think I'd—Robin, that's not—"

"Isn't it?" The words burst out sharper than she intended. "You've been here for over a month. You've slipped back into farm life like you never left. You've been incredible in Jake's care, in managing operations, with everything. But what happens when Jake improves enough that you're not essential anymore? What happens when your supervisor calls and says they need you back for fire season?"

"I don't know," Wyatt said honestly. "I haven't gotten that call yet."

"But you will." Robin wrapped her arms around herself. "And when you do, you'll have to decide. A Forestry Service career you've built for twelve years, or this temporary situation that became more complicated than you expected?"

"Is that what you think this is? A complicated temporary situation?"

"I don't know what to think!" The frustration she'd been holding back spilled over. "I don't know if you're questioning your career because you genuinely want something different, or because the crisis made you nostalgic for something we once had. I don't know if you're drawn to me because we have history and proximity or because what we had at eighteen is still there underneath everything else."

Robin started walking again, moving deeper into the grove. Wyatt fell into step beside her.

"And I'm terrified," she continued. "Because I did this before. We did this before. We chose practicality over possibility. Not only that, but we agreed that distance and different life paths meant ending what we had, and I've spent twelve years wondering if that was wisdom or cowardice."

"It was both," Wyatt said quietly. "We were eighteen. We made the best decision we could with the maturity and information we had."

"And now we're thirty, and I'm still trying to figure out if loving you is brave or stupid." She stopped walking and turned to face him. "Because I did love you, Wyatt, completely. And when you left for school and we ended things, I told myself it was the right choice. That we'd grow up and move on and find other people who fit our lives better. Except I never did."

"Neither did I."

Robin looked away, staring out at the rows of towering trees disappearing into the falling snow. "My ex-fiancée... Liam. He was—" She paused, gathering her thoughts. "Liam was practical. Safe. But he didn't love me enough to fight for us when his career took him elsewhere. He just—left. And I realized I'd been settling for someone who appreciated me but didn't treasure me."

"Robin—"

She held up a hand, still not looking at him. "I need you to understand what I'm asking. I'm partially worried that if you go back to your job in the future, the distance would be a difficulty between us, Wyatt. I'm afraid that if you stay here, you may resent me for being the reason you gave up a career you loved. I'm afraid that when things get hard here—and they will—you'll wonder if you made the wrong choice.

I'm terrified that I'll be the consolation prize while you're actually mourning the life you left behind."

Wyatt moved to stand in front of her, close enough that she had no choice but to look up to meet his eyes. His hands came up to gently touch her arms.

"You're not listening to what I've been trying to tell you for weeks."

"Then tell me clearly. Tell me what you want without hedging or leaving room for interpretation."

He held her gaze, snowflakes catching in his dark hair, his blue eyes intense with something that made her breath catch.

"I want this farm," he said. "Not because Jake needs me to manage it. Not because family obligation requires it. But working this land again has reminded me of satisfactions I'd convinced myself didn't matter. I miss Laurel Ridge. I miss this farm. I miss my family. I miss you being the center of my world."

"But your Forestry Service work—"

"Has been making me miserable for months. Maybe longer. I kept telling myself the isolation was temporary, that the adrenaline of fire season made up for the loneliness between deployments. But lately, watching my colleagues go home to families while I went home to an empty house ninety minutes from anyone I cared about here in Laurel Ridge—" He shook his head. "I've been questioning my career long before Jake's accident, Robin. I just didn't have the courage to admit it might be time for something different."

Robin's heart hammered against her ribs. "What are you saying?"

"I'm saying I've spent twelve years building a career that looks impressive but feels hollow when I'm living it. I'm good at wildfire suppression. I'm good at forest conservation. But being good at something doesn't mean it's what I'm supposed to be doing. I followed a path in life I thought I wanted. I succeeded and did very well. But it's not what I want anymore. It's not enough. I want more."

They started walking again, moving slowly between the towering trees. Robin needed the movement, needed something to do with the energy building inside her.

"Then what are you supposed to be doing?" she asked.

"Building something that matters with people I love in a place I've always called home." His voice was firm, certain. "I want children someday. I want a partner to share the work and the joy and the everyday moments that make life meaningful. I want to wake up next to someone and know I'm exactly where I'm supposed to be."

The words should have been a relief. Instead, they intensified the fear coiling in Robin's chest.

She stopped walking and turned to face him again. "But what if that changes? What if six months from now or a year from now, you wake up and realize you miss the forestry work? That you gave up something important for—"

"For you?" Wyatt finished. "Robin, I'm not giving up something I love for you. I'm choosing something I want more. There's a difference."

"Is there? Because from where I'm standing, it feels like you're making this decision in the middle of a crisis when emotions are heightened and everything feels intense and meaningful."

"You're right. Everything does feel intense right now. But this isn't about crisis intensity, Robin. This is about finally being honest about what I want instead of what I thought I should want. The farm work has always been in my blood. I left because I thought staying meant settling for less. But I've learned that sometimes what looks like less is actually more."

Robin wanted to believe him. Wanted to trust that his words represented a genuine decision rather than crisis-driven emotion. Yet the fear wouldn't quite release its grip.

"I can't be the reason you resent your life."

"You won't be. Because I'm not choosing you at the expense of something else I love—I'm choosing a life that includes you because that's what will make me genuinely happy." Wyatt's expression softened. "If I had to decide right now, today, between my career with the Forestry Service and building a future here with you—I choose you, Robin. I choose us. I choose this."

The certainty in his voice cracked something open in her chest.

"But I can't promise there won't be hard days," he continued. "Or moments when I miss aspects of my old work. Change is hard, even when it's right. What I can promise is that I won't blame you for choices I'm making freely. And I can promise that I've never stopped—" He paused, seeming to catch himself. "That my feelings for you didn't fade with time or distance. They just waited."

"I'm still scared."

"I know. So am I." His admission was somehow more comforting than false confidence would have been. "I'm scared I'll fail at running this farm. I'm scared I'll disappoint Jake by not living up to what he built. Scared that you'll realize I'm not worth the risk you're taking by trusting me again."

"I don't think that's possible."

"Then maybe we're both scared of the wrong things." He smiled slightly. "Maybe the real question is whether we're brave enough to be scared together instead of alone."

She looked away from him, staring out at the grove of massive trees surrounding them. "I don't have all the answers," she said softly.

"Neither do I." Wyatt moved to stand beside her, both of them looking out at the snow-covered evergreens. "I can't tell you exactly what the transition from Forestry Service to farm life will look like, or how long it'll take Jake to recover, or whether we'll face challenges that test this decision. But I can tell you that I've spent twelve years comparing every woman I met to a memory of you, and none of them measured up. Not because you were perfect at eighteen, but because what we had was real. And standing here now, I believe it's still real. Different, deeper, more mature—but real."

Robin couldn't speak past the emotion clogging her throat. She just looked up at him, seeing the man he'd become layered over the boy she'd loved.

"Can I ask you something?" Wyatt's voice was gentle.

She nodded.

"What does your heart tell you? Forget fear and past hurts and all the practical reasons to protect yourself. What does your heart want?"

The answer came without hesitation, rising from somewhere deep and true. "You. This. Us building something together that's better than what either of us could have alone."

"Then let's do that." His smile reached his eyes. "Let's be brave enough to trust that God brought us back together for a reason. That His timing—however confusing it seems—has prepared us both for something we couldn't have handled at eighteen."

"I don't know how to stop being afraid," Robin admitted.

"Neither do I, but maybe we don't have to figure it out alone." Wyatt took her hand in his. "Can we pray about it? Ask for wisdom and courage and whatever else we need to move forward?"

Robin nodded.

They stood there in the snow-covered grove, hands joined, towering evergreens surrounding them like silent witnesses.

"Father, we come to You with honest hearts and complicated feelings." His voice was steady, conversational—like talking to someone he knew well and trusted completely. "We're scared. We're hopeful. We're trying to make sense of what You're doing in our lives and whether this path forward is where You're leading us. Give us wisdom to make decisions that honor You. Give Robin courage to trust again when past hurts make that so difficult. Help me be worthy of the gift she's offering by trusting me with her heart."

He paused, and Robin squeezed his hand.

"Show us how to build something together that reflects Your love and faithfulness," Wyatt continued. "Not just romantic love, but the kind of partnership that serves our community and honors our families and makes our lives count for something beyond our own happiness. We're putting this in Your hands, trusting that Your timing and Your plans are better than anything we could orchestrate ourselves. In Jesus' name, amen."

"Amen," Robin whispered.

She opened her eyes to find him watching her, his expression open and vulnerable in a way that made her chest ache.

"Your turn," he said gently.

Robin took a shaky breath and closed her eyes again.

"Lord, I'm terrible at this kind of faith." Her voice wavered. "The kind that requires putting my heart out there without guarantees. I want to trust You, want to believe that choosing Wyatt won't end in the same pain I've felt before. Help me be brave. Help me stop protecting myself from the possibilities You might be offering. And if this is Your will—if we're supposed to build something together—then guide us through whatever challenges come. Don't let my fear sabotage what could be beautiful. Don't let either of our wounds prevent the healing You want to bring. Give us courage to take this next step, whatever it looks like. Amen."

When she opened her eyes, Wyatt was smiling—not his usual easy grin, but something deeper that suggested he understood exactly what that prayer said aloud in his presence had cost her.

"So what does the next step look like?" Robin asked, her voice barely above a whisper.

"I think—" Wyatt paused, seeming to consider his words carefully. "I think it looks like both of us agreeing to move forward together. No guarantees about timelines or how everything will work out. Just a commitment to trying, to being honest with each other, and trusting that what we feel is worth pursuing."

"Even though there are still unknowns?"

"Especially because there are unknowns. Faith requires uncertainty, right? If we had all the answers, we wouldn't need to trust God with it."

Robin grinned. "That's very theological of you."

"I have my moments." He pulled her into a hug, and Robin melted into his warmth, feeling his solid strength and the steady beat of his heart.

They stood like that for a long time, snow accumulating on their shoulders, the cold seeping through their coats.

When Wyatt finally pulled back slightly, he kept his arms around her waist, looking down at her with an expression that made her breath catch.

"We should probably head back," he said. "The crew will be wondering where I disappeared to, and Jake's probably watching those camera feeds trying to figure out what we're doing."

"Let him wonder." Robin said with a smile, feeling lighter than she had in weeks.

Chapter 23

The flatbed truck rumbled around the last curve, and Robin caught her first glimpse of Laurel Ridge's town square transformed into a scene of organized chaos. Police cruisers blocked both ends of Main Street, their lights flashing blue and red against the blue afternoon sky. Orange cones and barricades created a clear path down the center of the street, and clusters of townspeople lined the sidewalks, bundled in winter coats and scarves, their breath forming white clouds in the cold air.

Wyatt navigated the truck carefully through the detour route, following hand signals from Officer Davis, who directed them toward the square. Behind them, secured with heavy straps and still wrapped in protective netting, the twenty-foot Christmas tree rode like a herald of the season's magic.

Robin's pulse quickened as they approached. Through the windshield, she could see the familiar storefronts of Main Street—Martha's Diner with its cheerful red awning, Leslie's Blossoms with window boxes still filled with fall-colored mums, and The Book Nook's display windows already decorated with holiday themes. Business owners and customers alike had emerged to watch, lining the sidewalks in growing numbers.

"There's quite a crowd," Robin observed, watching families gather behind safety barriers near the white gazebo that stood in the square's center.

"Word travels fast about delivery day." Wyatt's hands were steady on the wheel, but Robin saw the tension in his shoulders, the way his jaw tightened slightly. "Dad used to say this was the most important delivery of the season. Not because of the size or the difficulty, but because it belonged to everyone."

Fire Chief Steve Johnson appeared in an orange safety vest, his hand raised to guide their approach. Wyatt slowed the truck further, following the chief's precise directions as they backed toward the square. The white gazebo stood freshly painted and decorated with evergreen garland, its traditional architecture a perfect backdrop for the towering tree that would soon dominate the space. Beside it, a massive steel stand had already been anchored into the ground, its adjustable braces and tightening bolts waiting to secure the tree's trunk.

Beyond the gazebo, the town square stretched toward the New River visible in the distance, its dark waters flowing steadily past the southern edge of Laurel Ridge. Seasonal planters lined the square's perimeter, and park benches—some already occupied by early spectators—offered views of both the river and the square's center, where tradition was about to unfold once again.

Wyatt brought the truck to a complete stop, setting the brake. He sat for a moment, both hands still on the wheel, staring through the windshield at the scene before them.

"You ready for this?" Robin asked.

He turned to face her, and his expression was a mix of pride, anticipation, and grief all tangled together, the weight of continuing a tradition his father had cherished for decades.

"Are you?" he countered.

"I chose the tree. You're the one who has to make sure it stands straight," she said with a grin.

His smile reached his eyes. "Then I guess we're both invested in this moment."

They climbed out into the crisp November air. The scent of pine from the tree mixed with the wonderful scent of delicious food drifting from Martha's Diner and the sharper smell of coming snow. Christmas music played from speakers mounted on lampposts—"O Come All Ye Faithful" carried across the square.

Robin wrapped her coat tighter against the wind as Sheriff Mark Baker approached, his hand extended toward Wyatt in greeting. The sheriff was in his mid-thirties, with close-cut brown hair and a smile on his face.

"Good to see you, Wyatt. I heard you have a pretty big tree this year for us." Sheriff Baker's handshake was firm, his smile genuine. "I'm sure you all chose one that's going to impress the whole town."

"Robin actually selected it," Wyatt said.

"Then Laurel Ridge owes you thanks, Miss Robin. The Gibson family has donated our town tree for as long as I can remember. It's one of those things that makes this town special."

"We're honored to continue that tradition," Wyatt said.

Tom Hartwell's voice cut through the ambient noise, calling out instructions to the crew. Robin watched as men she recognized from the farm—Caleb Morrison, Pete Norton, and several other workers—moved into coordinated action around the flatbed. They worked with the efficiency of people who'd done this before. Robin knew from conversations with Wyatt that while the Gibson family had donated the town tree annually, the actual delivery and installation had always been Dan Gibson's responsibility until his death six years ago. Jake had managed it in the years since, which meant this was Wyatt's first time leading the operation.

Robin watched him confer with Tom about the unloading sequence.

Heavy straps securing the tree were unfastened. Guide ropes were attached high on the trunk, their length carefully measured and tested for strength. The crane operator—a man Robin didn't recognize but who moved with the confidence of experience—positioned the machine's hydraulic arm directly overhead, his movements precise and unhurried.

Fire Chief Johnson approached Wyatt, gesturing toward the tree and then the crane. "Same procedure as always, Wyatt. We'll lift it from about one-third down from the top, guide it with the ropes, and lower it straight into the stand. Your dad had it down to a science. I've been doing this with the Gibson family for several years now, and we've never had a mishap."

"Let's keep that record intact," Wyatt said, and the chief laughed.

"That's the spirit. Now, do you want to coordinate with Tom, or do you want to work the guide ropes yourself?"

"I'll take a rope." Wyatt pulled work gloves from his jacket pocket. "Tom's got the coordination handled."

Robin stepped back onto the sidewalk, where a better vantage point allowed her to observe the entire operation. Around her, townspeople pressed against the safety barriers that kept spectators at a safe distance from the work zone. Children bounced on their toes in excitement. Parents pointed and explained what was happening. An elderly couple Robin recognized from church stood together, the woman's hand tucked in her husband's arm, both their faces bright with anticipation.

"Exciting, isn't it?" Martha said as she appeared at Robin's elbow, carrying a large thermos and a stack of paper cups. "I've watched this happen every year since I opened the diner, and it never gets old."

"It's incredible." Robin accepted a cup of steaming coffee gratefully, wrapping both hands around it for warmth. "The coordination required... it's just astonishing to see."

"The Gibsons make it look easy because they know what they're doing. Dan Gibson used to say that delivering the town tree was like conducting an orchestra. Every person has their part to play, and when everyone does their job right, you get something beautiful." Martha poured coffee for herself, steam rising from the cup. "Wyatt looks just like his daddy standing out there. Same stance, same way of moving. Same focus. It's like watching history repeat itself. I just wish Dan were here to see his boy taking over."

Robin watched Wyatt position himself at one of the guide ropes, testing its tension, his movements economical and sure.

"Dan and Marie would be so proud," Martha continued, her voice softening. "Those kids lost their parents too young. But they've done right by the family legacy. Jake and Lauren both built that farm into something special, and now Wyatt's come home to help. That's what family does."

The crane's cable descended with a mechanical whine, and several crew members worked to attach it to the lifting harness wrapped around the tree's trunk about seven feet from the top. The harness had been carefully positioned to distribute weight evenly, preventing damage to the branches while providing secure support for the lift.

Robin held her breath as the crane operator—responding to hand signals from Tom—began raising the boom. The cable went taut. The tree shifted, lifting slowly from the flatbed with a grace that seemed impossible for something so massive. Even wrapped in protective netting, its sheer size was apparent, and the crowd's murmur of appreciation grew louder.

A collective gasp rose from the spectators. Children pointed and shouted. Parents lifted smaller kids onto their shoulders for better views. Someone near Robin exclaimed, "It's huge!" and laughter rippled through the crowd.

The crane swung the tree gently through the air, rotating it into position above the waiting stand. Robin found herself clutching her coffee cup with both hands, watching as the tree she'd chosen moved into position. The guide ropes went taut as crew members on the ground controlled the tree's movement, preventing it from swinging too wildly in the wind that had picked up across the open square.

Wyatt's rope was one of three, each held by a different crew member positioned around the perimeter of the work zone. They moved in coordination, adjusting tension as the crane operator called out instructions Robin couldn't quite hear over the ambient noise and machinery.

Mayor Bill Wilson materialized beside Robin and Martha, his familiar face beaming with civic pride. The mayor was in his early sixties, with thinning hair and the kind of expansive personality that made him excellent at his job. "Miss Robin! I heard you selected our tree this year. Excellent choice—absolutely excellent."

"Thank you, Mayor Wilson." Robin managed a smile despite her nerves about the tree's ongoing installation.

"Sure is good to have Wyatt back home where he belongs. His father was a good friend and a pillar of this community. Dan believed in giving back, in being part of something larger than himself. I hope Wyatt knows he's following in remarkable footsteps."

"I think he does," Robin said softly, watching Wyatt adjust his rope as the tree descended toward the stand with painstaking slowness.

The tree lowered inch by inch, the crane operator working with determined patience. One mistake, one moment of carelessness, and the tree could be damaged, or the stand compromised.

Tom called out directions. "Easy now. Bring it down another foot. Hold there."

Two crew members positioned themselves at the stand, ready to guide the tree's base into the metal brackets. The trunk descended into position, and immediately workers swarmed around it, their movements coordinated through years of experience with similar installations.

"Is it straight?" Tom called.

Caleb Morrison stepped back about twenty feet, tilting his head to assess the tree's vertical alignment. "Little more to the left. No, too much. Back right, just a touch. Good. Hold it there."

The crane held the tree suspended while crew members tightened the stand's adjustable braces and attached stabilizing cables that would anchor it against winter winds. Each cable ran from the upper trunk to ground anchors that had been installed near the gazebo and hidden among the seasonal planters. These guy wires would remain in place throughout the holiday season, invisible to casual observers but essential for keeping the tree standing despite whatever weather West Virginia's mountains might deliver.

Pete Norton worked on one anchor point while another farm employee handled the opposite side. They moved with the kind of easy coordination that spoke to their experience working together, calling out to each other when they needed tools or help.

The crane's cable went slack as the tree's full weight transferred to the stand and stabilizing cables. Tom inspected every connection point, testing cables for proper tension, checking the stand's tightening bolts, and circling the entire installation with critical eyes.

"Looks good," he announced finally. "Disconnect the cable, and let's get the netting off."

The crane operator retracted his cable, and crew members moved in with cutting tools and ladders to remove the protective netting that had kept branches compressed during transport. As the netting fell away, released from constraint, the tree's branches sprang outward in their full glory—perfectly symmetrical, richly green, exactly as magnificent as Robin had envisioned when she'd chosen it from the special grove Saturday morning.

The tree towered above the gazebo, reaching toward the blue sky. Sunlight broke through the clouds for just a moment, illuminating the evergreen branches and casting long shadows across the square.

The crowd erupted in spontaneous applause. The sound washed over Robin like a wave, and she felt tears prick her eyes.

Wyatt appeared at her side so quietly she almost didn't notice his arrival until his hand found hers.

"It's perfect," she said, unable to tear her gaze from the tree.

"It is. You chose well."

"Your crew delivered it beautifully."

"That they did, I'm proud of them."

Around them, the square buzzed with activity and excitement. Tom supervised the final cleanup, directing crew members to gather tools and secure equipment. The crane operator began the process of retracting the boom and preparing his vehicle to exit the work zone. Pete and Caleb tidied the rope and checked the ground anchors one final time, their thoroughness ensuring the tree would stand securely despite whatever winter storms might blow through.

Martha distributed coffee to the workers, her cheerful voice carrying across the square as she offered sustenance and praise. The farm crew accepted cups gratefully, their faces flushed from exertion and cold, but their expressions satisfied. They'd done this job well, and they knew it.

Parents lifted children closer to the tree, wanting them to see its details up close. Robin watched a little girl—maybe four years old—reach out as if she could touch the branches, her face radiant with wonder. The child's mother snapped a photo, capturing that moment of pure Christmas magic that would probably end up in a scrapbook or family album, a treasured memory years from now.

Business owners emerged from shops along Main Street—Leslie Williams from her flower shop, carrying a gorgeous wreath she immediately offered to hang on the gazebo. Loretta and Mitch Dunbar from The Book Nook stood together on the sidewalk, Loretta wiping tears from her eyes as she watched everything. Even the employees from Talbot's General Store had come out to watch.

This was community. This was belonging. This was what Robin had loved about Laurel Ridge her entire life—the way people showed up for each other, celebrated together, built traditions that connected generations, and created the kind of memories that became the foundation of identity and home.

Fire Chief Johnson approached Wyatt, shaking his hand firmly. "Outstanding job, Wyatt. Your father would be proud of how you handled this. That's a textbook installation—safe, efficient, and the tree looks wonderful."

"Couldn't have done it without your coordination," Wyatt said. "And Tom deserves most of the credit. He's been managing this operation for years."

"But you led it today," the chief said. "That matters. Leadership matters."

Mayor Wilson had worked his way through the crowd and now stood before Wyatt with his hand extended. "Wyatt Gibson, on behalf of Laurel Ridge, thank you. Your family's generosity and commitment to this tradition bring joy to thousands of people every holiday season. Children grow up with memories of this tree. Families take their annual Christmas photos in front of it. It becomes part of our collective story, and we're grateful."

Wyatt shook the mayor's hand, clearly uncomfortable with the praise but accepting it with grace. "It's our honor, Mayor Wilson. This tradition meant everything to my father, and it means everything to Jake, Lauren, and me. We're just continuing what he started."

"Well, you're doing a fine job of it." The mayor clapped Wyatt on the shoulder before moving away to speak with Sheriff Baker.

Robin felt Wyatt's hand tighten around hers as the mayor walked away. She glanced up to find him staring at the tree with an expression she couldn't quite read—pride and grief tangled together, satisfaction and loss, and the complicated emotions that came from stepping into a role his father should still be filling.

"Your dad would be so proud of you," Robin said softly. "He would be proud of how you've handled everything—Jake's accident, managing the farm, and keeping traditions alive."

"I hope so." Wyatt's voice was rough. "I spent so many years running from this place, convinced I needed to build something entirely my own rather than just continuing what he created. And now that I'm back, standing here watching this tree go up—" He stopped, shaking his head slightly. "I keep thinking about all the years I missed. All the deliveries I could have helped with. All the times I chose my career over being present for moments like this."

"You're here now," Robin said. "That's what matters."

They stood together in silence for a long moment, hands joined, watching as the last of the crew secured their equipment and prepared to clear the work zone. The crowd began to disperse slowly, though many people lingered to admire the tree from different angles or take photographs.

The wind picked up, rustling through the tree's branches with a sound like whispered secrets. Above them, the clouds shifted, and snow began falling again.

"Dad used to say something every year when we'd finished the delivery," Wyatt said, his gaze still fixed on the tree. "He'd stand back and look at it, and he'd remind Jake and me that trees with strong roots can weather any storm. That what we build deep and true will stand when everything else shakes." He paused, and when he continued, his voice held quiet conviction. "I didn't understand what he meant back then. I thought he was just talking about literal trees and root systems. But standing here now, after everything that's happened—Jake's accident, coming home, finding you again—I think I finally get it."

"Tell me... what do you get?"

"That strong roots aren't just about staying in one place. They're about knowing where you come from, what you value, and who you love. They're about building something that goes deep enough to hold you steady when life tries to knock you down." He turned to face her, his blue eyes intense. "I've spent years with shallow roots, Robin. I was telling myself I was building a career when really I was just avoiding commitment to anything that might hurt if I lost it. But shallow roots can't hold a person through storms. They can't sustain real growth. They can't support the kind of life I actually want to live."

The snow fell steadily now, catching in Wyatt's dark hair and dusting Robin's coat. Around them, Laurel Ridge went about its business—the work zone being cleared, traffic barriers being removed, and townspeople heading back to warm shops and offices. But in this moment, standing beside the tree she'd chosen and the man she was learning so many new things about, Robin felt the rest of the world fade into background noise.

"What kind of life do you want, Wyatt Gibson?"

"One with deep roots," Wyatt said simply. "Here, in this place, with the people I love. Building something that will last not because it's easy or convenient, but because it's worth the work it takes to grow strong enough to stand."

He raised their joined hands and pressed his lips to her knuckles—a gesture so tender and deliberate that Robin's breath caught. He didn't look at her when he did it, his gaze still fixed on the tree reaching skyward, but the kiss felt like a promise sealed against her skin.

Chapter 24

"Hand me that box of clear lights—no, the other one. Yes, that's it." Robin reached for the cardboard container Megan Harlan passed her way, its contents rattling.

The town square spread before them in a winter wonderland. Six inches of fresh snow blanketed everything—the gazebo's roof, the park benches lining the perimeter, and the carefully maintained flowerbeds now sleeping beneath white quilts. City workers had cleared a wide path around the twenty-foot Fraser fir that dominated the square's center, exposing dark earth and dormant grass where volunteers could work safely. The tree itself stood magnificent against the darkening sky, its branches still dusted with snow that caught the glow from nearby streetlamps and the overhead lights the city had placed around the square that helped illuminate the entire area.

All around them, the decorating committee bustled with energy. Martha directed people near the gazebo, her clipboard in hand and reading glasses perched on her nose. Pastor Andrew and Lily worked together untangling a massive garland, their laughter carrying across the cold air. And dozens of other community and church members sorted through boxes, tested light strings, and coordinated the evening's carefully choreographed agenda.

Robin sorted through three large containers of lights that had spent the past year in storage at town hall. Her mother worked to her left, methodically checking each strand of lights for burned-out bulbs. Her father stood to her right, organizing extension cords by length and testing connections.

"I think we've got enough white lights to circle the tree at least three times," Megan said, crouching down to examine another box. She wore a puffy red coat and matching knit hat, her blond hair spilling out in waves.

"We're doing silver and blue decorations again this year, right?" Dottie asked, looking up from the light strand she'd been testing. "That was beautiful last year."

"Yep, that's what the committee decided on—with more blue accents this time," Robin confirmed. "Martha showed me her design plan last week at church. Very elegant, with blue ribbons and bows added to the tree and around the square."

Chuck chuckled, his breath forming white clouds in the cold air. "Well, maybe I should go and talk to Martha and ask her to consider adding some red to the color scheme. It could be more of a patriotic theme this year instead... but then again... maybe that's a bad idea. You know how she gets about her vision once she's set on something."

"Martha Kincaid doesn't compromise on aesthetics," Megan agreed. "Remember three years ago when she didn't like all those huge gold ornaments on the tree? She had every last one of us take them off and then add more green and red ornaments."

"I remember my arms being sore for days after that," Robin said, grinning at the memory. "But the tree was stunning when we were done."

Megan plugged in another strand of lights, watching them flicker to life before nodding with satisfaction. "So... is Wyatt joining us tonight?"

"He should be here any minute. He was going to town hall first and loading up his truck with more decorations, the tall ladders, extension cords, and some other equipment we'll need."

"Good. So... how are things going between you and Wyatt?"

Dottie's hands stilled on the light strand. Chuck's attention shifted from the extension cords to his daughter's face, his expression carefully neutral but clearly interested.

Robin felt heat climb her neck despite the cold air. "Things are... good. Really good, actually."

"Good?" Megan repeated, drawing out the word. "That's all I get? After watching you two at church last Sunday looking like the happiest couple in the world, all I get is 'good'?"

"What do you want me to say?" Robin asked, though she couldn't suppress her smile.

"Details! Specifics! The latest developments in the Robin and Wyatt saga that the entire town is watching with bated breath."

Dottie reached over and squeezed Robin's hand. "Sweetheart, we're happy for you. We can see something's different—something good. You're glowing."

"He's wonderful. He's the same Wyatt but different... more mature and focused," Robin said finally, the words feeling inadequate for everything she wanted to express. "Being around him again—it's like remembering who I was before I started settling for less than I deserved. He makes me feel..."

She trailed off, searching for the right description.

"Treasured?" Dottie supplied softly.

"Yes... that's a good word for it."

Megan made a small sound of satisfaction. "I knew it. I told David last week that you two were falling in love all over again, and he said I was being a hopeless romantic, but I was right."

"We're not—" Robin started, then stopped. Were they? Was that what this feeling was—this growing certainty that Wyatt Gibson represented not just her past but possibly her future?

"Robin." Chuck's voice carried the quiet wisdom that had guided her through thirty years of life decisions. "Sometimes, complicated things are worth the effort. Just enjoy yourself and put your trust in God. I promise... he has a plan for you."

"We're looking forward to seeing Wyatt," Dottie added. "It's been twelve years since he left for college. I'd like to tell him how proud we are of him coming home and taking care of the farm and his brother."

"And how grateful we are that he's making our daughter smile again," Chuck said.

Robin glanced up as his truck pulled up to the curb nearby, and her heart performed that now-familiar acrobatic routine that seemed to happen every time she saw him. Wyatt climbed out, dressed in jeans, work boots, and a heavy canvas jacket over a flannel shirt. His dark hair was slightly disheveled, and when his eyes found Robin in the crowd, his entire expression changed.

"Wyatt Gibson." Chuck said as he reached the truck first, extending his hand with genuine warmth. "Welcome home, son."

Wyatt's surprise was obvious, but he gripped Chuck's hand firmly. "Mr. Fitch. It's good to see you, sir."

"None of that 'mister' business. It's Chuck." Robin's father pulled Wyatt into a brief embrace. "We've missed having you around."

"I've missed being here."

Dottie stepped forward next, her smile bright despite the evening cold. "Wyatt, look at you. All grown up and still just as handsome as I remember."

"Mrs. Fitch—" Wyatt found himself pulled into another hug before he could finish the greeting.

"It's Dottie, and don't you forget it." She stepped back, keeping her hands on his shoulders while she studied his face. "You look good. Tired, but good. Taking care of Jake and managing the farm—that's a heavy load."

"I'm managing."

"You're doing more than managing," Chuck corrected. "Robin tells us you've kept everything running smoothly during an impossible situation. Your parents would be proud of how you've stepped up for your family."

"Thank you, sir."

"We're proud of you," Dottie said firmly. "And we're glad you're home."

The five of them made quick work of unloading the truck—three tall aluminum ladders, several boxes of additional decorations, multiple heavy-duty extension cords, and various equipment Martha had deemed essential. Other volunteers appeared to help carry items toward the tree, and soon the truck bed was empty.

Wyatt closed the tailgate and turned to find Robin standing beside him, slightly apart from the bustle of activity. Around them, the decorating committee was fully engaged with its tasks. Two firefighters worked from an extended ladder truck parked in the gravel lot west of the square, carefully wrapping lights around the tree's uppermost branches where it would be dangerous for civilians to reach. Below, volunteers stretched more light strands across lower branches.

The fire engine's flashing lights painted the snow in alternating shades of red and white. Laughter carried across the cold air—Martha's authoritative directions mixing with Pastor Andrew's good-natured responses, children's excited voices as they helped their parents, and the general hum of a community gathering for shared purpose.

It was beautiful. All of it.

Wyatt moved closer to Robin, and she felt the warmth of him beside her despite the December chill. He slipped his arm around her waist and pulled her against his side.

Robin leaned into him without hesitation, fitting against him as naturally as if they'd been doing this for years. They stood together, watching all the volunteers work their Christmas magic.

"This is nice," Wyatt said finally, his voice low enough that only she could hear. "Just watching everyone come together like this."

"I know. It's wonderful," Robin admitted. "The whole town working as one to create something beautiful."

"Your parents seem genuinely happy to see me."

"They are. They've always liked you, even after we broke up. They never blamed you for leaving—they understood that you needed to find your own path."

Wyatt was quiet for a moment. "I should have come back more often. Visited, kept in touch. I let twelve years slip away."

"Well... I'm glad you're here now. We can't worry about the past; we just have to move on."

They continued watching as more and more strings of light were added to the tree. Her parents were busy gathering blue bows and handing them to volunteers to start attaching to tree branches. Megan and several other volunteers were placing boxes of ornaments around the tree for the volunteers to begin hanging.

"Robin. Would you like to go out for dinner tomorrow evening? Somewhere nice. Just the two of us."

Her pulse quickened. "I'd like that."

"I'll pick you up at your house around five. And dress up—wear something you'd wear to somewhere special."

Robin turned to look at him, curiosity sparking. "Where are we going that requires me to dress up?"

His grin was boyish and mysterious. "It's a surprise."

"How dressed up are we talking? Like a nice Sunday dress or something fancier?"

"One of your Sunday dresses that you love the most."

Robin studied his expression, trying to read what lay beneath the careful neutrality. "You're not going to give me any hints, are you?"

"Where would be the fun in that?"

"The fun would be in not spending tomorrow afternoon agonizing over what to wear while wondering if I'm overdressed or underdressed for whatever mystery location you have planned."

Wyatt's laugh was warm and genuine. "Trust me. Whatever you choose will be perfect."

Robin wanted to press for more details, but something in his expression suggested this mattered to him—that wherever he'd planned to take her represented something significant. So instead of demanding answers, she simply nodded.

"Alright. Five o'clock. One of my favorite Sunday dresses. Mystery destination. Got it."

"You won't be disappointed."

"I'd better not be, Gibson."

She started to move away, intending to join the decorating efforts where Megan was waving them over with increasing urgency. But

Wyatt's arm tightened around her waist, drawing her back against him with gentle insistence.

"Just five more minutes," he murmured. "Let's just enjoy this for a few more minutes before we join everyone."

He pressed a kiss to the top of her head, and Robin let herself melt back against him. Around them, community members busied themselves transforming the town square into a Christmas wonderland. Laughter and conversation created a symphony of community connection. Stars were beginning to appear in the darkening sky.

But in this moment, wrapped in Wyatt's arms while the town she loved bustled with Christmas preparations, Robin felt nothing but pure happiness.

Chapter 25

Robin's hand fit perfectly in Wyatt's as they walked from the parking area toward the illuminated mansion rising before them. The December evening wrapped around them in cold clarity, stars scattered across the sky above while their breath formed white clouds in the frigid air.

"Wyatt." She stopped walking, pulling him to a halt beside her. "This is the Livingston Estate."

"It is."

"I've heard about this place for years. I've never been here before."

They climbed the wide stone steps together, their footsteps echoing in the quiet evening. The grand double doors were opened by a tuxedoed attendant as they approached.

"Good evening." A woman in an elegant black dress said. "Welcome to the Livingston Estate."

"Good evening." Wyatt said. "I have a reservation under Gibson."

The hostess consulted her leather-bound reservation book, then smiled warmly. "Mr. Gibson, party of two. We have you in one of our private alcove rooms this evening. If you'll allow me to take your coats, I'll escort you to your table."

Robin slipped out of her winter coat, grateful she'd agonized over every detail of her appearance. The soft blue wrap dress was her favorite—the color reminded her of mountain mornings, and the cut made her feel both elegant and comfortable. She'd styled her hair in loose waves that fell past her shoulders, applied makeup with more care than usual, and retrieved her grandmother's pearl earrings from the velvet box where she kept her most precious jewelry.

Wyatt handed their coats to the attendant. He wore dark slacks, a crisp white dress shirt, and a charcoal blazer that emphasized his broad shoulders. His dark hair was styled with care, and when he turned back to her, he smiled.

"You look stunning," he said softly.

"You clean up pretty well yourself."

The hostess led them through the foyer and into the Conservatory Dining Hall, where Robin's steps faltered slightly at the sheer beauty of the space. Soaring ceilings crowned with restored moldings stretched above them. Golden chandeliers hung from brass chains, their crystal prisms scattering soft light across tables draped in pristine white linens. Fresh flowers adorned each table—ivory roses mixed with sprigs of pine and holly, their arrangement both seasonal and sophisticated.

Around the perimeter of the main dining area, arched alcoves were enclosed by carved wood panels and glass-paned doors, offering intimate spaces that still allowed diners to feel connected to the larger gathering.

Robin glimpsed a string quartet setting up their instruments on a raised platform near the center of the dining area.

Their hostess guided them to one of the alcove rooms along the far wall, opening the glass-paned door. "This is your table, Mr. Gibson."

The dining space was gorgeous. A small round table set for two sat beside a tall arched window overlooking the estate gardens, where lanterns traced a snow-covered cobblestone path toward the river. The table was dressed with porcelain dinnerware trimmed in gold, flickering taper candles, and small arrangements of the same ivory roses and pine sprigs from the main dining area.

Wyatt held out Robin's chair, waiting until she was seated before taking his own seat across from her. The hostess handed them elegant menus bound in burgundy leather.

"Your server will be with you momentarily to explain this evening's dining experience and take your beverage order. Enjoy your evening at the Livingston Estate." She departed quietly, closing the glass-paned door behind her.

Robin looked across the candlelit table at Wyatt, emotion tightening her throat. "This is incredible. I can't believe you planned this."

"You deserve incredible."

A server appeared—a young man in a crisp white jacket and bow tie who introduced himself as Michael. He explained the evening's unique dining format with practiced elegance, describing how dinner would unfold in coordinated courses served simultaneously to all guests.

"The string quartet will begin playing shortly after appetizers are served," Michael explained. "Guests are welcome to enjoy the music from their tables or move to the main floor for dancing between courses. The evening progresses at a leisurely pace designed to allow you to savor both the cuisine and the company."

He took their beverage orders—sparkling water with lemon for Robin, coffee for Wyatt—and departed with a promise to return shortly.

Robin leaned back in her chair. "How did you even know about this place?"

"Tom brought his wife here for their twentieth anniversary. He was telling me about it last week, and it sounded interesting. I called and made a reservation yesterday."

Michael returned with their beverages, the crystal glasses catching candlelight as he set them on the table. Around them in the main dining hall, Robin could hear the gentle murmur of other diners being seated.

"So," Wyatt said once Michael had departed again, "tell me about last night. Were you and the decorating committee able to finish the town Christmas tree after I left?"

"We finished around ten. The blue and silver color scheme looks stunning, especially with the white accents we added this year."

"Your parents seemed to have a good time last night."

"He and Mom look forward to that evening all year. They seemed to really have a good time last night. They were so happy to see you. I don't think I realized how much they've missed having you around until I watched them light up when you arrived."

"I've missed them too. Your parents were always kind to me, even after we broke up. They could have blamed me for hurting you, but they never did."

"Because they understood you needed to follow your calling. They've always believed that God's path for people sometimes requires tough choices." Robin paused, gathering courage. "Speaking of your calling—have you decided about the Forestry Service... for sure?"

Wyatt nodded slowly, his expression thoughtful. "I'm planning to put in my two weeks' notice soon. Probably next week. I've already spoken with a supervisor informally about the possibility, and he's been supportive."

"How do you feel about that decision?"

"Certain. More certain than I've felt about anything in a long time. The Forest Service gave me important years and meaningful work, but it's not where my heart is anymore."

Robin started to respond, but Michael appeared with their appetizers—delicate portions of butternut squash soup garnished with toasted pumpkin seeds and a drizzle of sage cream. He explained each component before retreating once more.

They ate, savoring the rich flavors and the intimacy of the candlelit space. Through the glass-paned door, Robin could see other alcove rooms and the central open dining area filled with couples and small groups, everyone enjoying the evening's unhurried rhythm.

"I had a video conference today," Robin said eventually, setting down her soup spoon. "With Jake's care team—his hospital doctors and Dr. Morrison, his primary physician who's been managing his care since he came home."

Wyatt's attention sharpened. "How did it go?"

"I provided updates on his current status, and Dr. Morrison shared his observations from the past month. The team agreed that Jake's recovery is progressing, but more slowly now than those first few weeks. He's experiencing more frustration and fatigue, which is normal for this stage, but they want to ensure we're not missing any complications."

"What's the next step?"

"Dr. Morrison scheduled another video conference for Monday—just between the doctors this time. They'll review all the data and determine whether adjustments need to be made to his care plan. Then Dr. Morrison will do an in-home visit with Jake next Wednesday to go over everything."

"Do they think there's a problem?"

"Not a problem necessarily. Just recognition that recovery from this type of trauma is rarely linear. There will be plateaus and setbacks along with progress. They want to make sure Jake has the support he needs for whatever his recovery trajectory looks like long-term."

"Which might mean he doesn't regain full mobility."

"It might," Robin said gently. "Or it might mean his recovery just takes longer than initially hoped. The doctors are being cautiously optimistic but realistic. Jake's young and otherwise healthy, which works in his favor. But the damage was extensive."

Wyatt nodded, processing this information.

Michael returned to collect their soup bowls and refill their water glasses. As he departed, the string quartet in the main dining hall began playing, the soft notes drifting through the alcove's open archway.

"Enough talk about all the things going on in our lives," Wyatt said suddenly, his expression shifting from serious contemplation to something lighter. "Let's set everything aside and just enjoy the evening. We can worry about Jake's recovery and my job transition and all the practical complications tomorrow. Dance with me."

Robin's surprise must have shown on her face because Wyatt's smile widened.

"What? You thought I brought you to a place with a live band and a dance floor without intending to actually dance?"

"I wasn't sure if you'd want to dance," Robin admitted, standing and placing her hand in his.

He led her through the glass-paned door and across the main dining hall toward the polished parquet floor where several other couples had already gathered.

The string quartet was playing a gentle melody—something classical and romantic that Robin didn't recognize. Wyatt drew her into a proper dance position, one hand at her waist, the other holding hers with gentle firmness. They began to move, and within three steps, Robin discovered Wyatt was still a gifted dancer. Not flashy or showy, but confident and sure, leading her through the steps with a simple grace that made following him effortless. They moved together across the polished floor, his hand warm against her back, her dress swirling softly around her legs.

"You're a talented dancer." Robin said, looking up at him.

"I'm adequate. You make it easy because you follow my lead well."

"That's because you actually know what you're doing."

They turned in a smooth circle, passing another couple who smiled at them with the kind of knowing expression that suggested they recognized new love when they saw it. Robin felt heat climb her neck, but she didn't look away from Wyatt's face.

"I used to imagine this," Wyatt said quietly. "When we were teenagers. Taking you somewhere special, dancing with you somewhere elegant, treating you the way you deserved instead of just pizza and movies."

"I loved pizza and movies."

"I loved those things too. But you were always worth more than I was capable of giving you back then."

The quartet shifted to a new melody, slightly faster but still romantic. Wyatt adjusted their steps seamlessly, spinning Robin in a gentle twirl before drawing her back against him. She laughed, surprised by the movement and delighted by his simple confidence.

"Show off," she accused, but her smile took any sting from the words.

"I'm trying to impress you."

"It's working."

They danced through two more songs, moving from slower waltzes to slightly more energetic pieces that allowed Wyatt to show his skill with turns and dips that made Robin feel graceful and cherished. Other couples swirled around them, but Robin barely noticed anyone beyond the man holding her, guiding her, and looking at her like she was something precious.

The quartet concluded their set with a return to a slower, more romantic melody. Wyatt pulled Robin closer. Her arms slid around his neck while his hands settled at her waist, and they swayed together more than actually danced.

"Thank you for this evening," Robin said softly, her face close enough to his that she could see the subtle variations of green in his eyes. "For planning something so special. For making me feel—" She struggled to find adequate words. "Treasured."

Wyatt's hands tightened at her waist. "You are treasured, Robin."

She rose slightly on her toes, closing the small distance between them, and pressed her lips to his.

The kiss was soft and sweet.

Wyatt's arms tightened around her, drawing her closer as he returned the kiss with careful tenderness. When they separated, his forehead rested against hers.

Around them, the quartet continued playing. Other couples danced and laughed. Candlelight flickered across white linens and crystal chandeliers, and Robin knew with bone-deep certainty that she loved this man.

Chapter 26

Wyatt reached for Robin's hand, threading his fingers through hers. She glanced up at him with a smile that warmed his chest despite the cold evening.

"This is bigger than last year," Lauren observed, her voice carrying excitement as she scanned the gathering crowd. "I don't think I've ever seen this many people turn out for the tree lighting."

The town square spread before them, transformed into a winter wonderland that would have impressed even the most jaded observer. Snow blanketed the town in pristine white layers, carefully cleared from streets and pathways. The twenty-foot Christmas tree stood in the square's center near the gazebo, its branches decorated in blue and silver.

Beyond the gazebo, the New River drifted past, dark and unhurried, its snow-laced banks silent beneath the December sky. Seasonal planters marked the square's perimeter, decorated heavily for the holiday season.

A large white tent had been erected in the southwest corner of the square, its interior glowing with warmth and light. Through the open sides, Wyatt could see tables laden with refreshments—Taste of Heaven Bakery's signature cookies and pastries, Martha's Diner's famous hot chocolate and coffee, and Sugar Maple Sweet Shoppe's seasonal treats. Several street vendors had set up portable stations nearby, selling flavored coffees, cinnamon-roasted nuts, and other seasonal snacks that filled the air with tempting aromas.

Near the gazebo, a makeshift dance floor had been constructed from interlocking panels, and a local band was setting up their equipment on a small platform. The setup was modest but festive, designed primarily for children who would want to burn off energy dancing to lively Christmas music after the ceremony concluded.

"Over there." Robin pointed toward a spot near the gazebo with good sight lines to the tree. "Before someone else claims it."

They navigated through the crowd, exchanging greetings with familiar faces.

The elementary school choir had assembled on risers positioned to the left of the gazebo, their youthful voices already lifting in a cheerful rendition of "Jingle Bells." The children wore matching red scarves and white mittens, their breath forming small clouds as they sang with enthusiasm that more than compensated for any missed notes.

"This is so fun," Lauren said once they'd claimed their viewing spot. She pulled out her phone, her fingers moving quickly across the screen. "Jake needs to see this."

Within seconds, Jake's face filled her phone screen, and Lauren immediately switched to selfie mode, angling the camera to include both Wyatt and Robin in the frame.

"Hey guys," Jake said, his smile genuine despite the weariness Wyatt could see around his eyes. "How's the crowd looking?"

"Massive," Wyatt replied. "Probably the biggest turnout I can remember for a tree lighting."

"That's good. I wish I were there," Jake said. "How does the tree look?"

"The blue and silver scheme this year is beautiful," Robin said.

They chatted for a few more minutes, updating Jake on various community members they'd spotted in the crowd and describing the refreshment setup and the band's equipment. Then Lauren switched the camera to rear-facing mode, giving Jake a clear view of the scene unfolding before them.

"Can you see everything?" Lauren asked, keeping her phone steady.

"I can see the tree, the gazebo, and part of the crowd," Jake confirmed. "This is great, Lauren. Thank you."

Wyatt slipped his arm around Robin's waist, drawing her close against his side. Around them, the crowd continued to grow, children's laughter mixing with adult conversation and the choir's enthusiastic singing.

The elementary school choir transitioned to "Silent Night," their young voices creating a beautiful harmony that quieted some of the surrounding chatter. Wyatt found himself transported back to similar evenings from his childhood—standing in this exact square with his parents and siblings, watching the tree lighting with the same sense of wonder and anticipation he saw now on the faces of children around him.

His father had loved this ceremony and had always insisted the family attend, regardless of how busy the farm schedule might be. He'd claimed that taking an evening to celebrate community and tradition with neighbors was more important than any amount of additional work they might accomplish at home.

Wyatt understood that now in ways he hadn't as a youngster.

The choir concluded their set to enthusiastic applause, and Mayor Bill Wilson approached a microphone that had been set up near the gazebo. He wore a heavy coat and a festive red scarf, his breath forming white clouds as he waited for the crowd to settle.

"Good evening, Laurel Ridge!" His voice carried across the square, amplified by the sound system. "Welcome to our annual Christmas tree lighting ceremony. Thank you all for coming out on this beautiful December evening to celebrate the start of our holiday season."

Applause rippled through the gathering, punctuated by a few enthusiastic whistles from the teenage contingent.

"Before we light this magnificent tree," Mayor Wilson continued, "I want to take a moment to acknowledge the many people who made tonight possible. Our volunteer decorating committee, the vendor booth operators, our local businesses that sponsored the event, and, of course, Fire Chief Johnson and his crew for ensuring everyone's safety tonight. We owe tremendous gratitude to the Gibson family—Wyatt, Lauren, and Jake—for once again donating a lovely tree from their farm. This tree represents not just their family's generosity, but three generations of commitment to our community's Christmas traditions."

More applause erupted, and Wyatt felt dozens of eyes turn toward him. He kept his arm around Robin's waist, offering a modest wave of acknowledgment.

"Laurel Ridge is more than a town," Mayor Thompson continued, his voice taking on a more serious tone. "It's a family. And like all families, we support each other through challenges and celebrate together in moments of joy. This year has tested some of us, but it's also shown us the strength of community, the power of neighbors helping neighbors, and the blessing of faith that sustains us through all seasons."

"This town," Mayor Wilson continued, "is built on traditions like this annual tree lighting event. On neighbors who know each other's names and care about each other's families. On businesses that support community events and volunteers who give their time freely. I was born and raised here, and I've watched our town navigate challenges and celebrate triumphs, always with the same spirit of unity and mutual care that brings us together tonight. That's what makes Laurel Ridge more than just a place on a map—it's home in the truest sense of the word."

He paused, letting that sentiment settle over the crowd.

"After we light our tree, please enjoy the refreshment tent where Taste of Heaven Bakery, Sugar Maple Sweet Shoppe, and Martha's Diner have generously provided treats and warm beverages for everyone. The band will play for those who want to dance, and I encourage you all to stay and enjoy the evening with your neighbors."

The mayor stepped back from the microphone, and Pastor Andrew moved forward to take his place. His presence commanded immediate quiet, and Wyatt felt Robin's hand find his where it rested at her waist, her fingers curling around his palm.

"Let us pray," Andrew said. "Heavenly Father, we thank You for this community, for the gift of friendship and fellowship, and for the blessing of seasons that remind us of Your faithfulness. As we light this tree tonight, we're reminded that You are the Light of the World—the light that darkness cannot overcome. As we celebrate the coming Christmas season, remind us that Your greatest gifts cannot be wrapped or placed beneath a tree. The gifts of love, hope, and grace—these are the treasures that transform ordinary days into extraordinary life. Help us extend these same gifts to others, showing Your love through our actions and our words. Bless this gathering, protect those traveling home tonight, and help us carry the joy and peace of this season into every day of the coming year. In Your name we pray, Amen."

"Amen," the crowd echoed.

Pastor Andrew stepped back, and Mayor Wilson returned to the microphone with visible excitement. "It's time! Children, please gather near the tree for our countdown."

A wave of youngsters rushed forward, their eager faces turned up toward the unlit branches.

Lauren held her phone steady, ensuring Jake had a clear view of the proceedings.

Wyatt tightened his arm around Robin's waist, and she leaned more fully against him, her head resting on his shoulder.

"Ready?" Mayor Wilson called out, his voice filled with theatrical anticipation. "Let's count down together! Ten!"

"Ten!" the crowd shouted, children's voices carrying above the adults.

"Nine! Eight! Seven!"

The excitement built with each descending number, children bouncing on their toes, adults grinning at their enthusiasm, the entire gathering united in shared anticipation.

"Three! Two! One!"

Mayor Wilson pressed a button on a remote control, and the tree erupted into brilliant light.

Thousands of white lights blazed to life, transforming the tree into a luminous beacon that cast a warm illumination across the snow-covered square. The blue and silver ornaments caught the light, creating shimmering reflections that danced across the surrounding area. White accents sparkled between the colored decorations, and the overall effect was nothing short of magical.

The collective gasp of wonder that rose from the crowd was immediately followed by spontaneous applause and cheers. Children pointed and exclaimed, parents captured photos and videos, and grandparents wiped tears from their eyes. The tree stood magnificently against the dark winter sky.

"It's perfect," Robin whispered, her voice tight with emotion.

Wyatt looked down at her, watching the tree's lights reflect in her eyes, and felt something shift and settle in his chest. This—Robin beside him, his family's tree lighting up the town square, the community gathering in celebration and unity—this was what mattered.

He lifted her hand to his lips and pressed a kiss against her knuckles, holding her gaze as he did so. "It is perfect."

Around them, the crowd began to disperse into smaller groups, some heading toward the refreshment tent while others lingered near the tree for photos. The band struck up a lively rendition of "Rockin' Around the Christmas Tree," and children immediately claimed the dance floor with enthusiasm.

Several community members approached Wyatt, offering congratulations on the beautiful tree. Mayor Wilson shook his hand firmly, expressing his appreciation again for the Gibson family's continued generosity. Pastor Andrew and Lily stopped by to chat, Lily commenting on how the tree seemed even more spectacular this year than last. Martha hugged Wyatt and thanked him for carrying on his father's tradition with such dedication.

Through it all, Robin remained at his side, her hand in his, her presence grounding him even as the attention threatened to become overwhelming. Lauren kept the phone angled so Jake could enjoy every moment.

Eventually, the initial rush of congratulations subsided, and the crowd thinned as families with young children began heading home.

The dance floor remained active with the diehard revelers, and the refreshment tent still hosted clusters of adults warming themselves with hot chocolate and coffee while catching up on community news.

Lauren ended her video call with Jake after promising to bring him some of Taste of Heaven's cookies when she returned home. She tucked her phone into her coat pocket and turned to Wyatt and Robin with a tired but satisfied smile.

"That went well," she said. "Jake seemed to really enjoy being included, even virtually."

"It was a good idea," Wyatt agreed. "Though I suspect he's exhausted now, he had visitors all morning, and he fielded calls from vendors for most of the afternoon today."

"He'll probably sleep well tonight." Lauren said, then directed her attention to Robin. "So tomorrow evening, Wyatt and I are planning to decorate our family Christmas tree. But this year, we're putting it in Jake's room so he can enjoy it."

"That's a great idea," Robin said.

"Join us," Wyatt added, squeezing Robin's hand. "We're going to order pizza and just have a fun evening together."

"I'd love to," she said simply. "What time?"

"Six? That gives Lauren and me time to finish work and make sure the evening employees have everything covered."

"Six it is."

Lauren excused herself to join a group of friends near the refreshment tent, leaving Wyatt and Robin standing together beside the illuminated tree. The crowd had thinned considerably now; the square settling into a quieter contentment as the official ceremony concluded and people dispersed to their various destinations.

He kissed her forehead, letting his lips linger against her skin while breathing in the faint scent of her mixed with the cold winter air.

Standing here in the town square where his family's tree blazed against the winter darkness, holding the woman who'd once been his first love and was now his forever choice, Wyatt felt an absolute certainty that he was exactly where he belonged, with exactly the person his heart had been searching for all along.

Chapter 27

"Left—no, your other left!" Wyatt called out as he and Lauren maneuvered the five-foot Noble fir through Jake's bedroom doorway.

"I know my left from my right," Lauren protested, though her breathless laughter suggested otherwise as she shuffled backward with the tree's base gripped firmly in both hands.

"Could've fooled me," Wyatt said from his position at the tree's tip, guiding the uppermost branches through the door. "You just tried to take us through the wall."

"That was your fault. You shifted right when I said, Go straight."

"I shifted right because you were pulling left."

From his wheelchair positioned near the window, Jake watched his siblings with obvious amusement. "This is better than television. I should have recorded this."

"I agree; this would have been hilarious to watch again in the future." Robin said as she adjusted the tree stand's position slightly. "Okay, bring it straight back now. Slow and steady."

Wyatt and Lauren worked in tandem, lowering the tree into the stand's metal base. The noble fir settled into place with a soft rustle of branches.

"Perfect," Robin announced, tightening the stand's screws to secure the trunk while Wyatt held the tree upright. "Wyatt, you can let go now."

He released his grip cautiously, watching to ensure the tree remained steady before stepping back to assess their work.

"Not bad for a bunch of amateurs," Jake said with a grin. "I seem to remember Dad getting the tree in the house by himself and positioned in under five minutes. It took all three of you at least fifteen."

"Dad also didn't have Lauren's questionable sense of direction complicating matters," Wyatt replied.

Lauren swatted his arm. "My sense of direction is fine. You're just a terrible navigator."

"Children, behave," Jake said in a mockingly stern tone that made all three of them laugh.

Robin moved to Jake's wheelchair, adjusting the brake to ensure it was properly set. He'd been sitting upright for about twenty minutes now, and she could see the strain starting to show around his eyes despite his cheerful demeanor. His posture had shifted slightly, leaning more heavily on the chair's padded armrest than he had when they'd first gotten him settled.

"You doing okay?" she asked.

"I'm good," Jake assured her, but Robin caught the slight wince he tried to hide when he shifted his weight.

Lauren had already retrieved three large storage boxes from the hallway. She pried open the first container, revealing carefully wrapped ornaments nestled in tissue paper alongside coils of garland and strings of multicolored lights.

"Let's start with lights," Lauren said, pulling out a tangled mass that looked like it had been stored by someone in a considerable hurry. "Though I make no promises about untangling this disaster."

"That's my handiwork," Jake admitted without shame. "I was rushing to get them put away last January."

Wyatt took the tangled lights from his sister and began working on the knots with patient determination. Robin moved to help him, their fingers occasionally brushing as they separated strands and identified which bulbs belonged to which string.

"I've got the garland," Lauren announced, draping silver tinsel over her shoulders like a festive scarf. "Though I vote we skip it this year. Jake's room doesn't need to look like a department store exploded."

"Agreed," Jake said. "Just lights and ornaments. Let's keep it simple."

They worked together, Wyatt stringing lights while Robin tested connections and Lauren began unwrapping ornaments from their protective tissue. The bedroom filled with soft conversation and occasional laughter as they transformed the tree from a plain evergreen to something festive.

Robin watched Jake more closely than usual, her nursing instincts noting details she couldn't quite silence even during this social evening. His color looked slightly pallid despite the excitement. His movements when reaching for the ornaments Lauren handed him were careful in ways that suggested discomfort he was trying to minimize. When he adjusted his position in the wheelchair, Robin saw him grimace before quickly schooling his expression.

"This one's my favorite," Jake said, holding up a delicate glass angel with hand-painted features and gold-leafed wings. "Mom made it during a craft class she took the year before she passed."

"That one is also one of my favorites," Lauren said.

Jake nodded. "Put it somewhere I can see it. Front and center."

While Lauren positioned the angel on a prominent branch, Wyatt showed Robin other ornaments with stories attached—construction paper snowflakes from elementary school art classes, a wooden train engine Jake had painted when he was seven, and a photo frame ornament containing a picture of all three Gibson siblings standing in a Christmas tree grove with their parents.

"You were adorable," Robin said, studying the photograph where a young Wyatt grinned at the camera with a missing front tooth. "What happened?"

"Excuse me, I'm still adorable." Wyatt's mock offense made her laugh.

"Debatable," Lauren chimed in.

They continued decorating, each ornament revealing another piece of the Gibson family history. Robin learned Lauren collected snowflake ornaments and had been adding one new design to the tree every year since she was twelve. She learned Wyatt had hand-carved a wooden star when he was a freshman in high school that now occupied a place of honor near the tree's top. And Jake's girlfriend in high school had given him a ridiculous ornament shaped like a tractor that he'd insisted on keeping even after they broke up because it made him laugh.

The tree gradually transformed, becoming a visual representation of their family's journey through joy and loss, tradition and change, and the everyday moments that accumulated into a life well-lived.

Robin noticed Jake's fatigue increasing as they neared completion. His shoulders had hunched forward, and his grip on the wheelchair's armrests had tightened.

"Jake needs to lie down," Robin said to Wyatt, moving to position the wheelchair closer to the bed.

Wyatt set down the ornament he'd been holding and approached his brother. "Time for a position change, brother."

"I can sit a little longer—" Jake started.

"You've been up for forty minutes," Robin interrupted gently. "That's your limit for now, and you know it."

Jake sighed but didn't argue further as Wyatt positioned himself beside the wheelchair. The transfer had become routine over the past few days—Wyatt sliding his arm behind Jake's shoulders and under his knees and lifting carefully while Robin steadied the wheelchair. Jake's face tightened with discomfort during the movement, but he remained quiet until Wyatt had settled him against the pillows.

"Thanks," Jake said, his relief at being horizontal again clear in his voice.

Robin noticed how thin his legs looked beneath his sweatpants, muscle mass declining despite the physical therapy sessions. She'd seen this pattern in other patients—the slow erosion of strength when weight-bearing wasn't possible.

"The tingling's been worse today," Jake said, flexing his feet beneath the blanket. "In my toes and up through my ankles. It's driving me crazy."

"That's actually a good sign," Robin assured him. "It means your nerves are still communicating. Have you mentioned it to Dr. Morrison?"

"I will during my appointment on Wednesday."

"I'll just document it now in your chart, so that Dr. Morrison will have this information now," Robin said as she reached for her tablet.

The doorbell chime echoed through the farmhouse, and Wyatt glanced at his watch. "That'll be the pizza. Lauren, come help me get everything ready?"

"Only if you're paying," Lauren said, already heading toward the door.

"I paid last time!"

"No, Jake paid last time. Which means it's definitely your turn."

Their bickering voices faded as they left the bedroom, and Robin completed her note in Jake's chart. She moved to adjust his pillows, ensuring he was positioned comfortably, then settled into the chair beside his bed.

"You look tired," she observed.

"I am tired," he admitted. "But the good kind. The kind that comes from doing something normal instead of just lying here bored and staring at the ceiling."

Robin smiled. "How are you really doing? Not the version you tell your siblings or the doctors. The truth."

Jake was quiet for a long moment, his gaze fixed on the decorated tree.

"I'm scared," he said finally. "Scared that this is as good as it gets. That I'll spend the rest of my life watching other people do the work I used to love, being the person everyone has to accommodate and worry about." He paused. "But... let's not talk about that. It's too depressing. I'm happy seeing you and Wyatt back together. He seems like his old self these past couple of weeks."

Robin's chest tightened with emotion. "I never stopped loving him, you know. Even when I tried to convince myself I had."

"I know. Anyone with eyes could see that." Jake's smile was gentle. "You're good for each other. You make him a better man."

"He's changed. I mean, he's still that young, determined boy I remember, but now he's more complete. I'm not sure how to explain it really; he's the same but different. We've both changed, really. We're not the same kids who broke up twelve years ago."

"No, you're better." Jake shifted slightly, wincing at the movement. "I just hope—"

He stopped, seeming to reconsider his words.

"Hope what?" Robin prompted.

"I hope my situation doesn't complicate things for you two. My future's so uncertain right now. I'm coming to grips with the fact that my life on this farm is probably going to look a lot different from what I'd hoped for. And I keep wondering..." He trailed off, then continued quietly. "I keep wondering if Wyatt's going to leave his job and move home permanently to help run things. Someone has to ensure the farm survives, and Lauren can't manage everything alone."

The words hit Robin like cold water. She felt her expression freeze, confusion blooming sharp and immediate in her chest. Wyatt hadn't told Jake. He hadn't mentioned his decision to resign from the Forestry Service and to stay in Laurel Ridge permanently.

Why would he keep that from his brother?

She forced her features into what she hoped was a neutral expression, buying herself time to process. Jake was watching her with the kind of hope that made lying to him impossible, but she couldn't betray Wyatt's confidence by revealing plans he'd apparently chosen not to share with his own family.

"Wyatt loves you and Lauren," Robin said carefully, choosing words that were true without revealing what she knew. "He'll do whatever he needs to do to support you both. You don't need to worry about that."

"I know he will. That's what worries me. He's already sacrificed so much. I don't want him giving up the life he loves because I can't do my job anymore."

Robin wanted to reassure him, to explain that Wyatt's decision to stay wasn't a sacrifice but a choice. That he'd found his way back to the place where he belonged and the people who mattered most. But the words caught in her throat, tangled with her confusion about why Wyatt hadn't shared this crucial information with the brother who needed to hear it most.

Maybe he was waiting for the right moment. Maybe he didn't want to burden Jake during his recovery.

But the uncertainty gnawed at her, a small seed of doubt taking root in ground she'd thought was finally solid.

Chapter 28

"**B**lood pressure's 118 over 76," Robin said, recording the reading on Jake's chart while Josie removed the cuff from his arm. "Heart rate 72. Both well within normal range."

Lauren stood near the window, her arms crossed as she watched the morning assessment with the careful attention she'd developed over the past weeks. Jake sat propped against his pillows, looking alert and anxious.

Footsteps echoed in the hallway, and Wyatt appeared in the doorway with Dr. Morrison following close behind. The doctor carried a leather medical bag in one hand and a manila folder thick with files in the other. His weathered face wore the expression Robin had seen countless times—friendly warmth tempered with professional gravity, the look of someone who'd spent decades delivering news both hopeful and devastating with equal compassion.

"Good morning, Jake," Dr. Morrison said, his voice carrying the gentle authority that came from forty years of rural practice. He was in his early sixties, with silver hair and a steady presence that made patients trust him instinctively. "How are you feeling today?"

"Like a man about to get his report card," Jake replied. "Hopefully, I passed."

"Well, let's find out." Dr. Morrison set his bag on the bedside table and pulled up the chair Robin had vacated. "I had that video conference on Monday with your surgical team, your orthopedic specialist, and the neurologist who's been reviewing your case. We spent two hours going over every aspect of your recovery, comparing notes, and developing a comprehensive picture of where you are and where we expect you to go from here."

Robin moved to stand beside Wyatt near the foot of the bed, her professional instincts on high alert. She'd taken part in enough care conferences to recognize the careful phrasing that preceded tough news delivered with kindness.

Dr. Morrison opened Jake's file, reviewing several pages before looking up. "First, the good news—and there's plenty of it. Your surgical sites have healed beautifully. The work they did reconstructing your pelvis was exceptional, and you've had no complications with infection or improper bone fusion. Your lung function has returned to normal, and your general health markers are excellent."

"That is good news," Lauren said, her relief evident.

"Your upper body strength has improved significantly," the doctor continued. "The physical therapy has been incredibly effective there. You've worked hard, Jake, and it shows." He paused, his expression shifting to something more serious. "Now, let's talk about the more complex aspects of your recovery."

The room seemed to hold its breath.

"The spinal compression fractures at L1 and L2 have healed, but there's permanent nerve damage that we now understand better after monitoring your progress these past weeks. The tingling sensation you've been experiencing in your legs and feet is encouraging—it means the nerves are still communicating. However, the extent of the damage limits how much function you'll ultimately regain."

Jake's jaw tightened, but he nodded for the doctor to continue.

"Based on the comprehensive assessment from Monday's conference, we believe you will regain the ability to walk," Dr. Morrison said, and Robin saw hope flash across Jake's face before the doctor added, "with assistive devices. Likely a walker initially, potentially progressing to a cane or canes depending on your balance and strength development. But the weight-bearing capacity in your lower body will be permanently limited."

"What does that mean practically... in everyday words... not medical lingo?" Jake asked.

"It means modified activity levels for the rest of your life, more than likely," Dr. Morrison explained gently. "The reconstruction of your pelvis, combined with the spinal nerve damage, limits the amount of stress your lower body can safely handle. Heavy lifting, prolonged standing, climbing ladders, and operating farm machinery that requires significant leg strength—these activities carry too much risk of further injury or damage."

The implications settled over the room like a heavy blanket. Robin watched Wyatt's face, seeing the careful neutrality he'd adopted to hide whatever he was feeling. Lauren had moved closer to Jake's bed, her hand finding her brother's shoulder.

"So I can't do the physical work," Jake said.

"Not the heavy physical labor that traditional farm management requires," Dr. Morrison confirmed. "I'm sorry, Jake. I know this isn't what you hoped to hear."

Jake was quiet for a long moment. Robin recognized the visible effort it took him to maintain composure, the way his throat worked before he spoke again.

"What can I do, or what will I be able to do? Specifically. Give me the parameters."

Dr. Morrison's expression softened. "You can handle desk work, computer tasks, phone coordination, customer relations—anything that doesn't require sustained physical exertion. You can supervise operations, make business decisions, and manage planning and logistics. With proper adaptive equipment and workplace modifications, eventually you'll be able to take part in farm activities within reason. When you get to that point, we can talk about it further."

"So I become the brains while everyone else provides the brawn," Jake said, attempting humor that fell flat in the quiet room.

"You've always been the brains," Lauren said firmly. "The rest is just details we'll figure out."

Dr. Morrison spent the next twenty minutes going through specific recommendations—adaptive equipment options, workplace modifications, and physical therapy goals focused on maximizing mobility within safe parameters. He discussed timeline expectations, noting that Jake's progress over the next six to twelve months would give them better clarity about his ultimate functional capacity.

Robin took part in the discussion with a professional detachment that belied the ache in her chest. She'd suspected this outcome and had seen the pattern in Jake's recovery that suggested permanent limitations. But suspecting and knowing were different things, and watching Jake process the death of dreams he'd built his identity around hurt.

"I want to be clear," Dr. Morrison said as he prepared to leave, "this prognosis isn't a sentence to a meaningless life. I've worked with patients who've adapted to similar limitations and found tremendous satisfaction in modified roles. It requires adjustment, certainly, and grief for what's lost. But it doesn't mean you can't have a fulfilling, productive life that includes meaningful work on this farm."

"I appreciate that," Jake said quietly.

After Dr. Morrison departed with promises to follow up in two weeks, the room fell into heavy silence. Josie had retreated to the corner, giving the family space to process while remaining available if needed.

Robin moved to check Jake's side. His color looked good despite the stress, but his hands trembled slightly where they gripped the blanket.

"Jake—" Lauren started.

"I'm okay," he said, though his voice carried strain. "I mean, I'm not okay, but I will be. I just need to... get myself together and process all this. It's a lot. And besides... only God knows what my future looks like. Who knows? I could be a walking miracle in a few months and surprise everyone. But... just give me a few minutes to process Dr. Morrison's opinion about my future."

"We'll make whatever changes are necessary," Wyatt said. "We'll all adapt."

Robin waited for him to continue, to mention his decision to leave the Forestry Service and stay permanently, to reassure Jake that the physical labor wouldn't fall solely on Lauren's shoulders. But Wyatt remained silent.

Why wasn't he saying anything? Jake needed to hear that his brother was staying, that the burden of farm operations wouldn't rest entirely on Lauren's shoulders while Jake struggled to find a meaningful role within his new limitations. This was the perfect moment to share news that would ease at least some of Jake's worry.

Unless Wyatt had changed his mind.

The thought sent ice through Robin's chest. She pushed it away immediately, refusing to let doubt take root. There had to be a reason for his silence. Maybe he didn't want to make Jake feel like his injury had forced Wyatt's career change. Maybe he was waiting for a private conversation. Maybe—

"You know," Jake said, breaking the silence, "I've been thinking about something Dr. Morrison said. About how I can still be involved in planning and customer relations. We've always talked about expanding the agritourism side of the business—farm tours, educational programs, and seasonal events beyond just Christmas tree sales. That's all stuff I could coordinate without needing to climb ladders or haul trees."

Lauren seized on the idea with visible relief. "That's brilliant. We've had requests for years about spring events and fall harvest activities. You could develop entire programs."

"And the website needs a complete overhaul," Jake continued, warming to the topic. "Our online presence is stuck in 2020. I could manage that, coordinate social media, and handle digital marketing."

Robin recognized what he was doing—finding solid ground in the midst of devastating news and identifying ways to contribute that aligned with his new limitations. It was healthy and necessary, but it also carried an undercurrent of loss that made her throat tighten.

"Those are excellent ideas," Robin said. "And realistic. The key is giving yourself time to grieve what's changed while building something new... and never losing hope."

"How long does the grieving part take?" Jake asked, his attempt at lightness not quite masking genuine pain.

"As long as it takes," Robin said honestly. "There's no timeline for accepting major life changes. Grief will hit you at some point; don't fight it. Let it happen and work through it."

Wyatt had remained quiet throughout this discussion, his expression difficult to read. Robin wanted to shake him, to demand why he wasn't sharing information that would help his brother see a path forward. Instead, she maintained professional composure while frustration built beneath her calm exterior.

"We should probably let you rest," she said to Jake, noting the exhaustion creeping into his features. "It's been an intense morning, and you have physical therapy this afternoon."

"I am pretty wiped," Jake admitted. "Though I'm not sure if I can sleep after all this."

Josie stepped forward with a gentle smile. "How about I put on a movie? Something fun to take your mind off things for a couple of hours. You don't have to sleep; just relax."

"That sounds good, actually."

Robin gathered her supplies, making notes in Jake's chart about the morning's assessment and Dr. Morrison's visit. She'd need to update the care plan to reflect the new long-term prognosis and coordinate with the physical therapist about modified goals.

Wyatt touched her elbow as she prepared to leave. "Can you come with Lauren and me to the office? I'd like to discuss a few things with both of you."

Robin hesitated, suddenly uncertain about her role in this moment. "You and Lauren need to talk privately about everything you're facing. I shouldn't—"

"Please," Wyatt said, his voice carrying an urgency that made her pause. "I want you there."

Lauren had already moved toward the doorway, clearly expecting Robin to follow.

"Alright," she said finally.

They left Jake's room in silence, Josie's cheerful voice following them as she helped Jake get comfortable and scrolled through movie options on the television.

Robin followed Wyatt and Lauren down the hall, each step carrying her toward a conversation she wasn't sure she wanted to have, toward answers that might reshape everything she'd allowed herself to believe about their future together.

Chapter 29

The walls of the office felt like they were closing in on Wyatt. Dr. Morrison's words echoed in his mind—permanent limitations, modified activity levels, adaptive equipment—clinical phrases that translated into a fundamental restructuring of everyone's lives involved.

Lauren sat at her desk across from him, a concerned look on her face. Robin occupied the chair Wyatt had pulled close beside his own, her hands folded in her lap, her expression unreadable.

"I think it might be best to hire at least two more full-time employees," he said. "People we can train properly, who'll stay year round and learn the business inside and out. We have excellent employees already, but I'm talking about two more employees to take over part of our responsibilities."

"I've been thinking about that too. We need to consider that, probably for the next year at least, Jake is going to continue to need us as he recovers. Insurance will only pay for home health visits for so long. Wyatt... you and I are spread thin as it is already. Jake will need us even more in the future. Thinking ahead... if we restructure Jake's role to focus on planning, customer relations, and digital marketing like he suggested, we could justify the expense of additional labor by expanding operations. The agritourism ideas he mentioned could generate significant revenue if we develop them properly." Lauren said.

"It'll take capital investment," Wyatt said. "Infrastructure improvements, marketing budget, and possibly zoning approvals depending on what events we want to host."

"We have the capital. Dad and Mom were careful with the business finances, and Jake and I have been equally conservative. The question isn't whether we can afford to adapt—it's whether we can afford not to."

Lauren paused, looking down at the floor. "Jake was right about something else too. Only God knows what the future looks like. We can plan and prepare and make our best decisions, but ultimately we have to trust that we're being guided toward where we need to be."

Wyatt glanced toward Robin, who remained silent, watching them with an intensity that made him uneasy. Something in her expression carried questions she wasn't voicing, a careful neutrality that felt different.

"Robin," he said, turning his chair to face her directly. "You're awfully quiet. What are you thinking?"

She met his gaze, and he saw something flicker across her face—uncertainty and confusion. "I'm just listening. This is your family's business, your decisions to make. I really have no business being here."

"But you're part of this conversation for a reason," Lauren said. "You're not just Jake's nurse. You're—" She gestured between Robin and Wyatt. "Your family. Or as good as. Your perspective matters."

Before Robin could respond, Lauren's attention shifted back to Wyatt, her expression turning serious. "Actually, speaking of decisions—Wyatt, what are you planning to do? Long-term, I mean. Are you going to stay here and help us run the farm for the foreseeable future? Leave your job with the Forestry Service? Or are you planning to return to your position once your family leave runs out in a few weeks?"

Wyatt opened his mouth to answer, but his cell phone started ringing. The sudden sound jarring.

Frustration surged through him. Of all the moments for an interruption—

He grabbed the phone from his desk and silenced it without looking at the caller ID, setting it face-down with more force than necessary. "Sorry. Where were we?"

"Your plans," Lauren said.

"I've been meaning to have this discussion with you and Jake together. I wanted both of you to hear this at the same time, to make sure you both understood my reasoning."

"Understood what?" Lauren leaned forward slightly.

"I'm putting in my two weeks' notice with the Forestry Service. I'm staying here permanently."

Relief flooded Lauren's features so visibly that Wyatt felt guilt twist in his gut. She'd been carrying the weight of uncertainty about their future, wondering if she'd be managing everything alone.

"Wyatt—" she started.

"I need you to understand something. This isn't me sacrificing my career out of obligation. This isn't me giving up what I want because of Jake's accident or because the farm needs me. I'm making this choice because I want to be here."

Lauren's eyes glistened. "You're sure?"

"I'm sure. I haven't been enjoying my work with the Forestry Service these past several months the way I did before. The isolation, the wear and tear on my body during fire season, the way my life was... I just haven't been happy, sis." He paused, gathering his thoughts. "Coming home forced me to face all of that. This is home. This is where I want to be. And Robin—"

He turned to look at her, and the relief on her face stopped his words. Her eyes were bright with emotion, her careful neutrality crumbling into something that looked remarkably like joy mixed with residual uncertainty.

"Why have you been so quiet?" he asked her directly.

Robin's composure wavered. "Because I was getting upset. And confused. And trying not to show it because I didn't want to interfere in family business decisions."

"Upset about what?"

"You hadn't told your family about your decision to leave your job." The words came out in a rush. "You told me that you'd decided to stay, that you'd talked to your supervisor about it, and that you were planning to put in your notice. But then Dr. Morrison gave Jake his diagnosis this morning, and it was the perfect moment to tell them, to ease Jake's worry about the farm's future. And you said nothing."

Understanding crashed over Wyatt. "And you thought I'd changed my mind."

"I couldn't figure out why you hadn't told them already. Why you'd keep something that important from Jake and Lauren when they needed to hear it most. So I started wondering if maybe you'd reconsidered. If you were having second thoughts about giving up your career."

Guilt and regret twisted in Wyatt's chest. "Robin, I'm so sorry. I should have said something sooner to them. I should have had this conversation with Jake and Lauren already instead of waiting for some perfect moment that never came. Between the farm work keeping me busy and everything else happening, the conversation just never materialized."

"You really meant it?" Robin asked, her voice small. "You're staying?"

"I'm staying. My resignation letter is already drafted and saved on my computer. I just wanted to talk to Jake and Lauren together before I made it official." He reached for her hand, threading his fingers through hers. "That wasn't fair to you, and I'm sorry."

"Wyatt, check your phone. It's blinking, and someone obviously left a voicemail. It could be important—someone needing you out on the farm or a vendor or something," Lauren said.

Wyatt had forgotten about the interrupted call. He picked up his phone and checked the screen, his heart skipping slightly when he saw the caller ID.

"It's from Captain Rogers with the forestry division," he said aloud, surprised.

He pressed play on the voicemail, putting the phone on speaker. Captain Rogers' familiar gravelly voice filled the small office.

"Wyatt, it's Captain Rogers. I need you to call me back as soon as possible. It's important. Thanks."

The message ended, and Wyatt stared at the phone. His captain rarely called outside of official business, and the urgency in his tone suggested this was more than a routine check-in.

"Sounded important," he said as he pulled up Captain Rogers' contact information. He pressed the call button and waited through two rings before his supervisor answered.

"Wyatt! Thanks for getting back to me so quickly."

"Of course, sir. Your message sounded urgent. Is everything alright?"

"Everything's fine. Better than fine, actually. I wanted to call you personally before word starts spreading around." Captain Rogers paused. "I'm retiring, Wyatt. Effective April first. After thirty-two years with the Forestry Service, I'm finally hanging up my hard hat."

The news surprised Wyatt, though it probably shouldn't have. Captain Rogers had been talking about retirement for months now, but he'd always seemed too vital, too engaged with the work to actually follow through.

"Congratulations, sir. You've more than earned it."

"Thank you. But that's only part of why I'm calling." The captain's tone shifted to something more formal, more significant. "I just submitted my retirement request this morning, and along with it, I submitted a recommendation to district leadership. I recommended you for promotion to assume my position leading the Gauley Ranger District."

The words hit Wyatt like a physical blow. His breath caught, and he felt Robin's eyes snap toward him with alarm at whatever expression had crossed his face.

"Sir, I—"

"Before you say anything, let me finish." Captain Rogers said. "This isn't just me being sentimental about my favorite team member. You're the most qualified candidate for this position. You have all the necessary certifications, extensive field experience, demonstrated leadership during crisis situations, and the respect of every person in this district. Leadership has already indicated that my recommendation carries substantial weight, and barring any unforeseen circumstances, you're looking at a near guarantee for this promotion."

Wyatt's mind reeled. District supervisor. Leading the Gauley Ranger District. It was the position he'd been working toward since his first year with the Forestry Service, the culmination of everything he'd been building in his career. Increased responsibility, a significant salary increase, and recognition of his expertise in wildland fire management and forestry conservation.

Everything he'd ever wanted professionally offered at precisely the moment when accepting it would mean abandoning his family when they needed him most.

"The timeline would be tight," Captain Rogers continued, clearly interpreting Wyatt's silence as consideration rather than shock. "If you accept, you'd need to make your decision by January third. That would give us time to arrange your training—two months in Colorado starting in late January, focused on district management, advanced leadership, and administrative responsibilities. You'd assume the position officially on April first when I step down."

"Wyatt, this is the opportunity you've been working toward for years," Captain Rogers said, his enthusiasm clear. "Your expertise, your dedication, your proven ability to handle high-pressure situations—this is what you've been preparing for. I can't think of anyone I'd rather see leading this district."

Robin's face had gone blank, her earlier relief completely erased. Lauren looked stricken, clearly understanding the magnitude of what was being offered and what accepting would mean for their family.

Wyatt found his voice, though it came out rougher than intended. "Sir, I appreciate your confidence in me more than I can express. This recommendation means everything, and I'm honored that you'd think of me for this position."

"But?" Captain Rogers asked, hearing what Wyatt hadn't said.

"But I can't accept it." The words felt surreal even as Wyatt spoke them. "I need to give you my formal two weeks' notice. I'm resigning from the Forestry Service."

Silence greeted this announcement. Wyatt could picture Captain Rogers in his office, phone pressed to his ear, trying to process what he'd just heard.

"Wyatt, I don't think you understand what you'd be giving up."

"I do understand, sir. Believe me, I understand completely."

"This is the district supervisor position. This isn't just another field assignment you can walk away from and pick up again later. This opportunity won't come around twice. If you turn this down, you're closing a door that probably won't reopen."

"I know."

"Is this about your brother's accident? Because leadership would absolutely work with you on modified scheduling during his recovery. We could delay the training timeline, arrange for additional leave—"

"It's not about Jake's accident," Wyatt interrupted gently. "Or rather, it's not only about that. Sir, I've been doing some serious reflection these past months, and I've realized that the career I've been building doesn't align with the life I actually want to live."

"Wyatt—"

"I've already drafted my resignation letter. I'll send it to you via email this afternoon."

Captain Rogers was quiet for a long moment. When he spoke again, his voice had softened from professional authority to something more personal. "Can I speak frankly? Off the record?"

"Of course."

"I've watched a lot of good people make career decisions based on family obligations. Some of them handled it well, building meaningful lives around their choices. Others spent years resenting what they'd given up, wondering what might have been if they'd chosen differently. I want to make sure you're choosing this path for the right reasons, not just because circumstances have backed you into a corner."

"I appreciate that, sir. Truly. But I'm not being backed into a corner." Wyatt glanced at Robin, then at Lauren, then at the office walls covered in family photographs and farm records that represented generations of Gibson commitment to this land. "I'm choosing the life I want. The career I've had with the Forestry Service was valuable and meaningful, but it's not what I want anymore. This is where I belong—with my family, with my community, with the woman I love. That's not a sacrifice. That's finally getting my priorities straight."

Another long pause. Then Captain Rogers spoke with quiet respect. "Then I'm proud of you, Wyatt. Any man of honor would do the same given the circumstances. You've been an exceptional member of this team, and you'll be missed. But if you're certain this is the right path—"

"I am certain."

"Then I wish you all the best. Send that resignation letter when you're ready and let me know if you need anything during your transition out. And Wyatt? For what it's worth, I think you're making a brave choice. Not an easy one, but a brave one."

"Thank you, sir. That means more than you know."

They exchanged a few more words—logistics about paperwork, transition timelines, and final paycheck details—before ending the call. Wyatt set his phone down on the desk and stared at it, his mind struggling to process what had just happened.

The position he'd dreamed about since his first day with the Forestry Service. The culmination of a decade of training, certifications, deployments, and career building. The opportunity that would have represented professional validation and the recognition he'd worked so hard to achieve.

Offered to him at the precise moment when accepting it would mean walking away from everything that actually mattered.

And he'd declined without hesitation.

He'd given his two weeks' notice.

Pride swelled in his chest alongside something that felt remarkably like relief. He'd made the right choice. He knew it with bone-deep certainty that quieted every doubt and second-guess his analytical mind wanted to raise.

But underneath the certainty, another emotion stirred—something he couldn't quite name. Not regret, exactly. Not doubt. But a recognition of the magnitude of the door he'd just closed, the path he'd just turned away from, and the version of his future that had just evaporated with a single phone call.

The dreams he'd carried for years had just been offered to him gift-wrapped and guaranteed, and he'd said no without even a moment's pause to consider accepting.

He stood up, with a blank expression on his face, and turned toward Robin and said, "I need a moment."

And then he walked out of the office.

Chapter 30

Robin had watched Wyatt's expressions as they had shifted during the call from Captain Rogers—from surprise to shock to something that looked like a man watching his entire future split into two irreconcilable paths.

She had watched the color drain from his face after he had ended the call.

She had watched him stand abruptly, had heard the chair scraping against the floor, and had watched as he had turned toward her with eyes that seemed to look through her rather than at her.

"I need a moment," he had said.

Then, he had walked out of the office.

Robin now sat frozen, her hand still warm from where his fingers had been threaded through hers moments ago.

She heard the front door open and then close.

Robin stared at the empty doorway, her mind struggling to process the whiplash of the past fifteen minutes. Relief at learning Wyatt still planned to stay. Confusion about why he'd kept it from his siblings.

Then that phone call—Captain Rogers' voice filling the office with an offer that represented everything Wyatt had worked toward for a decade. District supervisor. The Gauley Ranger District. Training in Colorado. His dream job, offered at the worst possible moment.

And he'd turned it down without hesitation.

This is where I belong—with my family, with my community, with the woman I love.

The woman I love.

He'd said it so clearly, so deliberately, with all of them listening. Not "someone special" or "a relationship" but explicitly, undeniably—the woman I love.

Robin's throat tightened with emotion. Pride in his choice. Fear that he might come to regret it. Overwhelming gratitude mixed with guilt that his love for her had just cost him his professional dreams. Hope that his certainty was real and lasting. Terror that someday he'd look at her and see everything he'd given up.

She turned to Lauren, who sat at her desk with tears streaming silently down her face. Neither of them spoke. What words could be adequate for what they'd just witnessed?

Lauren wiped her eyes with shaking hands, then let out a breath that sounded like it had been trapped in her chest since Jake's accident. "He really did it. He just quit his job."

"He did," Robin whispered.

"Do you understand what that position meant to him?" Lauren's voice cracked. "And Captain Rogers just handed it to him. Guaranteed."

"I know." Robin's own voice was unsteady.

"And he said no, for us. For the farm. For—" Lauren stopped, fresh tears spilling over. "For you."

The words hung between them, heavy with implications that Robin wasn't sure she was ready to face. Loving someone was one thing. Being loved enough that someone would sacrifice their lifelong dreams—that was something else entirely. That was the kind of love that required her to be worth it, to justify the cost, to somehow make his sacrifice meaningful rather than merely tragic.

But it wasn't just about her. Wyatt hadn't turned down that promotion solely because he loved her. He'd made that choice because Jake needed him. Because Lauren couldn't shoulder everything alone. Because generations of Gibsons had poured their lives into this land, and Wyatt understood some legacies were worth preserving even at great personal cost. His decision reflected the kind of man he was—someone who showed up for the people he loved, who honored his parents' memory through action rather than sentiment, and who understood that being part of a family sometimes meant setting aside individual ambitions for the collective good. That depth of character, that bone-deep loyalty and sense of responsibility—those were the qualities that made Robin love him even more than his willingness to choose her.

"Where do you think he went?" Robin asked.

Lauren stood and moved to the window, looking out toward the farm buildings and the land stretching beyond. "When Wyatt needs to think—really think, not just sort through logistics but process emotions and big decisions—he disappears. He's always been that way, even as a kid."

"I remember," Robin said softly. "When we were together in high school, he'd sometimes just need space. He'd tell me he was going for a walk or that he needed to clear his head, and I learned not to take it personally. It was just how he worked through things."

Lauren nodded, still gazing out the window. "After Mom and Dad died—" Her voice caught, and she paused to steady herself. "We'd just come home from the funeral. The burial. Seeing them lowered into the ground beside the church where we'd worshipped our entire lives. It was the worst day of my life, and I think we were all just numb, moving through the motions because we didn't know what else to do."

Robin moved to stand beside her at the window.

"We pulled into the driveway here at the house, and Wyatt got out of the car with this look on his face—the same look he had just now when he walked out of this office. Like he'd seen something that fundamentally changed how he understood the world. Like he was standing at a crossroads, and every path forward led somewhere he didn't recognize." Lauren's hands gripped the windowsill. "He just walked away that day after the funeral. He didn't say where he was going, just that he needed to be alone."

"How long was he gone?"

"Two hours. Maybe a little more. Jake and I tried to give him space, but after a while we got worried. So we went looking for him." Lauren smiled slightly through her tears. "We found him down by the river, on that back portion of our property where the bank flattens out and there's a cluster of old oak trees. He was just sitting there, staring at the water."

Robin knew exactly where Lauren meant. The river spot. The place where massive oaks created a canopy of shade and the water ran steady and calm over smooth stones. Where the world felt quieter somehow, separate from the demands and noise of regular life.

"We used to picnic there on Sunday afternoons as a family," Lauren continued. "After church, when the weather was nice. Mom would pack a basket full of food. Dad would skip stones across the water and tell us stories about when he was young. Mom would spread out a blanket and read while we played. It was—" Her voice broke. "It was one of our family's special places. A place that was just ours."

"Wyatt took me there," Robin said quietly. "When we were dating. We'd pack sandwiches and go sit by the river for hours. We'd talk about everything—our dreams, our fears, what we wanted our lives to look like. Sometimes we'd just sit in silence and watch the water flow by."

Lauren turned to look at her. "I'm not surprised; he loves it out there."

"I always loved it out there too. It felt sacred somehow. Like the rest of the world couldn't touch us when we were sitting under those oak trees." Robin's eyes stung with tears she was trying not to shed.

Lauren reached for Robin's hand and squeezed it. "When Jake and I found him at the river that day after the funeral, we didn't say anything at first. We just sat down on either side of him. The three of us sat there for a long time—grieving, thinking, trying to make sense of a world where our parents were just... gone."

"What did he say when you found him?"

Lauren's expression grew distant with memory. "He said he'd been trying to pray, but he couldn't find the words. That everything he wanted to say to God felt too small for what he was feeling. So he'd just been sitting there, watching the river flow, thinking about how life keeps going even when it feels like it should stop."

Robin felt tears slip down her cheeks. The image of three young adults—barely more than kids themselves—sitting by a river trying to process the loss of both parents was almost too painful to bear.

"Jake started talking about all the memories we had of Mom and Dad at that spot," Lauren continued. "The Sunday picnics, the times Dad taught us to fish, the afternoon Mom brought her watercolors down and painted the oak trees. We laughed and cried and prayed together. Not eloquent prayers—just honest ones. Asking God to help us figure out how to keep living when everything had changed. How to honor Mom and Dad's memory while building our own futures. How to stay close as siblings even though grief makes you want to isolate."

"That must have been incredibly hard."

"It was. But it was also sacred. That moment by the river—the three of us choosing to face our pain together instead of separately—it became a turning point. We realized that we could survive this loss if we had each other. That family wasn't just about the people we'd lost but also about the people still standing beside us."

Lauren turned from the window to face Robin fully. "Wyatt's a deep thinker. He always has been. When something significant happens—something that requires him to process big emotions or make life-changing decisions—he needs time alone to work through it. Not because he doesn't trust others or doesn't value input, but because he has to understand his own heart before he can articulate what he's feeling."

"And you think that's what he's doing now? Processing?"

"I know it is. He just turned down the job he's dreamed about for years. Now the reality of what he gave up is hitting him. He's been so strong through Jake's accident. Stepping up immediately, taking on massive responsibilities, managing the farm, supporting me, and making decisions about his entire future. He's been carrying all of that without complaint, without breaking down, and without letting anyone see how much pressure he's under."

Robin nodded. "And now it's all caught up with him."

"He needs to grieve what he just gave up, even though he made the right choice. He needs to process the magnitude of turning down that promotion. He needs to reconcile the life he thought he'd build with the life he's actually choosing."

"And you think he went down to the river?"

"I do." Lauren said it with absolute certainty. "I'd bet anything that's where he went."

Robin's heart pulled her toward the door, toward finding Wyatt and somehow making this easier for him. But doubt crept in alongside the desire to help. Would he want her there? Or did he need the solitude Lauren described—the space to sort through his emotions without having to manage anyone else's reactions?

"Should I—" Robin stopped, unsure how to finish the question. "Do you think I should go after him? Would it help? Or would I just be intruding on something he needs to do alone?"

Lauren studied her face. "What does your heart say?"

Robin thought about the man who'd just walked out of this office. The man who'd turned down his dream job without hesitation. The man who'd told his supervisor—told everyone listening—that he was choosing to stay here and leave his career.

This is where I belong—with my family, with my community, with the woman I love.

She thought about eighteen-year-old Wyatt bringing her to his family's sacred place by the river, sharing something precious without ever telling her how much that spot meant to him. She thought about thirty-year-old Wyatt sitting there now, alone, processing the weight of choosing love and family over career and independence.

She thought about how many times in her life she'd held back, played it safe, and waited for perfect conditions before taking emotional risks. How Liam's rejection had taught her to protect her heart by not offering it too freely. How she'd spent years convincing herself that loving Wyatt was a teenage memory.

And she thought about what she'd learned in the past few weeks—that extraordinary love required extraordinary courage. That some moments demanded you stop waiting and start choosing. That the people worth loving were the people worth fighting for, worth showing up for, and worth finding when they needed someone beside them.

"My heart says to go after him," Robin said, her voice steady with certainty.

Lauren smiled, fresh tears brightening her eyes, and pulled Robin into a fierce hug. "Then go."

Robin hugged her back, grateful for this woman who understood her brother so completely and was generous enough to share that understanding. When they separated, Robin hesitated.

"Do you have a Bible I could borrow?"

Lauren's expression softened. She moved to her desk and opened the bottom drawer, pulling out a well-worn leather Bible with pages marked by colorful tabs.

"He loves you," Lauren said simply. "And you love him. The rest is just details you'll figure out together."

Robin nodded, unable to speak past the emotion clogging her throat. She turned toward the door, Lauren's Bible held against her chest like a talisman, and walked out of the office.

<h1 style="text-align:center">Chapter 31</h1>

The side-by-side's engine rumbled beneath Robin as she navigated the farm roads. Cold December air bit at her cheeks. Beside her on the passenger seat lay a thick quilt she'd grabbed from the hall closet, Wyatt's coat that had been hanging by the front door, and Lauren's Bible.

She drove with purpose, passing sections of the farm that bustled with midweek activity. A handful of customers wandered through the tree groves, their voices carrying across the crisp air. Two employees worked near the equipment barn, organizing tools and preparing for afternoon tasks. Tom directed a family toward the cut-your-own section, his familiar gestures visible even from a distance.

Life on Gibson's Tree Farm continued its steady rhythm, unaware that thirty minutes ago, one of its owners had turned down his dream job.

Robin steered past the customer areas, beyond the maintained groves, into the back sections of the property where the land grew wilder and the farm operations gave way to natural forest. Snow covered the ground in a blanket of white, pristine except for one clear set of tracks cutting through the landscape. Leading exactly where she knew they would.

Her heart steadied as she followed those tracks, the parallel lines in the snow like a path laid specifically for her to follow. Past the last row of nut trees, through a grove of mature oaks whose bare branches reached toward the blue sky, down a gentle slope where the sound of running water grew louder with each passing moment.

And there, parked beside the river under the shelter of ancient oak trees, sat a dark green side-by-side identical to the one she drove.

Robin pulled up beside him and cut her engine. The sudden silence felt profound, broken only by the rush of water over stones and the whisper of wind through bare branches.

Wyatt turned his head and looked at her. For a moment, neither of them moved. Then his face softened into a smile—tired but genuine.

Robin reached for his coat, opened her door, and walked the few steps to his side-by-side. She handed it to him without speaking.

"Thanks," he said, pulling the coat on and zipping it against the cold.

She climbed into the passenger seat beside him, bringing the Bible and quilt with her. She spread the quilt across both their laps, tucking it around their legs to trap what warmth they could generate between them.

Then she opened the Bible to Psalm 37 and found verses 23 and 24.

"The Lord makes firm the steps of the one who delights in Him," Robin read, her voice steady and clear in the winter air. "Though he may stumble, he will not fall, for the Lord upholds him with His hand."

She let the words settle between them, feeling their weight and meaning. Steps. Stumbling. Falling. Being held.

Jake, who might never walk unaided again but whose value to his family remained undiminished. Wyatt, whose carefully planned career path had just been abandoned for a future he was still learning to envision. Both of them stumbling through circumstances that had altered everything they thought they knew about their lives.

But not falling. Being upheld.

Robin closed the Bible. "I think we spend so much time trying to walk without stumbling that we forget the promise isn't about never losing our footing. It's about being caught when we do. God's not asking us to be perfect or to have everything figured out. He's just asking us to keep walking, to keep trusting that even when the ground shifts under us, He's still holding on."

Wyatt's response was physical rather than verbal. He reached for her, his arm sliding around her shoulders and pulling her against his side with gentle but unmistakable need. Robin went willingly, settling into his warmth, feeling his solid presence beside her as they sat together watching the river flow past.

She didn't push for conversation. Didn't ask if he was okay or demand explanations for his abrupt exit from the office. She simply sat with him, offering her presence as a gift without expectations, trusting that he would speak when he was ready.

The river moved steadily before them, its dark water catching occasional glints of pale winter sunlight that broke through the cloud cover. Ice lined the banks where the current moved more slowly, but the center flowed freely, carving its eternal path through the landscape.

Minutes passed. Maybe five, maybe ten. Robin lost track of time in the quiet communion of sitting beside the man she loved while he processed the magnitude of what he'd just done.

Finally, Wyatt spoke.

"I know I made the right choice. Putting in my two weeks' notice, turning down the promotion, committing to stay here permanently—I don't have a single doubt that this is where I'm meant to be."

"But when Captain Rogers told me I was practically guaranteed that position—that the district job was mine if I wanted it—" Wyatt's arm tightened around her shoulders. "It hit me hard. I'm only human, Robin. Hearing that everything I'd worked toward for a decade was finally within reach, and I was walking away from it—that reality crashed over me like a wave."

"Of course it did," Robin said softly.

"I never considered changing my mind. Not even for a second during that phone call." He turned his head to look at her, his green eyes intense with the need for her to understand this. "The entire time Captain Rogers was talking, trying to convince me what I'd be giving up, not once did I think about accepting. My answer was already decided before he even made the offer."

"I know."

"But after the call ended—" Wyatt's gaze returned to the river. "Everything started flashing through my mind like some kind of highlight reel. The years with the Forestry Service. The fires I'd fought, the forests I'd protected, the skills I'd developed. The reputation I'd built, the respect I'd earned from people I admired. All of it just—" He gestured vaguely toward the water. "Flowing away, like this river. Gone."

"And then other moments started flooding in," Wyatt continued. "Life-changing moments where everything shifted in an instant and I had to figure out how to keep moving forward when the path I'd been on disappeared."

He was quiet for a moment, gathering his thoughts before continuing.

"The first one was twelve years ago. Both of us were crying while we agreed to break up because we thought that was the mature, practical thing to do." His voice roughened with the memory. "I can still taste the salt of those tears. Still feel the weight of your hand in mine when you told me that was the right choice, even though it was breaking your heart. I convinced myself I was doing the right thing—choosing independence and career over love because that's what responsible adults do."

Robin's throat tightened with emotion, remembering that night from her own perspective. The ache that had lasted for months afterward. The way she'd second-guessed that decision for years.

"Then there was the day my parents died." Wyatt's jaw clenched, and Robin felt his pain as if it were her own. "Six years ago. Captain Rogers called me while I was out working in the forest... it had been just a typical day... and he told me to come to the station immediately. I got there... he told me I needed to call home. He sat by me as I made the phone call, and I learned they were gone." He stopped, his breathing uneven. "Everything I thought I knew about the world just shattered. The people who were supposed to be constants, who I'd always assumed would be there—just gone in an instant."

"And then Jake's accident. October fifteenth. I was supervising a controlled burn, everything routine, when Captain Rogers called me again and pulled me from the burn. That call—the drive to Charleston not knowing if my brother would survive—that was another one of those moments where life just splits. Before the accident and after the accident, and you can never go back to before no matter how much you might want to."

He turned to face Robin more fully, his expression open and vulnerable.

"And then today. Dr. Morrison told us that Jake will probably never regain full mobility. That the brother who built his entire identity around physical work and hands-on farm management has permanent limitations that will reshape his entire future." Wyatt's eyes glistened. "Followed immediately by Captain Rogers offering me the position I've dreamed about since my first day with the Forestry Service. The culmination of every certification I've earned, every fire I've fought, and every goal I've pursued. And me turning it down without hesitation because I finally understand what actually matters."

"Life can change in the blink of an eye," Wyatt said quietly. "I've witnessed it over and over. Moments where everything you thought you knew gets turned upside down, and you have to figure out how to keep breathing, keep moving, and keep trusting that somehow there's still a path forward even when you can't see it."

"When I walked out of the office earlier, I wasn't having second thoughts about my decision. I wasn't questioning whether I'd made a mistake or wondering if I should call Captain Rogers back and accept his offer." His voice carried absolute conviction. "I just needed a moment to let myself feel the full weight of what I'd given up. To acknowledge that turning down that promotion cost me something real and significant, even though it was the right choice."

"Sitting here, watching this river, remembering all the times I've experienced life-changing moments—I realized something. Every single one of those moments felt like an ending at the time. Like something precious was being taken away, and I had no choice but to accept the loss and move forward. But they weren't endings at all. They were redirections. God's way of saying, 'Not that path, this one. Not that timing, this timing. Not that version of your life, but this version.'" He looked at her with such tenderness that Robin's eyes filled with tears. "Breaking up with you twelve years ago felt like the end of the most important relationship I'd ever have. But it was just... God's way of saying not yet. We both needed those twelve years to grow into people capable of building something that lasts."

"I think you're right," Robin whispered.

"My parents' death devastated me. Still does, in ways I'll probably always carry. But it also brought me home more often, kept me connected to Jake and Lauren, and reminded me that the farm is part of who I am." Wyatt's voice was thoughtful rather than bitter. "And Jake's accident—as terrible as it is, as much as I wish it had never happened—it forced me to face what I'd been avoiding. That I wasn't happy. That my life was hollow. That coming home didn't mean I'd failed—it meant I'd finally figured out where I actually belong."

Robin felt tears slip down her cheeks, moved by his ability to find meaning even in tragedy.

"So when Captain Rogers offered me that promotion today—the opportunity that would have represented the pinnacle of everything I'd worked for—turning it down didn't feel like sacrifice. It felt like choosing. Like finally having the courage to stop pursuing what I thought I should want and start claiming what my heart has been telling me I need."

"And I need this." He gestured toward the farm visible in the distance. "The land my family has cultivated for three generations. Work that matters not because it's prestigious but because it connects me to something bigger than myself. Jake and Lauren as partners rather than people I visit a few times a year."

He turned to face her fully again, his hands coming up to cup her cheeks with tenderness.

"And you," he said simply. "I need you, Robin. Because loving you makes me want to be the best version of myself. Because coming home to you at the end of every day would make even the hardest work meaningful. Because building a life with you is worth more than any promotion or career achievement could ever be."

Robin couldn't speak past the emotion clogging her throat. She'd spent years believing she wasn't enough for any man to fight for, convincing herself that she was destined to be appreciated but never loved and treasured.

"I love you," she said. "I never stopped loving you, even when I tried to convince myself I had. Even when I thought we'd missed our chance and I needed to move on. My heart has always been yours."

"And mine has always been yours," Wyatt said, his thumb wiping away the tears on her cheek.

They sat in silence for a moment, the magnitude of everything spoken and unspoken settling between them like a blessing. The river continued its steady flow, indifferent to human drama but somehow comforting in its constancy. The winter wind whispered through bare oak branches overhead, and somewhere in the distance, the farm continued its rhythms of work and life and tradition.

"Do you think you'll ever wonder 'what if'?" Robin asked, needing to hear his answer. "Years from now, when the choice you made today feels less immediate—will you look back and question whether you gave up too much?"

Wyatt considered the question with the careful thought he gave to everything important. "Honestly? I'll probably have moments where I wonder what the other path would have looked like. I'm human, and it's natural to occasionally think about roads not taken." He smiled at her. "But wondering isn't the same as regretting. I can acknowledge that the district supervisor position would have been professionally fulfilling while still knowing with absolute certainty that I chose the better path. The path that leads to a life I actually want to live rather than a life that looks impressive on paper."

He paused, then turned the question back to her. "What about you? Do you ever wonder what if we'd tried to make it work twelve years ago? If we'd refused to break up and attempted long distance instead?"

Robin thought about the girl she'd been at eighteen—idealistic and romantic but ultimately too immature to sustain the kind of relationship that required real sacrifice and compromise. She thought about the years between then and now, the lessons learned, and the growth that came through pain and disappointment.

"I think if we'd tried to force it twelve years ago, we would have failed," she said honestly. "We were too young, too focused on becoming who we thought we should be rather than discovering who we actually were. The distance would have strained us. The different directions our lives were taking would have pulled us apart eventually, and we might have ended up resenting each other instead of loving each other."

"You think God brought us back together when we were finally ready?"

"I know He did." Robin's voice carried quiet conviction. "Everything that happened between then and now—your career with the Forestry Service, my work as a nurse, my engagement to Liam and the lesson that taught me about my worth, your years of building independence and finally recognizing it wasn't fulfilling—all of it shaped us into people capable of this. Capable of choosing love even when it requires sacrifice. Capable of building something that lasts instead of something that just feels good in the moment."

Wyatt pulled her close, and Robin rested her head against his shoulder, feeling the steady rhythm of his breathing and his solid presence beside her.

"I'm not afraid anymore," Wyatt said quietly. "For years, I've been afraid of losing people I love, so I kept everyone at a distance. Afraid of commitment because commitment means vulnerability. Afraid of putting down roots because roots mean you can't run when things get hard." He pressed a kiss on the top of her head. "But sitting here with you, having just walked away from my dream job to choose this life—I realize that being afraid of loss meant I was also avoiding real connection. And a life without real connection isn't actually a life worth protecting."

"No," Robin agreed. "It's just existence."

They sat together in comfortable silence; the quilt keeping them warm despite the December cold, the Bible resting in Robin's lap as a reminder of the faith that had guided them both through their separate journeys and was now guiding them toward a shared future.

Finally, Wyatt shifted slightly and let out a laugh.

"What?" Robin asked, lifting her head to look at him.

"I'm freezing," he admitted, his grin sheepish. "And I know you have to be too. We've been sitting out here for probably over an hour together. I can't feel my toes anymore."

Robin laughed, the sound breaking through the emotional intensity with welcome relief. "I was trying to be supportive and let you process without rushing you."

"I appreciate that. Truly." Wyatt's eyes sparkled with affection and amusement. "But I think I've processed everything I need to process for now, and if we stay out here much longer, we're going to get frostbite."

"That would be a terrible way to end such a meaningful conversation."

"Terrible," he agreed. Then, before she could move, he cupped her face in both hands and kissed her.

The kiss was soft and sweet and carried the weight of everything they'd just shared—promises made and received, futures claimed, and love chosen deliberately.

When they finally separated, Wyatt rested his forehead against hers.

"Let's go home," he said simply.

Robin nodded, then reluctantly pulled away from his warmth to climb out of his side-by-side and return to her own. She folded the quilt carefully, tucking it beside her on the seat along with Lauren's Bible.

Wyatt started his engine, and Robin started hers, the twin rumbles breaking the quiet that had sheltered their conversation. He pulled forward, turning his vehicle back toward the farm buildings visible in the distance, and Robin followed, her tires tracking in the path he created through the snow.

As they drove away from the river, Robin glanced back once at the spot under the oak trees where so many significant moments had unfolded. Where a family had picnicked on Sunday afternoons. Where three siblings had grieved their parents and found strength in each other. Where teenage sweethearts had dreamed about futures, they couldn't yet imagine. Where a man had just grieved his professional dreams and claimed his personal ones instead.

The river continued flowing, steady and constant, just as it always had and always would. Unmoved by human drama but somehow bearing witness to it all, a reminder that some things endure regardless of the changes happening on the banks.

Robin turned her attention forward, following Wyatt's side-by-side as it navigated the farm roads. Ahead, Gibson's Tree Farm spread across the landscape—groves of evergreens, equipment barns, and the main farmhouse where Jake recovered and Lauren and Wyatt managed operations and life continued despite every challenge thrown its way.

She smiled as she followed Wyatt. The December afternoon was cold but bright with possibility; her heart settled and certain in ways it hadn't been back when she was eighteen years old. Back then, she didn't yet understand what real, lasting love required.

Now she knew. And so did he.

Epilogue

The torn wrapping paper scattered across Jake's bedroom floor told the story of the evening—bright reds and greens and silvers, crumpled ribbons, empty boxes that had held thoughtful gifts exchanged between people who'd become more than friends, more than patient and caregivers, more than even the family bonds that already connected three of them.

Robin sat cross-legged on the floor near the Christmas tree, its lights casting a warm glow across her face as she laughed at something Lauren had just said about the fuzzy socks Jake had given her—each pair featuring a different farm animal with increasingly ridiculous expressions. The socks were spread across Lauren's lap now, and she held up a pair with googly-eyed chickens that looked slightly deranged.

"I'm wearing these to church," Lauren declared, her blue eyes sparkling with mischief. "Pastor Andrew will get a kick out of them."

Jake laughed from his wheelchair positioned near the tree. "Those socks are a masterpiece," he said. "I spent hours shopping online trying to find the most ridiculous pairs possible."

"Mission accomplished," Wyatt said from his position on the floor near Robin. He'd been quieter than usual tonight, Robin had noticed—not withdrawn, but distracted a little.

Robin surveyed the gifts surrounding her. The leather-bound journal from Lauren with "Robin, Registered Nurse Extraordinaire" embossed on the cover in elegant script. The collection of gourmet hot chocolate mixes from Jake, each flavor more decadent than the last, with a note that said, "For the woman who brought Christmas to a man stuck in bed." The soft cashmere scarf from Wyatt in a gorgeous soft blue color that he'd said would bring out the color of her eyes.

She'd given them thoughtful gifts too—a first edition copy of a forestry manual from the 1940s for Wyatt that she'd found at an antique shop, its pages filled with hand-drawn illustrations of tree species native to Appalachia. For Lauren, a custom photo album she'd been assembling secretly for weeks, filled with images of the farm through this past winter. The album held dozens of images of The Christmas Shop at its most beautiful and images of Wyatt helping customers out in the fields. There were also various photos of church members enjoying time together on the farm and candid shots of the Gibson siblings working together with Jake here in this room while they were planning for the future of Gibson's Tree Farm. For Jake, she had given him a framed photograph she'd taken of the town Christmas tree standing magnificent in the special grove, before it had been cut down, dusted with snow, representing both the tradition he'd entrusted to her and the recovery journey he'd traveled with courage and faith.

Robin drew her knees up to her chest, wrapping her arms around her legs, and let contentment wash over her. This was what Christmas was supposed to feel like: filled with love and laughter and peace.

"This has been perfect," she said, her voice filled with gratitude that went deeper than wrapping paper and gift tags. "Thank you for including me in your Christmas Eve."

Lauren's expression softened, and she reached over to squeeze Robin's hand. "You're family, Robin."

Wyatt shifted beside her, and when Robin glanced at him, she found him watching her with an expression that made her pulse quicken.

"What are you thinking about, Wyatt Gibson?" she asked.

"I'm thinking there might be one more gift."

Robin blinked. "No, we already exchanged everything. There's nothing left under the tree."

"Are you sure?" Wyatt's smile was slow, secretive, and devastatingly handsome. "Maybe you should check again. Thoroughly."

Lauren had gone very still, Robin noticed, her phone suddenly in her hand with the camera angled toward Robin in a way that seemed too deliberate to be accidental. Jake's expression had shifted too—anticipation replacing the relaxed contentment he'd worn moments before.

Robin's heart began a peculiar rhythm against her ribs—too fast, too hard, like her body understood something her mind hadn't quite caught up to yet.

"Wyatt Gibson, what did you do?"

"Go look," he said simply, gesturing toward the tree. "Check the branches. Carefully."

Robin unfolded herself from the floor, her legs slightly unsteady as she approached the tree. The lights cast shadows through the branches, making it difficult to see clearly into the deeper layers where ornaments hung in careful arrangement. She leaned closer, her fingers carefully moving aside branches, searching.

Nothing on the right side. Nothing obvious on the left.

She moved around to the back of the tree, where branches pressed close to the wall, and there—tucked deep within the evergreen needles—was a small velvet box.

Robin's breath caught.

Her fingers trembled slightly as she reached for it. The velvet was soft beneath her fingertips, deep navy blue, and small enough to fit in her palm. The kind of box that held jewelry. The kind of box that held—

No, she wouldn't let herself think it.

She turned back toward the others, holding the box up. "This?"

Wyatt had moved. He wasn't sitting on the floor anymore. He was standing close enough that she could see the rapid pulse at his throat, the careful control in his expression that suggested he was working very hard to appear calm when he felt anything but.

"That's it," he said, his voice rougher than usual. "Open it."

Robin's hands shook as she carefully lifted the lid.

The box was empty.

Confusion flooded through her, followed immediately by disappointment that she tried desperately to hide.

She looked up at Wyatt, a question forming on her lips as he dropped to one knee in front of her.

The velvet box tumbled from Robin's suddenly nerveless fingers, landing on the floor. Her hands flew to her mouth as shock rippled through her entire body, stealing her breath, stopping her heart, and freezing her completely in this moment that couldn't possibly be happening but was.

Wyatt knelt before her, his green eyes steady on hers despite the emotion she could see swimming in their depths. His right hand emerged from behind his back, and he was holding a ring.

Not just any ring. The most beautiful ring Robin had ever seen.

The center stone was a magnificent marquise-cut diamond that caught the Christmas tree lights and threw them back in brilliant fragments—white fire dancing across its faceted surface. But it wasn't alone. On each side of the diamond, set into the elegant band, was a ruby. Deep red, gleaming, and perfect.

Robin couldn't breathe. Couldn't think. Could only stare at the ring and the man holding it and try to process that this was real, this was happening, this was Wyatt on his knee offering her—

"Robin." His voice cut through her spiraling thoughts, anchoring her. "Look at me."

She dragged her eyes from the ring to his face, and what she saw there—love and certainty and vulnerable hope—made tears spill over her cheeks.

"Twelve years ago," Wyatt began, his voice steady despite the emotion clearly working through him, "I let you go. The moment I saw you walk into this bedroom weeks ago to take care of my brother, the moment you looked at me with those beautiful hazel eyes... I realized that not a single day had dulled what I felt for you. You've shown me what home really means. It's not a place on a map or a job title or an accomplishment I can put on a resume. Home is wherever you are. Home is the way you laugh at Jake's terrible jokes and the way you collect Christmas ornaments like some people collect stamps. Home is watching you care for my brother with skill and compassion that humbles me. Home is the way you fit into my family, like you were always meant to be there. Home is the way loving you makes me want to be the best version of myself because you deserve nothing less than everything I have to give."

Robin's legs trembled, her entire body shaking with the force of her emotions.

"This ring," Wyatt said, lifting it slightly so the diamonds and rubies caught the light, "I chose it by myself, though Jake and Lauren helped me via FaceTime when I was at the jewelry store last week. The center diamond represents the life we're going to build together—something beautiful and strong and lasting. The rubies on each side represent our hearts. One for mine, one for yours. Two hearts that have belonged to each other since we were teenagers, that never really stopped belonging to each other. Two hearts that are finally coming home to where they've always belonged."

Robin dropped to her knees. She couldn't stand anymore, couldn't maintain the physical distance when everything inside her was screaming to be closer to him. Her hands found his face, cradling it with trembling fingers, feeling the slight stubble on his jaw and the warmth of his skin and the realness of him kneeling before her, offering forever.

"I love you," he said. "I have loved you since we were kids. And I will love you every single day of whatever life God grants us together."

He drew a shaky breath. "Robin Elizabeth Fitch, will you marry me? Will you let me spend the rest of my life treasuring you the way you deserve? Will you build a home with me, raise a family with me, and grow old with me? Will you be my wife?"

The sob finally broke free from Robin's chest, emerging as something between a laugh and a cry. Joy and disbelief and overwhelming gratitude crashed over her in waves that threatened to pull her under.

"Yes." The word came out rough, thick with tears. "Yes, Wyatt. Yes to all of it."

His hands shook slightly as he took her left hand in his, sliding the ring onto her finger. It fit almost perfectly, settling into place as if it had been waiting its entire existence for this exact moment.

Robin stared at it through her tears—the marquise diamond throwing light across the room, the rubies gleaming like promises kept, the band cool against her skin. It was the most beautiful ring she'd ever seen.

"Oh my goodness, Wyatt," she whispered, her voice breaking.

"Choosing you is the easiest decision I've ever made," Wyatt said, and then he was pulling her closer, his hands framing her face.

When he kissed her, it was soft and sweet and reverent—the kind of kiss that spoke of promises and futures and love that would last beyond this lifetime into whatever eternity God granted them. Robin kissed him back with her whole heart. She knew with certainty that this was right, this was God's plan, and this was the answer to her prayers.

"I got pictures!" Lauren's voice broke through the bubble surrounding them, and Robin looked over to find her weeping as well while holding up her phone. "I got everything—the moment you found the box, the confusion when it was empty, Wyatt on his knee, the ring, the kiss—all of it!"

"Lauren Gibson, you're a genius," Robin managed through her tears.

"I know," Lauren said, grinning through her own emotional overflow. "I'm also an excellent secret keeper. Do you know how hard it's been not to say anything for the past week?"

Jake was smiling so widely his face looked like it might split. "We watched via FaceTime while Wyatt went over approximately forty-seven different options in that jewelry store and had an existential crisis about whether the marquise cut was too dramatic."

"It's perfect," Robin said, extending her hand to admire the ring again. "Wyatt, it's absolutely perfect."

"You're perfect," he corrected, helping her to her feet and immediately pulling her back into his arms. "The ring is just a symbol of what I already knew—that you're the most precious thing in my life."

Robin buried her face in his chest, letting herself feel the steady beat of his heart beneath her cheek, breathing in the familiar scent of him. His arms tightened around her, holding her close, and she thought about the journey that had brought them to this moment. Young love as a teenager. Her own broken engagement had taught her she deserved to be treasured rather than tolerated. Wyatt's years of running from the very thing his heart needed most. Jake's terrible accident. The slow, careful rebuilding of trust and the discovery that sometimes the greatest love stories require patience, pain, and perspective before they can reach their proper conclusion.

Thank you, God, she prayed silently, her heart swelling with gratitude too big for words. *Thank you for bringing him home. Thank you for teaching us both what we needed to learn before we could do this right. Thank you for second chances and perfect timing and love that endures.*

"Come here, you two," Jake said, his voice thick with emotion. "I want in on this family moment."

Robin and Wyatt turned toward him, and Lauren was already moving, crossing the small distance to Jake's wheelchair. Robin and Wyatt followed, and the four of them came together—Lauren wrapping her arms around Jake from behind his chair, Wyatt and Robin flanking them on either side, all of them leaning in until their heads touched and their arms tangled, and they formed a circle of connection that felt sacred and unbreakable.

"You're gonna be my sister," Lauren whispered, her voice muffled. "Officially. No take-backs."

"I wouldn't dream of it," Robin said, reaching out with her right hand to squeeze Lauren's arm.

"Wow... another sister," Jake said, his tone suggesting he was smiling even though Robin couldn't see his face from this angle. "The Gibson sibling gene pool is improving dramatically."

They laughed, the sound mingling with tears, joy mixed with the remnants of grief that would always be a part of their story but no longer defined it. Dan and Marie Gibson weren't here to witness this moment, but their legacy surrounded them—in the farm they'd built, in the values they'd instilled in their children, in the Christmas traditions they'd established, and in the faith they'd modeled that sustained this family through tragedy and triumph.

Robin looked at her ring again. The symbol of forever with Wyatt. The promise of a future filled with Christmas mornings and farm work and family dinners and the everyday sacred moments that built a life worth living.

She thought about the girl she'd been at eighteen, heartbroken when she and Wyatt parted ways. She thought about the woman she'd become in the twelve years since—a skilled nurse, a faithful believer, and someone who'd finally learned through pain and disappointment that her worth didn't depend on someone else's recognition of it. She thought about how God's timing was perfect even when it felt impossibly slow, how sometimes the greatest gifts required the longest wait, and how the love that lasted was the love that endured through separation and growth and transformation.

This Christmas Eve—this perfect, impossible, miraculous Christmas Eve—had given her everything she'd ever wanted and more than she'd ever dared to hope for. Not just the ring, though it was beautiful. Not just the proposal, though it had been everything she could have dreamed. But the promise of forever with the man who'd finally come home. The certainty of belonging to this family who'd claimed her as their own. The knowledge that she was treasured, chosen, and loved with the kind of depth and permanence she'd stopped believing existed.

God's plans were always, always better than anything any of them could orchestrate themselves.

She was home.

And home, she now understood with perfect clarity, wasn't just a place or even a person.

Home was this: being held by the man who loved her, surrounded by the family who'd chosen her, wrapped in the faith that had sustained them all through the darkest valleys, and knowing undoubtedly that the future stretching before them would be filled with more joy than sorrow, more laughter than tears, and more love than any of them could possibly contain.

Home was Wyatt Gibson's arms around her, his lips against her temple, and his whispered words of love and forever.

Home was Christmas Eve in a bedroom transformed into a celebration space, where a recovering man sat in a wheelchair and his sister cried happy tears, and wrapping paper littered the floor like confetti.

Home was the ring on her finger—two rubies representing two hearts that had finally, finally found their way back to each other.

Home was now and always would be wherever faith flourished and wherever love triumphed over fear and hope conquered despair.

Robin tightened her grip on the people surrounding her, memorizing this moment, this feeling, this absolute certainty that God's timing was perfect and His plans were good, and sometimes the very best gifts required the longest, hardest wait before they could be properly received and appreciated.

Merry Christmas, she thought, joy rising in her chest like a hymn. *Merry Christmas to us all.*

And truly, it was the merriest Christmas she'd ever known.

Leave A Review

If you enjoyed this book, please consider leaving an honest review on Amazon

Visit Our Website:

www.tarabaisden.com

Visit Our Amazon Author Page HERE

Find Us On Social Media:

Facebook

Facebook Author Page

Instagram

Also by Tara Baisden

<u>Laurel Ridge Series</u>

#1. Season of Hope

#2. Finding Grace

#3. His Perfect Plan

#4. Love Redeemed

#5 Snowbound Blessings

#6 Sheltered Hearts

#7 Restoring Faith

#8 Love Rekindled

#9 Where She Belongs

#10 Shelter in His Arms

#11 Where Love Stands

#12 The Pieces We Mend

#13 Where Love Grows

#14 Where Hearts Heal

#15 Harvest of the Heart

#16 Season of Forgiveness

#17 Heart of the Season

#18 Threads of Grace

<u>Riverbend Valley Series</u>

#1 A Cowboy's Second Chance

#2 Wanderlust & Wild Horses

#3 Heartstrings on the Horizon

#4 Runaway in Riverbend Valley

#5 Mended Hearts

#6 Healing Hearts

#7 Home to Lost Creek

<u>Mistletoe Falls Series</u>

#1 Whisk Me Under the Mistletoe

#2 Once Upon a Christmas

#3 The Mistletoe Express

#4 Candy Canes & Sweet Dreams

#5 Wrapped Up in Christmas

#6 Jingle All the Way Home

About The Author

Tara Baisden is a Contemporary Christian Inspirational Romance author who proudly calls the beautiful state of West Virginia her home. Nestled on a sprawling mountainous property, she is surrounded by the peace and serenity of nature. Her days are happily spent in the quiet of country life, writing heartwarming stories of love, faith, and second chances. Tara also enjoys quilting, working in her garden, tending to her beloved pets, and soaking in the beauty of her surroundings.

With deep roots in West Virginia, family is everything to Tara. One of her favorite pastimes is gathering on the front porch with loved ones, sharing stories, laughter, and enjoying the simple, meaningful moments that life offers. When she's not crafting her novels, Tara can often be found exploring the rich history of her home state, visiting local historical sites, and, of course, stopping by every bookstore she passes! Her passion for reading and discovery always fuels her next adventure.

Tara is the author of the Laurel Ridges series of novels, as well as the Riverbend Valley series of novels, of which have been beloved by fans of inspirational romance. Her novels reflect her love for faith, family, and the timeless beauty of the world we live in.

Known for her sweet and clean romances, she creates characters that feel like family and settings that make readers want to visit again and again.

You can find out more about Tara and her latest releases at www.tarabaisden.com or follow her on social media for updates and behind-the-scenes glimpses of her writing process. Stay connected—you won't want to miss the heartfelt stories of love and family she has in store!

About Laurel Ridge

Welcome to the fictional town of Laurel Ridge, West Virginia!

Nestled deep in the heart of the Appalachian Mountains, Laurel Ridge is a place where time slows down, allowing visitors and residents alike to enjoy life's simple pleasures. With its quaint, brick-paved streets, historic storefronts, and the ever-present backdrop of rolling hills and dense forests, Laurel Ridge is a hidden gem that attracts tourists looking for both serenity and adventure.

A Rich History

The town was founded in the early 1800s by pioneering settlers who were drawn to the fertile land and abundant natural resources of the region. Laurel Ridge began as a small logging community, relying on the towering forests that covered the surrounding mountains. The New River, one of the oldest rivers in the world, provided an essential transportation route for lumber, as well as a lifeline for the early settlers.

As the years passed, the town evolved from a logging outpost into a thriving hub for craftspeople and artisans. By the late 19th century, it had developed a reputation for its hand-crafted furniture, textiles, and pottery, all made by skilled locals. The town's proximity to the New River also made it a destination for adventurous souls seeking to kayak, fish, or hike along the riverbanks.

A Place of Renewal

Though the logging industry faded by the early 20th century, Laurel Ridge adapted to the changing times. Its natural beauty and deep connection to West Virginia's mountain heritage drew travelers from near and far, transforming it into a beloved tourist destination. Local shops, run by generations of the same families, line the town square, offering handmade goods, locally sourced foods, and, most of all, warm hospitality.

The town's signature event, the Harvest Festival, began in the 1930s, celebrating the craftsmanship, music, and traditions passed down through the generations. Each year, visitors flock to enjoy live Appalachian music, taste locally grown produce, and witness demonstrations of old-world techniques like blacksmithing and weaving.

A Town of Faith and Community

At the heart of the town stands Laurel Ridge Community Church, a small, white clapboard building with a steeple that reaches toward the sky. Built in 1876, the church has been a pillar of faith and strength for the community for over a century. Its bell, crafted by the town's original blacksmith, has been ringing on Sunday mornings ever since, calling townsfolk to worship and reminding everyone of the enduring values of faith, hope, and love.

The church's history is intertwined with the town's, serving as a refuge in difficult times and a gathering place in moments of joy. Over the years, the church has grown to include an outreach center that supports local families and tourists in need, providing everything from free meals to spiritual counseling. The church's welcoming atmosphere reflects the town's deep sense of unity and service.

A Growing Tourist Haven

Today, Laurel Ridge has grown to a population of around five thousand people, yet it has managed to retain its small-town charm. Its thriving tourist industry draws visitors year-round. Tourists can stroll through mom-and-pop shops, and dine at the beloved Martha's Diner, famous for its homemade pies and retro charm. The town square, with its white gazebo surrounded by flowering bushes, is often the site of outdoor concerts and farmers' markets, creating a sense of nostalgia and small-town pride.

For nature lovers, the New River offers breathtaking views and the thrill of adventure, whether it's fishing in its crystal blue waters or hiking along the rugged trails that weave through the wilderness. Tourists and locals alike cherish the scenic beauty, often finding peace in the simple pleasures of watching the river flow or taking in the panoramic vistas of the Appalachian Mountains.

Laurel Ridge, with its rich history, strong community spirit, and natural beauty, is more than just a tourist destination—it's a place where past and present blend seamlessly, offering everyone who visits a chance to experience the best of West Virginia's mountain heritage. You'll find that Laurel Ridge is a town that captures the heart.

Welcome to Laurel Ridge. I hope you fall in love with this charming small town and its residents.